SPARE THE CHILD

Mack Molloy

ISBN: 0692477861
ISBN 13: 9780692477861
Library of Congress Control Number: 2015910259
Mary Malloy, Atlanta, Ga

Dedicated to Diane, Donna, Jay, Darryl, and Kevin

PROLOGUE

The four men shifted uncomfortably in their chairs as the eldest man, well into his seventies, reviewed the details of the plan. Collectively, they represented the political elite of Savannah, Georgia. Don Abbott, the school superintendent, could trace his roots in the city back four generations, making him practically aristocracy. Had the South prevailed in the "war of northern aggression," he would no doubt be running the family's textile business from Bangalore instead of devising creative strategies to keep thick, recalcitrant students from being left behind. Robert Murphy, the gruff old Irishman, had served as chief magistrate longer than most folks could remember and treated the election process with the same disdainful air in which his colleagues in law treated continuing education. Sam Katz, the CEO of the local hospital, sat on the board of no less than six corporations, from aerospace to insurance. Being Jewish in a sea of fundamentalist Christianity, he was used to sticking out in a crowd and wore it like a badge of honor. Charles Mosely, the police commissioner, was born and raised in Savannah, the great-grandson of a freed slave. Mosely worked his way up through the ranks of the police department before he entered and subsequently won the last election by a narrow margin, thanks in large part to the support of the mayor, and maintained a tenuous hold as the city's top cop.

Each was lost in his own thoughts as the old man spoke with a presence and authority that came only from years of experience in leading others. They were all successful in their own right, yet they deferred to him out of respect for his personal accomplishments as well as a profound appreciation for the wealthy and influential benefactors he represented.

Six months ago, he approached each of them individually and related the basic scheme. It seemed a bit far-fetched at first but feasible, definitely feasible. The biggest hurdle would be the money. Raising one hundred fifty million dollars for what was essentially a grand social experiment seemed beyond reason. No one in his right mind would throw that kind of money at a scheme like this. Or would they? Surely he wouldn't have brought them together as a group if funding was an issue.

The plan was simple enough in concept. They would create a charitable trust offering any resident of the county between the ages of sixteen and forty the sum of fifteen thousand dollars to voluntarily undergo a sterilization procedure—either a tubal ligation for women or a vasectomy for men—and would reimburse the cost of the surgery. The devil, of course, was in the details.

"You are all aware," the old man continued, "of the case histories of forced sterilization or eugenics programs in turn of the century America, Nazi Germany, Sweden, Japan, Finland and even modern-day Australia, Africa and Peru. These programs were either misguided attempts to improve the gene pool by targeting specific groups such as the mentally ill or population-control strategies. Most of the world today views forced sterilization programs as human rights violations. Our program, on the other hand, is a voluntary one. No one is forced to participate, and no specific group will be targeted. The offer is open to anyone provided they meet the age and residency requirements."

Mosely and Katz made eye contact. They'd heard this part before. Voluntary or not, there were bound to be repercussions.

"I met with our friends in New York on Monday, and they've given us the green light," said the old man. "The funds are sitting in a Cayman Islands bank account as we speak."

"How much?" asked Robert Murphy. He seemed more self-assured than his three colleagues, having less than three years remaining on his final term on the bench before retirement. They all understood this program would be controversial. Each knew that the fifteen thousand dollar stipend was more likely to attract individuals lower on the socioeconomic scale than affluent citizens. And that is why a simple plan became more complex.

"One hundred fifty million dollars."

"That's an awful lot of money to be throwing away," said Charles Mosely.

"They don't think of it as throwing money away," the old man replied. "I told you already, they see this as an experiment. If it works here, they believe it can be duplicated anywhere in the world. These people are forward thinkers. They have the power and the resources to take this blueprint and implement it on a global scale. What we're talking about doing—right here in this room—could eventually change the course of history. We're talking about wiping out poverty and hunger in our lifetime and minimizing crime. What more dramatic outcome could anyone possibly imagine?"

"I'm still curious," said Don Abbott. "Just who are these people? I know you have to protect your sources, but are they politicians? Business people? Public figures?"

"They are individuals with more power and money than you or I can imagine. Beyond that, I'm afraid I'm not at liberty to say."

"And their motives?" asked Sam Katz.

"Complicated, as I'm sure yours and mine are," replied the old man. "Overpopulation, hunger, the increasing scarcity of natural resources, illiteracy, poverty, violence, crime and child abuse are all subjects which concern these people on a global scale.

Almost all of these problems can be traced to one common underlying factor—the birth of children to parents who are unwilling, untrained or lack the proper economic or human resources to properly care for them. And in so many of these cases, the pregnancies are actually unintended and could have easily been prevented. The cost to society of these children born to incompetent or disinterested parents is immense. Those costs manifest every day in our hospitals, schools and prisons."

"I agree with that," said Katz. "Some of the mothers who give birth at our hospital are essentially children themselves. They've got no clue what it means to be a mother and care for a child."

"And once they have the baby, the odds are pretty good that they'll be dropping out of school," said Abbott. "Pregnancy is a major reason for drop-outs in our school system today. Imagine what it must be like to face a life with practically no hope of success by the time you're sixteen years old."

"I send kids away to prison every day," said Murphy. "I used to feel sorry for them in my younger days, but now I look into their eyes and see that cold hard stare. No remorse, no fear. I'm just the guy stamping their ticket to the next stop on their long and inevitable journey to hell."

"The world is full of do-gooders who want to help these kids, and I don't mean that as a snide remark. They have good intentions and want to make a difference in the world. I think all of us can relate to them because we want to make a difference too, but the hard facts say that their batting averages are well below average. It's usually too late by the time they get involved. It's not too late for us. Gentleman, we stand here on the brink of a shift in the very fabric of our society. We mustn't turn back now."

"I don't think any of us want to turn back," said Abbott. "Obviously this could turn out to be a very controversial program. I think maybe we're all a little nervous about publicity at this point.

If our names were to be connected to a program like this, it could ruin our careers."

"All the more reason for having a front man," interjected Murphy.

"Exactly," said the old man.

"Do you think he'll do it? What if he refuses?" asked Mosely.

"First of all, I don't think he'll refuse," replied the old man. "You just need to be careful how you present it to him. I'm counting on you all for that. If he does refuse, however, we can always find someone else. The kind of money we'll be offering will be too tempting for most attorneys to turn down. It's critical, however, that we find someone we can trust. Confidentiality is the key to the success of the entire program. That's why I suggested him in the first place. He's the perfect candidate."

"This whole thing makes me nervous," said Mosely. "I'm up for re-election next year, and if word got out that I was involved in something like this, I wouldn't stand a chance in the election."

"I think we all agree that we're taking a big chance here," said Abbott, but if this thing works the way we think it might, we'll have a healthier, safer, better-educated population, and we can take credit for it. We'll be able to write our own ticket in this town."

"Sounds to me like you're getting ready to run for mayor," Mosely sneered. "I just want to keep my job."

"What voters are you worried about losing if word got out?" asked Abbott.

"At least half of the religious voters would be opposed to this, the fundamentalists, Catholics, Mormons and Muslims. They're generally against any kind of birth control. And the women's rights groups would probably be upset, though it sure doesn't take much to piss them off. And the minority voters might feel targeted. Those are some of the same folks the good judge here sends away to prison on a regular basis."

"But you're African-American," said Murphy. "I wouldn't think you'd need to worry about the minority vote."

"Why does everybody think just because I'm black that all black people will automatically vote for me? If one of my officers uses excessive force in restraining a poor brother in the community, I might as well be a white, right-wing republican come Election Day."

"Just think how much easier your job would be if the population in the housing projects was cut in half over the next twenty years by our program," said the old man. "That's where half the city's crime comes from, isn't it?"

"More like sixty percent," admitted the chief, "and there's no doubt that a lot of those people would be better off without children, at least until they could get themselves out of the projects and stand on their own two feet. Still, by the time any of this has any effect on the population, I'll be long gone and retired. Personally, I don't see any upside here, in the short term anyway."

"I hope we'll see a drop-off in the number of crack babies born at the hospital, if nothing else," said Katz. "I've been tempted to have a few of the mothers sterilized as we're delivering their babies while they're high on crack cocaine, but you just can't do that sort of thing at a public hospital. If just a few of those mothers voluntarily submitted to sterilization and that prevented them from conceiving, abusing and mistreating future fetuses, then that's enough of a short-term solution for me."

"Gentlemen," the old man said, resuming control of the conversation, "are we all in agreement here as to what must be done? It's important that we have no dissension. If anyone has any doubt or uncertainty concerning their involvement in Fresh Start, it's critical that we discuss it now." He looked into the eyes of each man, searching for signs of hesitancy.

"I'm in," said Murphy.

"Me too," said Katz.

"Count me in," chimed Abbott.

All eyes turned to Mosely. He was the most conflicted and had the most to lose. "I think this is crazy, but I'm tired of living in a country where young black men are feared by white society just because of the actions of some gangster punks. Count me in too."

"Very well then," said the old man rising to leave, "we start tomorrow. Good luck, gentlemen."

CHAPTER ONE

R. Tyler Marshall IV rose on a clear Savannah spring morning to the chirping of birds outside his bedroom window. "Hold down the goddamned racket would you?" he shouted out the open window. "Can't you see a man's trying to sleep in here?" The morning sun cast intense rays of light through the curtains, illuminating the bedroom of the three-story brick, federal-style home. The house, a wedding gift from his parents, was originally built in 1820 and restored in 1876, a product of Reconstruction as the South moved to salve its wounds from the ravages of the Civil War. The sunlight cast shadows on the heart-pine flooring, the four-poster bed and the tiger-maple night stand on which rested an empty bottle of eighteen-year-old Glenfiddich Scotch Whiskey and an alarm clock. "Shit! It's eight-thirty!" he groaned, with the sudden realization that he was supposed to be meeting a client at nine o'clock at the office.

Since his divorce was final a year ago, he found himself settling into a disturbing pattern most mornings—waking up hung over and alone. He hit the bathroom like a trained commando attacking a target as he pressed the "on" button to the steam shower, while simultaneously swallowing three aspirin, then rinsing with mouthwash. *At least I'm not drinking the stuff.* He thought of a saying one of his old drinking buddies had, "I can't be an alcoholic because I don't go to the meetings." It comforted him somehow to imagine that the sweat running from his pores in the steam bath was actually Scotch, and, once certain that he had sufficiently sweated off at least a pint of the stuff, he rinsed off and dressed— light cream suit with fuchsia tie. He didn't look the part of the conservative southern lawyer but come to think of it, he didn't feel like one either.

From his house, he had a view of the old cemetery at Colonial Park, the tree-lined resting place of many of the town's deceased. He lived just six blocks from his law practice, located on Drayton Street, nestled in between two of the city's twenty-two public squares. It was a beautiful walk past well-manicured lawns lined by stately oaks, their clinging Spanish moss forming a natural roof-top overhead. The azaleas and dogwoods were in full bloom, their perfumed aroma wafting through the air producing a scent that was distinctivyely southern. Today, with his head throbbing from the effects of the prior night's alcohol, the flowers' scent made him retch. Wisely, instead of walking, he drove the six blocks in his Mercedes and cranked up the air-conditioning until he felt goose bumps form on his arms and beads of perspiration crystallize on his forehead from the mechanically-induced chill.

Tyler pulled into the main entrance of the office building at nine twenty-two and instinctively parked the car in back of the two-story brick building bearing a tastefully hand-painted sign out front which read: "Marshall & Marshall Attorneys at Law. Established 1956." The Marshall & Marshall was actually a reference to his grandfather, who founded the practice and his father, who joined the firm, as Tyler had done, immediately upon completion of law school. His grandfather was now deceased, and his father semi-retired, so the day-to-day operations of the firm were left to him. He entered the building through the back door and sneaked up the stairs to his office on the second floor. He tried to picture either of the elder Marshalls, stoic, resolute men sneaking through the back door after a long night of carousing, but the image just wouldn't come to him.

He immediately dialed his assistant, Darlene Frazier, while he removed his suit coat. "Hello Tyler, Mr. and Mrs. Wellbourne are waiting for you here in the reception area."

"Of course, I'll be right down. I got held up on another call," he lied.

There was barely a second of hesitation. Darlene was well accustomed to covering for him by now. "Yes, I explained that to them already."

His office looked like it had been ransacked by a gang of thieves searching for hidden treasure. Somewhere in this mess, he was confident, was the Wellbourne file. Paul and Ashley Wellbourne were there to establish an irrevocable trust for their three children. He had already done most of the prep work and just needed their signatures and some follow up documentation, if he could just find the file.

"Looking for this?" Annie Burriss, his associate, stood in the doorway, holding a thin manila file.

"Where'd you get that?" I've been looking everywhere for it."

"Darlene was worried that you might not make your meeting this morning, so I took the liberty of looking for it myself. I found it on the floor behind your desk under last month's issue of your sailing magazine. You have a very unique filing system, I must say."

"What? It's under S for stupid, boring trust documents."

"You know, sometimes it sounds like you don't enjoy practicing law, Tyler."

"Whatever gave you that idea? Was it my complete indifference and chronic absenteeism that tipped you off?"

"I just don't get it. I worked my way through college and law school to get where I am today, and you act like you'd rather be doing something else."

"You see, Annie, that's the difference between you and me. I was born a lawyer. You got to choose."

"You were born with a silver spoon in your mouth is what you were."

"And you were born the daughter of a maid—sorry, domestic assistant—my parents' domestic assistant since before we were even born. Is this the part where you assert your superiority over me by reminding me of how ungrateful I am for all the advantages I've been given and how I'm wasting my life?"

"Not really. You seem to be doing a good enough job of that on your own. Rough night last night?"

"No more so than the night before. They all kind of blur together after a while."

"It's been a year since Deborah left. Don't you think it's time you moved on?"

"I hear she's engaged already. A doctor. Maybe I should have been born a doctor."

"Honestly, Tyler, why do you even miss her? She pretty much represents everything you seem to despise about your own upbringing. She's a blueblood, a social climber and a world class, money-hungry snob. You seem to forget that you didn't even like her that much during your entire five years of marriage."

"That's why we were so perfect for each other."

"Your father should have told me to get a psychology degree instead of helping me through law school, so I could have worked on fixing his whacked-out son!"

"Thanks, Annie. You always know how to cheer me up."

"I'm just worried about you, that's all. I do love you, you know."

"I love you too, Annie. Maybe **we** should get married?"

"I'd love to be there to see the look on your mother's face when you broke that news to her," Annie cackled. "Tyler, you know I love your parents, but I don't think they're quire ready for an African-American daughter-in-law. Besides, I don't think I could ever marry a man who eats earthworms."

"I was six years old!"

"Doesn't matter. There's bound to be some of that leftover worm shit in there somewhere. Tyler?"

"Huh?"

"The Wellbournes?" she said holding up the legal file.

"I almost forgot! Thanks Annie."

"Don't mention it. Meet me at O'Brien's after work tonight for a drink? There's someone I want you to meet."

"Not another one of your fix-ups, Annie!" he groaned.

"You need to get out more."

"The last woman you fixed me up with had six cats named after the kids on the Brady Bunch, and she looked kind of like Alice, the housekeeper."

"She did not—she was nice!"

"I hate cats, and I'm allergic to boot."

"Don't be such a bore. I'll see you at O'Brien's. The Wellbournes?" she said, dropping the file in his lap.

As Tyler finished his meeting with the Wellbournes and escorted them out the front door, Darlene waited expectantly for him at the reception desk. Annie's nickname for her was Mrs. Doubtfire as she bore a striking resemblance to the cinematic title character played by Robin Williams. She wore large, round eyeglasses much too big for her narrow, delicate face, making her look insect-like, and matronly blouses buttoned to her chin, covered with flowers of every genus. He wasn't sure if he could ever forgive Annie for the nickname because it made him laugh every time he looked at her. Fortunately, Darlene mistook his ever-present smile to mean that he was in a good mood most of the time.

"Good morning, Darlene."

"Good morning, Tyler. How are we doing today?"

Tyler was convinced that Darlene was a nurse in a former life based on her insistence on using "we" in the second person singular tense. "We couldn't be better thanks. Do I have any messages?"

Marshall & Marshall was one of the last firms in America yet to use voice mail for messaging services. Tyler's father was old-school and insisted that the firm's clients be directed to a live person every time they called during business hours. It was a quaint custom, and the clients seemed to like it, plus it gave Darlene something to do.

"Yes, you've got a couple here," she said. "Your father called and wants you to call him at home, and Tom Grier from First Bank of Savannah called—something about your mortgage."

He had no idea what his father wanted, but it was unlikely he was calling to congratulate him on the stellar job he was doing running the family business. Some of the older clients initially brought on board by his father were retiring or selling their companies to larger corporations that preferred to use their own law firms out of Atlanta or New York, and several of the Atlanta firms were opening branches in town, further diluting the pot. That, in addition to Tyler's growing indifference to work, created business conditions that might best be described as "challenging." Tom Grier was calling because he was two months behind on the mortgage payment for the building, having refinanced it the day after his divorce was final in order to buy a new sailboat, a forty-six foot Morgan.

"Tear those up and bring me some better messages, would you, Darlene?" Tyler joked.

"There's one more, Tyler. Don Abbot called and wants you to call him back. He says it's urgent." Don Abbott was the superintendent of schools and a city councilman who Tyler knew casually. Don was a fourth-generation Savannahian and a rather pretentious sort with serious political aspirations. Tyler also found him to be somewhat of a bore.

"Hmmm, I wonder what he's calling about? Thanks, Darlene." Once back in his office, he dialed his parents' house first, hoping for voice mail but his mother picked up on the second ring.

"Hey, Momma. It's me."

"Hey, son. How are you?"

"I'm good. Busy," he lied. "I'm returning Dad's call. Is he around?"

"You just missed him I'm afraid. He's gone over to the club to play golf. I'll have him call you when he gets home."

Not only did his father not believe in voice mail, he was the last man in America, Tyler was convinced, not to take incoming calls on his cell phone, something he was grateful for at the present moment. "Thanks, Momma."

"Have you heard the news about Deborah?"

"News travels fast around this town. She's engaged I hear."

"To a doctor."

"I guess all the good bus drivers and construction foremen were taken."

"It still hurts me that you two weren't able to work out your differences."

"That's what Obama said to Israel and Palestine."

"You always were such a cynical boy, Tyler. Your father and I haven't seen you in ages. Why don't you come for dinner tomorrow night, and I'll have Bitty make your favorite dish, crawfish etouffee?"

"I don't know. My schedule's pretty full right now..."

"I spoke to Darlene, and it just so happens you're free tomorrow night. I took the liberty of asking her to put it on your calendar. So, we'll see you tomorrow night then?"

"Looking forward to it," he lied again.

Tyler hung up the phone and found the number for Don Abbott, the school superintendent. He dialed the number absent mindedly, moving the piles of scattered papers from the left side of the desk to the right side and vice versa. A recorded message greeted him.

"Welcome to the Savannah-Chatham County Public School System. Press one for English, dos por Espanol."

After wearing out the keypad with automated choices, he found a live operator. "Don Abbott, please."

"One moment, I'll connect." Tyler waited for what seemed like an interminable amount of time before a second lifeless female voice answered.

"Schools."

"Don Abbott, please," Tyler repeated patiently. There is something worse than being a lawyer he decided. He could be working for the city government. How about an attorney for the city government? *That job would really suck…*

"Don Abbott."

"Don, Tyler Marshall returning your call."

"Tyler, thanks for getting back to me so quickly. I was wondering if you and I could get together this afternoon. I have a proposition which might require the use of your services."

"Let me check my calendar." A quick glance revealed the calendar to be empty for the remainder of the afternoon. "How about three o'clock?"

"I can't do three o'clock. We have a staff meeting. Can you make it later, say four?"

"Sorry, I've got a conflict then." Tyler had no such conflict, but if there was anything he learned from his father is that for an attorney, the next best thing to being busy was to appear busy, especially to a prospective client. "I could do five-thirty if it won't take too long. I have a dinner meeting with a client." It was more like drinks with Annie, but why split hairs he thought to himself.

"It shouldn't take more than an hour or so."

"That sounds fine. So, I'll see you here at my office."

"If you don't mind, can we pick a place with a little more privacy? Tyler, what I want to talk to you about is strictly confidential."

"That's not a problem, but you don't have to worry about that here in this office."

"I know that, Tyler, but just the same, there are other people with me."

"What other people?"

"I'd rather not get into it over the phone. I don't mean to be melodramatic. It's just that this is a sensitive issue, and we want to be as discreet as possible. I'll explain it when we talk."

"How about my house? I only live a couple of blocks from the office."

"You're single now, right?"

"Yep, have been for a year now."

"Have you heard about Deborah?"

"Yes, Don, I've heard about her and the good doctor."

"Oh, sorry, that wasn't very tactful on my part. We'll see you at your house at five-thirty."

Tyler hung up the phone feeling slightly annoyed that Abbott had something so confidential that he couldn't share it over the phone. It never ceased to amaze him how clients could be so dramatic sometimes.

CHAPTER TWO

Tyler arrived home that afternoon slightly after five-thirty to find a four-door black SUV parked in his driveway with the motor running. The temperature had begun to cool a bit as the sun sank slowly into the horizon, but the four suited gentlemen in the car elected to remain under the protection of tinted windows and air-conditioning. Tyler recognized each of the car's occupants as they climbed out to greet him: Charles Mosely, the Savannah-Chatham County police commissioner; Sam Katz, the CEO of Savannah Regional Hospital and a prominent fund-raiser in the city's large and prosperous Jewish community; Robert Murphy, one of four magistrates for Chatham County and an old friend of Tyler's father; and Don Abbott, the superintendent of Savannah-Chatham County public schools.

"Gentlemen, if this is about my lapsed membership in the Chamber of Commerce you could have just sent me a friendly reminder in the mail," quipped Tyler. The four men stared back at him uneasily. "That was a joke guys," he said to the stone-faced men. They didn't seem to be in a joking mood. "Forget about it. What can I do for you gentlemen?"

"Tyler, do you mind if we go inside first?" asked Don Abbott.

"Of course. Sorry to jump the gun. I'm just not used to having such distinguished company." He led them into the house and past the kitchen, hoping they wouldn't notice the empty scotch bottle resting on the kitchen counter or the dead soldiers of Corona in the trashcan, until they arrived at the study, which was located in the back corner of the house overlooking the garden. The azaleas were in full bloom, bursting with vibrant hues of red, white and pink, intermingled with one another to form one continuous blanket of spectacular color. The room itself reeked of masculinity—judges paneling stained a deep mahogany formed the perimeter walls and leather-bound copies of various legal texts and original collectors' editions of rare books worth a small fortune lined the bookshelves.

"Can I get anyone a drink?" Tyler asked as he ushered them to a small conference table at the center of the room. "I'm having a scotch, myself."

After pouring bourbon for the judge and three ice waters for his associates, Tyler took a seat behind his desk, a restored eighteenth-century Chippendale.

"Now, what is it that I can do for you gentlemen?"

It was evident by the way the others deferred to him that Don Abbott was in charge. Abbott's father had once been mayor of Savannah with the full support and political backing of Tyler's father, and it had been rumored for some time that he was positioning for a run at the office himself in the upcoming election. He was a frail-looking man with a pasty white complexion and long slender hands that looked almost effeminate. His eyes were sunken in their sockets, and he had a long, aquiline nose on which rested a pair of wire-rimmed glasses, giving him the appearance of a schoolteacher, which in fact he was before his recent tenure as superintendent. He reminded Tyler of Ichabod Crane.

"Tyler, I think I expressed to you how important confidentiality is in this matter. It's critical that this conversation is kept in the strictest confidence. None of what we say here should leave this room."

"You've all known me for a long time. I'm sure that won't be a problem."

"That's why we're here talking to you instead of someone else," said Robert Murphy. Tyler didn't know Bob Murphy all that well, but he knew that Murphy supported his father many years ago in his unsuccessful bid for governor, and his father had repaid that debt by helping him in his election for magistrate. A portly man in his early sixties, he had a large, bulbous red nose that comes only from years of hard drinking. Murphy was a tough old Irishman from one of Savannah's original Irish-Protestant families and last year was Grand Marshall of the St. Patrick's Day parade, one of the largest St. Patrick's Day parades in the country and a long-standing Savannah tradition. He was also a no-nonsense judge, extremely capable and well regarded in the town's legal community.

"Tyler, your firm specializes in trusts, isn't that correct?" asked Abbott.

"That's one of our areas of expertise. We've helped a lot of folks in this town with their estate planning needs—wills, children's trusts, that sort of thing."

"Great. We want to set up a sort of a trust, if you will—a philanthropic trust. We're also looking for someone to act as the administrator or trustee."

"That sounds like something we might be able to help you with. What kind of philanthropy is it?"

"It's a bit unique. We're pretty sure it's something that's never been done before, but we're not aware of any legal implications which might prevent us from accomplishing our goals, are we Bob?"

"There are no legal concerns whatsoever," replied Murphy.

Tyler was confused. "I don't get it. Why would there be legal concerns over a philanthropic venture?"

Abbott leaned forward in his chair. "I think it's important that we get right to the point, so here it is. We propose to offer any male or female citizen of Chatham County the sum of fifteen thousand dollars to voluntarily undergo a vasectomy or a tubal ligation in addition to paying the cost of the operation itself. This offer will be made available to the first ten thousand qualified applicants. To be considered, the individual must be between the ages of sixteen and forty, live in Chatham County and supply documentation that the surgery was successfully performed. Applicants under eighteen will be required to have a permission form signed by their parents. We propose to set up an account at First Bank of Savannah with a balance of one hundred fifty million dollars to initially fund the project, although we may increase the investment as the success of the project dictates. As executor of the trust, your duties would involve the disbursement of monies, marketing, advertising and any and all public relations duties that may arise. In no event is anyone under any circumstance to learn of the involvement of the men here in this room with this project. You would be the sole contact to the public in all cases."

"One hundred fifty million dollars! Where in the world did y'all get that kind of money?" Tyler was conscious of his southern drawl, which manifested itself whenever he got excited.

"Where we got the money is a subject that falls under the category of classified information, and we're not able to share that with you, I'm afraid. Suffice it to say that some very influential individuals are behind this and support our efforts."

"I don't understand. Why in the world would you want to do this?"

"Because of our different backgrounds, we each have our own unique perspective. I thought maybe we could speak individually to you about our motives, so you can get a clearer picture. Is that okay with you?"

"That sounds like a great place to start," said Tyler, puzzled.

"Then I'll start off," said Abbott. "We believe that many of the societal problems we are experiencing in Savannah—crime, poverty, illiteracy and child abuse—place a hefty financial burden on the taxpaying citizens of our county. We also believe those problems can be traced to one root cause—unfit parents. When I use the word unfit, I mean financially or psychologically unfit. Numerous studies have shown that children who are victims of child abuse are very likely to become abusers themselves—that would fit the definition of a psychologically unfit parent. Then there are the studies showing causation between crime rates and income inequality rates, which may indicate parents who are financially unfit. Income inequality is obviously caused by many different factors including racism and sexism, but without question illiteracy and lack of education contribute greatly to income inequality in this country. As a lifelong educator, I'm concerned about these last two in particular. The world is becoming an increasingly competitive place with countries like China and India putting a huge emphasis on education with a specific focus on science and technology. Meanwhile, fourteen percent of Georgia's high school students drop out before graduating even though their education is being provided free of charge. I'll spare you the statistics on joblessness and expected wages for high school dropouts, but it's not a pretty picture. Based upon my experience as a school administrator, many of the students who drop out come from households where educational achievement is not valued. In many cases the parent or parents never graduated from high school themselves. The other big factor for dropouts is pregnancy. Girls withdraw from school to have a baby, and we never see them again, which leaves them in the job market with no skills and a child to support. And so the cycle of economic hopelessness begins again for the next generation."

"So you would be okay sterilizing a sixteen year old girl just to keep her from getting pregnant? Isn't that a little drastic?"

"I would be okay with it, providing she and her parents both agreed. If it keeps her in school and helps her make a decent life for herself, why not? She could always have surgery to reverse the procedure later when she's in a better position to start a family."

"There's no guarantee that surgery would be successful, is there?"

"No there's not, but I believe the reward is worth the potential risk, and she would have to understand that risk up front. We would obviously want people to have the necessary information in order to make informed decisions. That's pretty much it from my perspective," he said, turning his head in the direction of Murphy. "Bob, why don't you share with Tyler some of your thoughts?"

"Don's already touched on the crime factor. That's the part that concerns me the most. Crime today drains about five percent from our economy when you factor in the cost of prisons, the court system, security guards, insurance premiums, higher retail costs due to theft and things like that."

"Haven't crime rates been coming down the past few years?" asked Tyler.

"They have. There have been numerous studies that have tried to explain why crime rates are falling: more prisons, greater police presence, harsher sentences, healthier economy but each of these factors don't hold up under scrutiny. There is one study though that provides a fairly radical explanation for the recent drop in crime."

"What's that?"

"Legalized abortion."

"I'm not following you."

"Two researchers, Steven Levitt and John Donahue, reported some years ago that the national drop in crime came around the time when the first generation of terminated pregnancies would have entered the peak ages of criminal activity, eighteen to twenty-four, in the early 1990s after the Roe v. Wade decision in 1973. California and New York both legalized abortions prior to 1973 and experienced a drop in their crime rates before the rest of the nation. The premise was that women who were more at risk of having children who might later engage in crime might opt for abortions. These women may be teenagers, they might be living at or below poverty level, their pregnancies might be unwanted or they may fall into some combination of these situations. While teenagers and those near the poverty level could potentially be described as unfit parents, it's the parents of unwanted children I'm most concerned about. Don spoke to you about psychologically and financially unfit parents, but the group he didn't mention was disinterested parents, parents that give birth to unwanted children. You see, I believe that a woman or a man can still provide love and nurturing to a child regardless of age or social stature, though the odds may be against them, but I can't imagine what it must be like for a child to grow up with a parent or parents who regret their very existence. That is, assuming they're not put up for adoption. Today there are about four hundred thousand American children in foster care facilities. You're well aware of the controversy over abortion that still rages on today, more than thirty years after the Roe v. Wade decision, but this project we're talking to you about in many ways is a viable alternative. In our opinion, the prevention of pregnancies is a much less controversial subject than the termination of them."

"But if the goal is to prevent pregnancies, why not just promote abstinence or birth control? That seems a lot easier and cheaper too."

"I'll take that one," said Sam Katz, the hospital CEO. His small stature, protruding ears and round, animated eyes combined with an inexhaustible supply of energy gave one the impression of a mouse. "You're right Tyler, abstinence or birth control are cheaper and easier solutions but they're not always practical or effective. Various religious groups have been very proactive in attacking any attempts to promote birth control among today's youth. In some cases they have initiated their own campaigns to discredit the use of condoms, birth control pills and other forms of contraceptive drugs and devices. They are constantly pressuring the federal government to limit funding for family-planning initiatives and to make it easier for insurance companies and Medicaid to deny coverage for prescription contraceptives. In place of birth control initiatives, they want to promote abstinence, which is just not practical. If you tell them 'Don't do drugs,' or 'Don't have sex,' you've made it all the more likely that they're going to do just that."

"That makes sense I guess," admitted Tyler. "Some of those religious groups you're talking about, though, have a lot of power in this country. If they're putting up that much of a fight against birth control, what are they going to say about this voluntary sterilization idea?"

The four men shifted uneasily in their chairs. He had obviously asked the right question, one for which they didn't have a ready-made answer. Abbot was the first to speak. "It's in all of our best interests to keep this under the radar as much as possible, but generally speaking, these religious groups have pretty much conceded an individual's right to use birth control methods. They may try to discredit the use of condoms, but you don't see them picketing against the sale of them outside of local drug stores or, for that matter, local vasectomy clinics. They may not like our program much, but we don't expect aggressive opposition."

"Charles, what about you?" asked Tyler. "It seems I have everyone's two cents except for yours."

Mosely's three compatriots eyed him warily. They knew he was the weak link in the chain, the least enthusiastic of the four. They had even considered excluding him from the meeting with Tyler, but the old man had insisted they stick together.

"I admit I had some reservations when I first heard about the idea," Mosely said. "But I've been a cop for a long time. Unfortunately, a lot of the criminals I send to prison are the children of criminals I've dealt with in years past. Deep down, I know these kids never really had a chance. They were born to be criminals like you were probably born to be a lawyer, and there's not a whole lot that Don or Sam or Bob or I or anyone else for that matter could have done to help them. In our society we require people to have a license to hunt, fish, drive a car and own a handgun, but anyone can make a baby at any time without a second thought as to how they're going to care for it. For the unlucky few, the ones that I deal with on a regular basis, they're pretty much on their own."

The plan seemed so outrageous to Tyler that at first he thought it might be a joke. Their determined resolve convinced him otherwise. They were dead serious. "I think I pretty much get the drift here," he said. "Let me summarize what I think I heard, and you guys tell me if I'm off base. You want to offer fifteen thousand dollars to any citizen who agrees to a vasectomy or tubal ligation. This amount is probably not enough to attract white-collar, college-educated types but is a pretty strong incentive for someone who is socio-economically less fortunate. The money is coming from some deep-pocketed source or sources that want to try to limit certain undesirables, people who fit a profile of being potentially unfit parents, from having children in the future. If successful, society gains by having less crime and poverty and, on average, better-educated and more well-adjusted youth."

"For one hundred words or less, I'd say that's a very good summary," said Abbott.

"So what happens if it doesn't work?" asked Tyler. "What happens if the people you think would make unfit parents want children so bad, they don't take your money?"

"That's okay, Tyler," said Murphy. "Remember, it's not our decision, it's theirs. And if they really want to have children, they'll probably make good parents someday. It's those who don't feel strongly about having children who would be our most likely candidates, and that could be a good thing."

"Wouldn't women be better off becoming egg donors? That pays good money these days."

"Recipients of those types of programs are looking carefully at the donor's educational background, skill sets and certain traits or characteristics which not everyone has," answered Katz. "This is an experiment, Tyler. It's possible that our assumptions are all wrong. We really won't know until we try."

"And if your assumptions are wrong?" asked Tyler.

"If our assumptions are wrong, then this ends as nothing more than a failed experiment." said Katz, smiling. "A very expensive failed experiment."

"And if your assumptions are right?"

"I'm not sure that the lines between success and failure will be so clearly defined," said Abbott, "but depending on the end results, I assume our benefactors would try something like this in other cities here in America and possibly abroad. As Sam mentioned, we won't know until we try."

"This all sounds controversial to me. How can you be sure I won't have a bunch of demonstrators in my front yard? It seems like some religious groups or maybe civil rights groups would jump all over something like this. That would not be good for business. We're an old, staid, conservative law firm."

"That's one of the reasons we picked you as our first choice," said Abbott. "You and your firm have an excellent reputation in this town, and you're known for your discretion. Believe me, none of us want to see this turn into some sort of public spectacle. Of course, we would compensate you handsomely for your services."

"It's not an issue of money," Tyler lied. "I'd have to get comfortable with this proposition before I'd be prepared to discuss financial arrangements."

"We're prepared to pay you a retainer of thirty-five thousand dollars per month."

"That's very generous of you, but I just can't ignore my practice." The irony of that statement seemed to hang in the air, naked and exposed. Ignoring his practice was all he had been doing for the past twelve months. *Annie would've had a good laugh over that one!*

"You don't have to ignore anything. We don't expect you to devote all of your time to this. Just put some feelers out in the community, verify that the operations were performed, collect the data and cut the checks. That's all you have to do."

Tyler couldn't help but think about the money. Thirty-five thousand dollars a month would get the creditors off his back. He could bring the mortgage current and have money to spare within a few months. He would have to discuss this with his father, who was still a partner in the firm. What would his reaction be? This proposal seemed way too radical and potentially controversial for his father's conservative viewpoint. In that event, would he dare go against his father's wishes? He'd done it before, and, as managing partner, the decision was ultimately his. Still, the whole idea seemed crazy and more than a little dangerous.

"I don't know guys. I'm going to need some time to think about this."

"That's fine," said Murphy. "You don't have to give us an answer today. This is a big decision, and we don't expect you to take it lightly. It's important that you're fully committed because there may be some bumps down the road, and we don't want you having second thoughts once we've begun. It takes a certain kind of man to accomplish extraordinary feats, and we all believe that you're the right man for the job. That's why we're here today. We have a lot of faith in you, Tyler."

Tyler looked into the eyes of Robert Murphy and saw a man completely at peace with himself. He envied his serenity. "I'll think about it."

"That's all we ask."

The four men filed out of the study, stopping to shake Tyler's hand. Last to leave was Murphy. "Remember what I said about being the right man for the job. Your father would be proud of you."

Tyler wasn't so sure about that.

It was close to seven-thirty by the time Tyler made it to O'Brien's, a quaint Irish pub located down on the riverfront with distressed brick walls, giving it the look of the old dock-front warehouse it once was. That was until some enterprising Irishman figured it was more profitable to sell beer to the crews of the visiting shipping vessels than it was to stow their unloaded cargo. Annie was well into her second drink when Tyler spotted her at a table toward the back. With her was a very attractive woman, late twenties, with jet black hair tied in a bun and iridescent blue eyes behind black, thick-rimmed glasses. She wore a long skirt and Birkenstock sandals giving her a certain bohemian look, definitely not his type but a significant improvement over Annie's last stab at matchmaking.

"Tyler, this is a friend of mine, Mara Dressler," said Annie.

"Nice to meet you, Mara."

"Likewise, Tyler," she said extending her hand in a firm handshake. She had a warm, intoxicating kind of smile, and her eyes locked intently on his, causing him to momentarily look away. His first impression of her was of someone highly aggressive, very open or both. Either way he felt slightly intimidated by her.

"You don't have cats, do you?" he asked, as Annie kicked him sharply under the table.

"I'm afraid I'm allergic to them. Why do you ask?"

"No particular reason. It seems we have something in common. I'm allergic to them as well."

"I dated a guy one time who thought I was his soul mate because we both used the same kind of toothbrush. You're not weird like that are you?"

"I hope not," he said, laughing.

"Annie's told me so much about you," Mara said.

"That puts me at a severe disadvantage I'm afraid. I know nothing at all about you. What do you do for a living?"

"Mara works for the Division of Family and Children Services, better known as DFACS," Annie interrupted. "I was doing some pro bono work, and one of my clients was lucky enough to have Mara as her caseworker. The client worked two jobs and had to leave her two youngest children unattended for three hours a day after school before their grandmother came home from work. A jilted boyfriend turned her into the agency, and I ended up representing her. Mara found her a higher paying job, which allowed her to quit the second job, so she could be home with the kids."

"I'm impressed," said Tyler. "No offense Mara, but all you read about DFACS in the paper are articles about the number of cases that go uninvestigated. I don't think I've ever read a single story like the one Annie just described. Maybe you could use a good publicist?"

"Every now and then, we're lucky enough to make a difference in people's lives, but that doesn't sell newspapers, I'm afraid," Mara said. "We're woefully understaffed and underpaid, and it can be a very depressing job at times. Too often, when we get involved, it's too late to help."

"So you're a masochist then?"

"I prefer the term, hopeless optimist."

"A genuine do-gooder! I didn't know there were any of you left in the world, besides Annie here of course."

"There are a few of us left, believe it or not. Of course, we hold clandestine meetings to protect our identity from the cynics for fear of being exposed and publicly ridiculed. Tell me Tyler, what do you believe in?"

"Tyler doesn't believe in anything," said Annie.

"That's not true. I believe I'll have a drink. A Corona and a shot of Don Julio please," said Tyler, flagging the waitress. "So tell me Mara, how exactly did you end up at DFACS?"

"I graduated from the College of Charleston with a degree in Sociology, which I soon found as useful as snow tires in South Carolina. I was engaged to a terribly dull guy from The Citadel who was going to work for his daddy in Charleston and make piles of money. I could see my life all laid out so clearly in front of me—a nice home on The Battery, two spoiled but beautiful children, dinner at the club on Friday nights with his parents and a summer home in the North Carolina mountains. As we got closer and closer to the wedding, I started feeling claustrophobic, like I couldn't breathe. One night I had a dream that I was living in this beautiful historic home facing the harbor with bars on the windows. I tried to leave through the front door, but it was locked from the outside. I checked the back door, but it was locked from the outside as well. I picked up the phone to call for help, but the line was dead. It seemed that I was a prisoner in my own home. I woke up the next morning and called off the wedding. I figured it wasn't a very healthy sign that I viewed my upcoming nuptials as a prison sentence of some sort. After our break-up, he became reacquainted with a girl he knew in high school and was married within a year. He was determined to cross that one off his to-do list no matter what, I guess. Married—check. Finding myself suddenly single, I had to get a job, and this was about all my degree qualified me for, besides waiting tables that is. Come to think of it, waiting tables probably pays better."

"Any regrets?"

"Not a solitary one. I think everyone has a need for a purpose-driven life, a reason for being if you will, in order to feel fulfilled or satisfied. I would never have had that if I stayed in Charleston. My job is plenty frustrating, don't get me wrong, but I really do feel like I can make a difference in people's lives, and that's enough for me."

"I envy your conviction. Not everyone is so lucky."

Mara shrugged. "Luck doesn't have anything to do with it. Sometimes you just have to be prepared to make sacrifices in order to reap the rewards."

"Like working for minimum wage?"

"Could be. Everyone has his or her own hot buttons. Making a career out of something you're passionate about, that's pretty much what you describe as luck. Only it's not luck. It's having the self-awareness to recognize and understand your passions."

"Tyler's not passionate about anything," said Annie.

"Annie, remind me not to call you as my character witness if I'm ever on trial for murder," said Tyler testily. Annie smiled sweetly back in response.

"So what's *your* story, Tyler?" asked Mara.

"I assume Annie has already filled you in on my numerous deficiencies?"

"Most of them," Mara admitted. "At least I hope that was most of them."

"Just for curiosity's sake, what was my most glaring weakness on Annie's top ten list?"

"She says you're a lost soul, drifting along aimlessly in life, with no sense of purpose. Would you agree with that assessment?"

"Wouldn't matter if I agreed or not. If Annie says it, then it must be so. Not something that looks very impressive on a resume is it?"

"There's nothing wrong with being lost as long as you're smart enough to realize it and aren't afraid to stop and ask directions every now and then."

"That's not something that the male species is all that adept at unfortunately."

"Which? Admitting you're lost or stopping to ask directions?"

"Either one. My story is probably the opposite of yours. Your fiancé—that was me. Like my father before me, I graduated from the University of Georgia, went to law school at Emory and started working in the family practice right after graduation. I married a girl with what my parents considered the right pedigree, someone who wasn't so frightened at the idea of being locked in prison. Actually, I think she rather liked the idea. We went to our club on Friday nights—they have a delicious beef tenderloin on Fridays—attended parties hosted by those she deemed socially acceptable. She became secretary of the Junior League while I concentrated on work, and we grew completely bored with each other. Anyway, she married me for better or worse, at least until she found something better, which as it turned out, was a doctor. I was never upwardly mobile or ambitious enough for her."

"How sad," Mara remarked.

"Who me?"

"No, your ex-wife. She sounds very shallow from what you say and from what Annie has told me."

"Maybe so. I can't be too critical though. I did marry her."

"Why?"

"I don't know. It seemed like the right thing to do at the time. We grew up in the same social circles, and our families were friendly. Everyone expected us to get married."

"Have you always done what people expected you to do?"

"I don't know if I would go that far..."

"Excuse me?" asked Annie.

"Well maybe a little…"

"Come again?" pressed Annie.

"Yeah, I've pretty much done what people expected of me my entire life, and that's why I'm so fucking miserable. There, are you satisfied now, Annie? Jesus, sometimes it's like I'm walking around with this great big angel on my shoulder whispering in my ear. Who do you think you are—my conscience or something?"

"Be glad you have a conscience," said Annie. "Otherwise, you'd be beyond hope."

"Maybe that's the key, Tyler," said Mara. "Perhaps the next time you're faced with a big decision you should do the opposite of what everyone else expects. It worked for me."

"Me too," said Annie. "If I did what everyone else expected when I was in high school, I'd probably be a housekeeper today like my mother. And unlike some people I know, I actually enjoy being an attorney."

"To each his own," said Tyler. "Mara, I appreciate the advice, but contrary to what Annie may have told you about me, I'm really pretty happy with my life. I have a nice house, a decent job, good health, good friends, and I've never been arrested for anything. What's so wrong with that?"

"Nothing's wrong with that, if that's what you want."

"What's that supposed to mean?"

"Tell me, Tyler, are you bored?"

He started to respond but shot a quick glance at Annie and thought better of it. No use denying it with the conscience police on patrol. "Yeah, maybe a little bit, but that's not so bad."

"Really? I can't imagine anything worse. If you're not passionate about what you do, then you're just checking things off a list like you do when you shop for groceries. That's what my fiancé did. And once you fill up the cart all you have is a bunch of food. That food may provide you basic sustenance, but it doesn't bring you happiness. To find true happiness, you need to feed your soul, not your body. And to feed your soul you must first find the passion that's inside you. Boredom is the enemy. It inhibits passion, deprives the soul of nourishment and makes each of us less human, less alive. Once you've accepted boredom as part of your life, you may as well start counting down your remaining days until death because there's not much else to look forward to."

"Did you learn that in sociology?"

"Some of it. I figured most of it out on my own. I see the same vacant stares every day in the faces of the people at work. They long ago abandoned their dreams and surrendered their passions. Now they're just going through the motions like the walking dead, human zombies. They don't believe in anything any more, and that's the point when they become most dangerous...to themselves."

"This is starting to feel a bit like a lecture. Why are we having this conversation?"

"Because I recognize that same look on your face, Tyler," said Mara.

Tyler recalled little else of the conversation after that. He sat and suffered the infuriating banality of polite conversation just long enough to finish his drink before making up some lame excuse like needing to catch up on some work at home. He felt frustration and anger building inside and needed to leave before he said or did something he would regret later. Public demonstrations were not part of his genetic make-up. Where did this woman get off psychoanalyzing him? She didn't even know him! He was furious with Annie for setting him up with this amateur shrink and feeding her a detailed list of his supposed deficiencies. It was one thing for Annie to criticize him. They'd known each other since childhood, but it was quite another to be subject to the barbed scrutiny of a complete stranger. He didn't understand or pretended not to acknowledge the one thing that upset him most. Mara's words stung not because of the source or the conspiracy behind them but because they were grounded in truth.

Once home, he turned on a baseball game on TV. There was no beer in the kitchen refrigerator or the one in the garage, and he'd apparently finished the last of the Scotch the night before. The only alcohol he could find was a bottle of cooking sherry in the pantry. The high salt content made him grimace at first, but after a few sips and a bag of chips to wash it down, he grew accustomed to the taste. He felt his anger subside as the wine doused the fire raging inside of him and smoothed the sharp, prodding edges of his resentment. As he found the bottom of the bottle and the game rolled into the late innings he drifted off to sleep and dreamed of human zombies.

CHAPTER THREE

Tyler confronted Annie the next day in her office. The salt in last night's sherry had left him dehydrated, while the sugar lent an acute edge to his hangover, giving him a piercing headache and making him more irritable than usual.

"What the hell was that about last night?"

Annie looked up from a large file on her desk, distracted. "What do you mean?"

"You invited me for drinks, Annie. You didn't say anything about the free, unsolicited psychological evaluation from some goth social worker who thinks she's got all the answers to the world's problems."

"She's not goth—they wear all black."

"Whatever. You ambushed me. I expected more from you."

"What did I do? I thought you might like to meet an attractive, single, self-assured woman with more than half a brain. Excuse me if that's not what you're looking for. Next time I'll take you to Hooters for chicken wings. I'm sure all the girls there will tell you how smart and good-looking you are. Is that what you want?"

"That's not what I meant, and you know it."

"Really? What did you mean, Tyler?"

"Last night felt like the Spanish Inquisition, and I was the one on the rack. All we talked about were my inadequacies, and you could have stood up for me."

"Why do you think she was there in the first place? Do you think I told her I had some deadbeat boss with no personality that she just had to meet?"

"Then what did you tell her?"

"I told her you were a great guy with everything going for you, but you were struggling with some…internal demons, and you needed some help finding your way."

"Ah, yes, the lost-soul campaign. Really, Annie, don't you think that's a bit much?"

"You are a lost soul. You're sleepwalking through life, and everyone seems to know it but you. You don't like your job, your family, your now ex-wife, and you're drinking entirely too much. You're obviously unhappy right now, but most people would kill to be in your shoes. If that's not lost, I don't know what is."

"So you thought this sociology major could fix me?"

"I thought it might be good for you to meet someone who would challenge you. Someone who could bring you out of that man cave you've been hiding in. Lord knows I've tried and failed."

"I appreciate your efforts at reforming me, Annie, but tell me, how's your love life these days?"

"We're not talking about me."

"Maybe we should. When was the last healthy relationship you were in?"

"It's different for me. The pool of eligible college-educated black men with decent jobs in this town is about as shallow as your ex-wife and besides, I'm happy with all other aspects of my life. I'm focused on my career, and I love being an attorney. I've worked my ass off to get where I am today, and I don't take that for granted for one second like you seem to. I don't need a man to bring me happiness."

"And who says I need a woman to make me happy?"

"No one, but if you're not willing to change your attitude, then you should probably find something else that does—other than Scotch."

"At least Johnny Walker doesn't point out all of my shortcomings to the single women I meet."

"He doesn't have to. With his help, you do a good enough job of that on your own."

"Very funny. Just cut me a little slack, Annie. I'm going through a tough time right now, that's all. I'll bounce back before long. I always do."

"I hope you're right, Tyler. I'm rooting for you. And for what it's worth, Mara's interested, if you want to call her."

"Between you and my mother, I already have enough women in my life trying to fix me, thanks."

"Suit yourself," said Annie, "it's your life."

Tyler arrived that evening at his parents' house, which was an hour south of town. The house was located in an area known as The Marshes of Glynn, named after a poem by the Georgia poet, Sydney Lanier. The area served as a luxurious suburb for several grand plantations dotting the Low Country, as the locals refer to the vast, open low-lying terrain etched by tidal creeks and endless marshes that line the Atlantic Ocean from Charleston, South Carolina to St. Marys, Georgia, south of Savannah. The plantation houses in the area are relics of the day when cotton was king in the South.

The house itself was typical of ante-bellum construction throughout the South, its stately white columns buttressing the high, steeply-pitched black shingle roof and widow's walk from which one could, on a clear day, view the sea and the passing ships making their way in and out of the port to the north. The house was constructed entirely of clapboard, restored to its original condition, with black hurricane shutters silhouetted against a snow-white background. A row of rocking chairs was arranged on the spacious veranda, so one could sit quietly and stare out over the vast expanse of land on which the house is situated. With over twenty acres of gently rolling, arable terrain surrounded by soggy marshland, the house could best be described as a gentleman's estate as there were no horses or cattle grazing on its premises, nor had crops of any form been seen since before the Civil War.

Approximately thirty yards off to the side of the main house was a smaller, quaint brick house surrounded by a clean, freshly painted white picket fence. Built as slave quarters by its original owner, the house had served as a guest house for several years until guests became less and less frequent, and Bitty, Annie's mother, began having trouble commuting from her house in town due to her increasing frailness. The decision was made to move Bitty out to the estate permanently, and the small brick house had served as her home for the past five years. Tyler's parents and Bitty, living together in relative seclusion, made for an odd piece of imagery, fading remnants of the South's once proud aristocracy. The wealthy landowners and lifelong servant lived side by side in blissful harmony, a nostalgic ode to a bygone era, as they shared the fading evening of their lives together while the rest of the modern world rushed past them, too busy to notice.

Finding the door locked, Tyler rang the doorbell of the great old house and was greeted by Bitty. Her legal name was Flora Mae Burris, but people had called her Bitty for as long as Tyler could remember. Bitty was short for Itty Bitty, which aptly described her appearance—five feet tall and a hundred pounds soaking wet. She had a head of closely cropped gray hair and deeply etched crow's feet at the corners of her eyes, which still glimmered dark with mischief. Bitty had eight children by four different fathers but steadfastly refused to marry any of them, saying she didn't need a man to take care of her or her children. She was perfectly capable of doing that on her own. Annie was the youngest of the siblings and the only one who had never known her father. Bitty encouraged her children to maintain relationships with their respective fathers but simply refused to even talk to Annie about hers. Tyler always assumed this was the primary driving forces behind Annie's relentless ambition, like she had something to prove to a man who had repudiated her. In fact, Annie was the first and only of her brothers and sisters to graduate from college.

"Look what the cat dragged in. It's my little Ty!" said Bitty smiling. "We don't see you around here much anymore, baby. I reckon you've gone and holed up with some pretty young thing and don't have time for us old folks anymore. Is that it?"

"You know that's not true, Bitty," said Tyler. "I've always got time for the woman who taught me how to fish and hit a curve ball—fat lot of good either of those ever did for me."

Bitty's mouth turned up at the corner in a wry smile. "I suppose I shoulda been schoolin' you on some other things instead. I take that to mean there ain't no pretty young thing in the picture?'

"Don't start on me, Bitty. I'm already taking enough crap from Momma and your daughter."

"My daughter needs to be lookin' after her own self. Girl's bright as a country sunrise but treats men like they got a disease or somethin'. I suppose she's afraid a man's gonna slow her down from gettin' to the top, though for the life of me, I can't figure out why she's in such an all-fired hurry."

"For some reason we've been butting heads more than usual lately. I don't know why she's been on my case so much."

"Been like that since you both were kids, I suppose. She always wanted what you had and never could understand why it was you didn't."

"I'd say that's pretty descriptive of our relationship today. She really needs to get over that. Can't you talk to her?"

"You think she listens to me? Ms. College-Educated Lawyer is gonna listen to old Bitty, the housekeeper?"

"Forget it. I can handle Annie. I just let her lecture me until she tires out. Speaking of lecturing, where are they?"

"Your parents? They're in the parlor havin' a cocktail before dinner. You want one?"

"Bitty, have you ever known me to join my parents for a night of stimulating conversation without having a couple of shots first?"

"Scotch on the rocks comin' right up."

Tyler made his way to the parlor, which was located directly off the large spacious hallway that ran the length of the house. The parlor functioned as a sitting room with a couple of high-backed Queen Anne wing chairs and a stiff, uncomfortable Sheraton sofa with accompanying sideboard, facing a fireplace made of Italian marble. The floor was the same original random-planked wood found throughout the house, a light beige bleached yellow by years of sunshine that streaked through the massive open windows. Covering the floor was an eighteenth century Persian Sarouk rug, lending an international flavor to the traditional décor of the room. Above the fireplace was a portrait of Tyler I, Tyler's great-grandfather, glaring fiercely down upon the occupants of the room. Tyler I ran booze through several of the southern ports during Prohibition in the 1920's earning the small fortune that his heirs would later parlay into more respectable pursuits. The menacing portrait and the stiff, formal furniture lent the room a feeling that could hardly be described as comfortable.

"Hello, Momma, Dad," Tyler said, entering the room. "How y'all doing?"

Cecil Marshall rose to greet him with a stiff hug and a peck on the cheek. The former Cecil Pennington, daughter of the pulp and paper Penningtons, was Savannah society through and through and still dressed for dinner, wearing a St. John textured knit suit and a strand of cultured pearls around her neck. Tyler's father was wearing a blue blazer and tan dress slacks with a long-sleeved shirt. When in their presence, Tyler continually found himself reminded of the generational gap between his parents and himself. An only child, his parents were in their early forties when they had him. Bitty had once told Tyler that after years of trying to conceive, a doctor informed Tyler's father that he was likely sterile due to exposure to toxins as a result of his service during the Korean War. Believing that a successful pregnancy was impossible, his parents simply quit trying until one day a miracle occurred, and they found themselves expecting.

"Hello, son," said his father, offering a firm handshake.

Tyler could not remember his father ever hugging him.

"So how are things at the office? I'm afraid I don't have that many opportunities to stop by anymore. I feel like I've been neglecting my duties, but I just don't get around as well as I used to these days."

"That's okay. Everything's fine."

"Good to hear. I played golf with Arnold Worthington at the club yesterday. He said you did a top-notch job handling that labor problem for him."

Tyler handled a wrongful termination claim against Worthington's company, Fiber Con, which manufactures fiber optic cable. It was really only a matter of filling out a couple of forms and presenting documentation to the court, something a first-year law student could have easily handled. False praise from his father always put Tyler on edge. It usually meant he was setting him up for something else. "That was nice of Arnold to say."

"I hope you're still being challenged in the practice, Tyler. One should guard against letting things get too stale."

"I agree. So far, that hasn't been a problem. Every now and then I fall into a rut and wonder what I'm doing there, but for the most part I'm happy."

"Your happiness is all your mother and I ever wanted for you, Tyler. We still have very high hopes for you. There's nothing you can't accomplish once you set your sights properly."

Tyler suddenly had the feeling of a rat caught in a trap with a piece of stinky cheese in his hands. "I appreciate your confidence in me."

His father cleared his throat and stiffened in his chair. "I have noticed that billings for the firm are down substantially."

"Yes, well…"

"And I spoke with Tom Grier at the bank. He told me you were two months behind on the mortgage payment for the building. You know I was against refinancing the property in the first place. The old mortgage would have been paid off in five years."

"I know, Dad, but…"

"Tyler, I'm sure I don't need to remind you of the sterling reputation that Marshall and Marshall has built here in the community over the past fifty years. I can't…I won't allow anything to jeopardize that reputation. If it was a matter of money, why didn't you come to me for help?"

"I think I'm going to go in the kitchen and see if Bitty needs any help," said Cecil Marshall, excusing herself. She found it crass to discuss business and quickly disassociated herself from such conversations.

"Look, Dad, everything's under control. We just have a few cash flow problems, that's all. I'm working on a couple of things right now that stand to bring in substantial revenue to the firm. I'm confident that we'll be back on our feet in no time. I appreciate your offer to help, but I can handle it."

"What kind of things are you working on exactly?"

"Well there's the…I've got a contact at…"

"Just what I thought. You don't have a plan at all, do you? Honestly, Tyler, when are you going to grow up?"

The words stung like freezing rain. His father always showed his impatience by treating him like a child. Tyler could handle yelling, but when his father adopted that patronizing tone it made the hairs on the back of his neck stand at attention. "I do have an opportunity that I need to speak to you about. It's highly confidential."

"May I remind you that I'm your father, not to mention your business partner?"

"Of course." Tyler instinctively knew his father would reject the proposal immediately. He wasn't even crazy about the idea himself, but it was the only plan he had for bringing new business to the firm, so he dutifully related the details of the charitable trust to his father.

Once he finished explaining the concept, his father showed no hesitation. "I don't like it. That's not the kind of business we're looking for, son. It's too contentious. That kind of publicity we can do without. Best leave that sort of business to the ambulance chasers of the world."

"It would bring in a substantial amount of revenue to the firm."

"Money is not everything, Tyler. A man must stand on principle, or he has nothing left to stand on. The reputation of the firm is not for sale."

His father's predictability irritated Tyler. He was so set in his ways, so completely close-minded to anything new or different.

"Times are changing, Dad. If we're not willing to change with them, we won't survive. Our sterling reputation is not going to do us any good if we're out of business."

"There are better alternatives."

"Such as?"

"I spoke with Henry Lassiter the other day. He asked about you. It seems he's considering retiring from politics. He's decided not to run for re-election this fall." Lassiter was a four-term state senator for Savannah's second district as well as a long-time political crony of the elder Marshall.

"That's your old seat. Let me guess, the two of you think I would make a great candidate."

"To be honest with you, it was Henry's idea. He wants to make sure his seat falls into capable hands, and you're his first choice for a successor. I'd say that was quite an honor."

"Quite an honor indeed."

"Of course I told him of your reluctance to get into politics."

"And what did he say to that?"

"He thinks maybe you can be persuaded. The organization is all in place to back you, and if we have the right team…"

"We? How did it get to we all of a sudden?"

"Representation in the state legislature is good for business. You'll be exposed to contacts throughout the state who may be in need of our services. You'll also have something everyone else wants—influence."

"Dad, no offense, but the days when you served in the legislature are long passed. The good old boys playing cards and smoking cigars in the back room while they cut deals to line their pockets are dying off. Things don't work like that any more."

"Of course they still work like that. Only the players have changed. Some of those good old boys you speak of have been replaced by men and even women with, how should I say it, darker complexions?"

"You mean African-Americans? What does that have to do with me?"

"If you were a member of the legislature and we promoted Annie to partner, you would both have the inside track to bid on state business, which could open many doors that are closed right now."

"Annie?"

"Why not? She's a damn fine lawyer, and it's about time I recouped my investment in her education."

"She is a great lawyer—better than me. Why don't you run her for public office instead?"

"Someday that may be a possibility, but she's not ready yet. You are, Tyler. It's time you did something with your life, time you made a difference in the world."

"That's what this is really about, isn't it? You don't care about the extra business to the firm. You've already got more money than you know what to do with. This is about me fulfilling some destiny you've got in mind. Well I'm not like you, Dad. Power and influence are two things I don't crave. Why can't you just accept me for who I am instead of trying to make me into someone I can never be?"

"So what do you propose to do? You're not making enough money as a lawyer to support even yourself, let alone a family. That's the real reason Deborah left, wasn't it?"

"You said yourself, Dad, money's not everything. Maybe I don't want a family. I'd say there's already been enough Tyler Marshalls in the world. I'm through doing what you and everyone else expect of me. So far I don't have much to show for it. I will not run for public office. If I have to take the occasional unsavory business to get by, I'm prepared to do just that."

"You know I've never stopped you from running the practice as you saw fit. I've only offered my advice."

"I know that."

"I won't start now. If you choose not to listen to me, so be it. But I will tell you right now, son, if you take that charitable trust on as a client, you'll be making a big mistake."

"I appreciate the advice, Dad. I'll take it under consideration."

Dinner proved to be more tense than usual. Tyler's father hardly spoke throughout the meal, brooding over his failure once again to sway his stubborn son to the side of reason. He stared silently down at his plate throughout dinner rarely looking up while his wife took over as sole inquisitor.

"Tyler, tell us are you seeing anyone special these days?" she asked in a sugar-sweet voice. He caught Bitty's eye, and she winked at him knowingly. *Another scotch!*

"Not really, Momma."

"I spoke with Barbara Andrews yesterday, and it seems her daughter, Alice, is divorcing that doctor from San Francisco and moving back here. You remember Alice, don't you dahlin'?"

"Yes, Momma, I remember Alice. She was cross-eyed and had a nervous twitch that made her head jerk sideways like a parrot. And she kept a stuffed panda bear buckled in the back seat of her car at all times, which she spoke to in the voice of a four-year-old child."

"She wears eyeglasses now Tyler, and she was just a little high strung, that's all. Why do you always have to exaggerate things so? She really is a charming young girl, and I thought the two of you could get reacquainted."

"I appreciate your interest in my love life, but really I'm doing fine on my own. Besides, Alice is just not my type. Thanks anyway though."

"If you're doing so fine on your own Tyler, why is it you don't seem to have a regular lady friend?"

"Because I choose not to at this point in time, that's why," Tyler said, with a touch of irritation in his voice.

"You're not getting any younger, son. Before you know it, there won't be any available women left out there."

"First of all, I'm sure there will always be available women out there. People don't stay together their entire lives like they did when you and Dad were younger. And second, what makes you think I want to find someone to settle down with anyway?"

"You can't go through your life alone. Life is so much more enjoyable when you have someone to share it with, right dear?" she said looking over to Tyler's father who mumbled something unintelligible under his breath.

"I'm sure you and Dad are very happy together, but right now I'm happy being single. You don't need to worry about me."

"I can't help it, son, I worry about you all the time. I don't care what you say, you need to find someone to take care of you."

"I can take care of myself just fine, Momma. Why do people believe that you have to be married to live a fulfilling life? Not all single people are lonely and depressed. So many people get married because they think it's the right thing to do and then spend the rest of their lives in misery. I've already made that mistake once, and I don't intend to repeat it."

"What about children? Don't you want children?"

"Not particularly."

"Sometimes when I think of you throwing your life away, it just makes me sick to my stomach! How can you be so selfish as to not want children?"

"How is not having children selfish? Because I'd be depriving you of grandchildren?"

"Of course your father and I would love to have grandchildren. It's only natural that one would want to leave a legacy behind. Don't you want someone to carry on the family name?"

"Momma, if I don't care about making a name for myself now like Dad says, why would I care about it when I'm gone?"

"I can't believe you can be so flippant about this. Your father and I were heartbroken when we thought we couldn't have children until your father...until we found out that we could. It was one of the most joyous times of our life. I just wish there was some way I could convince you that having children would make your life so much richer."

"It would be nice if just once I could come over here and spend time with the two of you without leaving with the feeling that I'm a total disappointment."

Tyler's father looked up from his plate.

"What are you talking about?" asked his mother.

"Dad's disappointed that I won't run for public office, and I'm not a famous statesman like he was, and that the law firm is struggling under my leadership, and you're disappointed that I'm divorced with no children and no prospects for marriage. I feel like

I'm letting you both down somehow, but the funny thing is I'm where I am today because I tried so hard to do what you both expected of me. I went to law school and joined the family firm without thinking twice about whether that was really the right career for me, and I married Deborah because she was from the right family and you both approved, even though I never loved her. Today all three of us are dissatisfied. That's one hell of a tragic irony, don't you think?"

"We're not disappointed in you, son. We just see your potential," said his father. "Don't sell yourself short."

"That's right, honey," said his mother. "We want you to be happy."

"I know that, but the problem is we all have different definitions of happiness. Someday I hope you'll both accept that mine is the only one that counts."

Tyler thought back to his conversation with Mara. Something she said stuck in his mind. *Maybe the next time you're faced with a big decision, you should do the opposite of what everyone expects.* Subconsciously, he felt himself gravitate to any position opposite his parents, like a rebellious teenager. It was at this moment that he resolved to take on Fresh Start as a client, and he would be its first participant. He might not fit the target profile, but he wouldn't ask of anyone something he wasn't prepared to do himself, and besides, there were already enough Marshalls in the world.

CHAPTER FOUR

Annie finished her morning run at 6:23 A.M. She did the calculation in her head—five miles, averaging less than ten minutes per mile—not too shabby. She covered the same route along the river every day, rain or shine. Annie believed in discipline above all else. Without discipline, she wouldn't be where she was today. Instead, she'd be cleaning toilets and washing windows, like her mother. Not that there was anything wrong with hard work. If anything, Bitty had taught her the importance of giving maximum effort to anything she did, but the discipline—that came from somewhere else. It was discipline that allowed her to study four hours every night after school, despite coming home to a tiny, four-room shotgun style house full of eight kids and the five-by-eight foot bedroom she shared with three sisters. It was discipline that made her avoid the sexual advances of the boys in her neighborhood—a discipline that her three older sisters didn't share, each of them getting pregnant and dropping out of high school before graduation. It was discipline that enabled her to graduate at the top of her class at Fort Valley State, despite having to work a full-time job to pay her expenses, and it was discipline that saw her through law school at Mercer University in Macon despite being one of a select few African-Americans accepted to the school.

Despite this, she knew discipline and hard work would have taken her only so far. She knew she would never have made it to law school without Mr. Marshall's help. He called in a few political favors to guarantee her acceptance to Mercer and helped her financially along the way. Upon graduation from law school, she felt indebted to him and agreed to take a position with his firm despite having received better offers from law firms in Atlanta, practically fighting over themselves to hire capable minorities. It was an interesting dichotomy. The odds were stacked against a black female being accepted into and surviving law school, but once she did, opportunities abounded.

Her early struggles in life and subsequent success made her less tolerant of others' misfortunes. Of her seven older half-brothers and sisters, two brothers had served prison time for various offenses, and one sister was living on welfare, a single mother trying to raise four kids. They grew up in the same environment as Annie with strikingly different results. It all came down to choices, Annie believed, and she didn't feel much sympathy for people who made bad choices in life. She didn't believe in luck—we each make our own luck she liked to say—only hard work and discipline.

She showered and dressed for work and eyed herself in the mirror. She was thirty-two and more than a little self-conscious about her appearance. The five miles of daily roadwork clearly showed on her taut, lithesome body. Every day she looked for signs of wrinkles on her face but the image reflecting back at her showed none yet. She looked closely at the light-complexioned face in the mirror and found her thoughts wandering to the white father her mother had refused to discuss until the day Annie graduated from law school. "I guess you got a right to know," she had said reluctantly. "Maybe it'll help you understand why you are who you are."

"Oreo!" the kids had teased her as a child growing up. She was painfully aware of being different for as long as she could remember. In the South there were two worlds—one black, one white. Sometimes it felt to Annie that she really didn't belong to either.

As she walked out of the door of her apartment, her cell phone rang. Mara.

"Hey, Annie. Guess who I just heard from? Delphine Jackson."

"Who?"

"Your client, Tamara Whitfield's mother. You know that job I got Tamara so she could quit the second job to be home with her kids and keep me…DFACS… off her ass?"

"Sure, my pro bono case."

"Delphine said she got a call from Tamara's employer last night. She hasn't shown up to work now for three days, and she's officially fired. Seems she's been on some three-day meth and booze bender with an old boyfriend. Delphine's been taking care of the kids in the meantime, but if she doesn't get back to work soon, she'll lose her job too."

"Shit! I can't believe Tamara would do that after all the trouble we went through to help her."

"Welcome to my world. One step forward, three steps back."

"What happens next?"

"The case was closed when Tamara quit the second job, but since Delphine called me I can't look the other way. If I have knowledge that the kids are going unsupervised, I've got to take action. If I can't find another solution, a babysitter or something, odds are the kids will become wards of the state."

"That's terrible, Mara! That just doesn't seem fair that the kids have to pay the price for their mother's incompetence."

"Unfortunately, Annie, it's always the kids who pay in the end. Life's not always fair."

"What can I do?"

"Nothing right now. I'm going over there this morning to assess the situation. I just thought you'd want to know."

"Thanks. I appreciate the heads up."

"So how is your friend, Tyler? Is he going to call me?"

"I doubt it. Like most men, he doesn't take criticism well."

"That's too bad. He was kind of cute."

"It's my fault. I shouldn't have given you the trouble-shooting manual before the sale was finalized."

"I don't mind being the help desk."

"That doesn't work if the customer doesn't think he needs help, and this customer is totally clueless."

"What's the deal with you two anyway? It sounds like a bit of a love/hate relationship. Are you sure there's not something going on?"

"Between Tyler and me? No, we're more like brother and sister. My mother is his family's domestic assist…maid. When I was a kid, I used to fantasize about being Tyler's kid sister and growing up white and rich. It was my way of escaping the bleak reality of my own life at the time. He had everything I wanted. I guess I was probably jealous of him in some way. Things have always come easy for him, while I've had to bust my ass to get ahead. It just frustrates me that he doesn't appreciate what he's got. He acts so cavalierly, like he's willing to throw it all away. I don't get it."

"One man's burden is another man's gain. That doesn't make one right and one wrong. It simply makes them different."

"How philosophical. I thought you were a sociology major?"

"I took all that liberal crap. I didn't know at the time I was actually going to have to work for a living."

"Speaking of, let me know what I can do to help with Tamara."

"Will do. Bye."

Annie was in the office working on a divorce filing and property settlement for a friend of the Marshalls. The client's wife saw him at a downtown hotel restaurant with his secretary, a young, attractive woman with a penchant for short skirts and rich men, on a night when he was supposed to be out of town on business. Annie inherited the case from Tyler as juries tended to be more sympathetic toward men represented by female counsel, particularly when the man in question was caught red-handed. Out of the corner of her eye, she saw Tyler hovering hesitantly by her door.

"Do you need something, Tyler?"

"I've got something I'm struggling with. I'm not sure what to do. I could use your help. It could take a while. If you're busy, I can come back."

"For you, anytime," she said, motioning him into her office. "What's on your mind?"

"I need your opinion on something. I've got these clients— potential clients right now—who wish to remain anonymous. They want to set up a charitable trust and they want me to act as the administrator."

"That's right up your alley. What's the catch?"

"The catch is that they propose to pay fifteen thousand dollars to any full-time resident of Chatham County between the ages of sixteen and forty who agrees to undergo voluntary sterilization— vasectomies for men, tubal ligations for women."

"I don't get it. Why would anyone want to do that?"

"They loaded me up with reasons, but the capsule summary is that they believe the people most likely to take advantage of this offer are those who may have a disposition to be unfit parents, either economically or psychologically. They believe society would benefit by preventing pregnancies from the segment of the population that typically produces maladjusted children."

"Like poor people, or minorities."

"Could be. It could also be drug users or people who don't want children and have them by accident or someone who could use the cash. They didn't specifically mention race, but reading between the lines I got the feeling class distinction was definitely a factor."

"Fifteen thousand dollars is a lot of money. How do they intend to fund this?"

"With one hundred fifty million dollars to start."

"One hundred fifty million!"

"That's what I said. They're also prepared to pay the firm a retainer of thirty-five thousand dollars a month."

"That's crazy! Who are these people?"

"I have no idea who is behind the money. The clients I met with are intermediaries. I doubt they're anyone we know. So what do you think?"

"What do you think?"

"I was hesitant at first I have to admit, but lately I've been coming around to the idea. Frankly, we could use the money."

"Your father will never go for it."

"I've already talked to him about it. He thinks it's a terrible idea that would damage the firm's reputation."

"Knowing you, that probably pushed you off the fence."

"Bingo. He did say, however, that the decision was mine, and he wouldn't stand in my way."

"So you've already made your decision then?"

"No, not yet. I wanted to get your take on it first."

Annie paused to consider the question. "I guess I don't see anything wrong with it, Tyler. It's not like you're putting a gun to anyone's head. There's a whole mess of people out there who have no business having children. I just got a call this morning from Mara. Remember that pro bono client of mine? After Mara found her a higher paying job so she could take care of her kids, she went on a three-day bender and left the kids with Grandma. Now it looks like the state's going to take her kids from her, and at this point, they might be better off without her. I guarantee you she would take that fifteen thousand dollars in a nanosecond. She would probably blow it all on drugs, but the world would be a better place if she stopped reproducing today."

"What about the racial component?"

"What do you mean?"

"I mean, what would you think if the majority of applicants were minorities?"

"I assume you're asking me that from an ethical standpoint and not a legal one. As long as the offer was made available to all citizens, I don't see how you'd have any issues. I'd be surprised if that were the case though."

"Really? I would think that minorities would be more likely to apply since the money would be more...meaningful."

"You're saying that minorities are poorer than whites, so the money would be more tempting to them?"

Tyler started to speak, but she held up her hand to stop him.

"That's okay, let's assume for the sake of argument that's true. I don't have anything but life experience to back me up on this, but most of the poor black women I know would never trade the cash for the baby. For most of them, a child is the only precious thing they'll ever possess. For some of them, it's a badge of honor. I had three sisters that got pregnant and dropped out of high school. I promise you, none of them was an accident. My mother never married but had eight kids and treasured every single one of them. She wouldn't trade them for anything. Black women love their babies as much as white women do—maybe more."

"But surely teenage girls would be better off staying in school and postponing parenthood until after graduation at least?"

"Sure, and people would be better off if they didn't drink or do drugs, but they still do. You can't change human nature, Tyler, no matter how much money you throw at them."

"What about the men?"

"That I'm not so sure about. A lot of men see a child as the woman's responsibility. They don't plan on taking care of the child in the first place, so they don't worry about birth control. It's possible that some of them might be drawn to the money, but I still don't think it would be a significant number. I certainly don't see this as a potential race issue. Personally, I think your clients are wasting their money, but that's not your problem, is it?"

"I don't suppose it is," said Tyler, lost in thought. "So if you were me, you would do it?"

"If I were you, Tyler? That's a whole 'nother question unto itself."

Tyler showed up unannounced at Savannah Regional Hospital and headed for the fourth floor, which housed the administrative offices. He found the reception desk off the elevator lobby. "Excuse me, is Sam Katz in by any chance?" he asked the receptionist, her head buried in paperwork.

"Do you have an appointment?"

"No, I'm afraid I don't. I'm a friend of his. My name is Tyler Marshall."

"Hold on a minute. I'll see if he's available." Tyler waited as she dialed a number. "There's a Tyler Marshall to see Dr. Katz. Uh-huh. Sure, I'll hold." She went back to her paperwork, cradling the phone in her neck. "Okay, thanks," she said hanging up. "Dr. Katz will be with you in a minute," she said. "Please have a seat."

"Thanks." He found a hard plastic chair and sat down. He never could understand why hospitals had such cheap and uncomfortable furniture when they charged more for a night than the Four Seasons Hotel.

After a few minutes, Katz appeared. "Tyler, what a surprise! What brings you down here?"

"I'm sorry to barge in on you, Sam, but I was in the neighborhood and thought I'd take the chance that you'd be available. I was thinking about what you were telling me the other day and I wanted to see for myself. If this is a bad time I could come back..."

"Not at all. Now is as good a time as any. I'm glad you're interested in our program," he said with a nervous sideways glance toward the receptionist. "Sarah, I'll be taking Mr. Marshall on a tour of our maternity ward. I should be back in fifteen minutes or so. Shall we?" he said to Tyler, motioning toward the elevator.

The maternity ward was located on the third floor of the hospital. It was a cheerful place, full of crayon-colored art, inspired floral arrangements and celebratory balloons with happy faces, smiling down at the proud parents. Katz led Tyler around the entire floor as if he were an expectant parent coming to inspect the premises.

"We're very proud of this section of our hospital," Katz beamed. "It's been recognized nationally, and our staff does such a great job with the patients. Most of them have been with us for years. We have very little turnover here."

"You sound like you care very much for your work."

"This hospital is like a second home to me, and our staff is like my extended family. We all take a great deal of pride in our work."

The last stop as they neared the end of the tour was the incubator room, which housed the premature babies and those suffering complications from birth.

"Tyler, you are now standing in the saddest room in the hospital. This is what we call the NICU—Neonatal Intensive Care Unit. These children, for various reasons, are getting a rough introduction into the world. Some of the babies are born prematurely, like this one here," he said pointing through a plastic bubble at an incredibly tiny human form that weighed three pounds at the most. "This is Courtney Chambliss. Her mother had complications during her pregnancy, and we had to perform a Cesarean in the sixth month. She's one of the lucky ones. When she leaves here, she'll go home to a nice, loving family and will most likely grow up to be perfectly healthy and normal. Some of the other babies here may not be so fortunate."

He led Tyler to an incubator in the back corner of the room. Through the bubble, Tyler could see a baby approximately the same size as the last one with one very noticeable exception. This baby was deformed in every manner possible, it seemed. There was a pronounced forehead that jutted prominently from the skull, and the baby's eyes were focused in two opposite directions. The outstretched right hand contained only three fingers—the pinkie and ring finger were stubs. The name card on the incubator read, "Jane Doe."

"This baby doesn't have a name?"

"Her mother was strung out on crack cocaine when she came in here. At birth, the baby had approximately two grams of cocaine in her system, which should have been enough to kill her, but somehow she survived. The mother apparently didn't want her. She disappeared in the middle of the night and left the baby behind. Seems she didn't even know she was pregnant when we got her. She thought it was an ulcer or a tumor or something. She had no prenatal care, no proper diet and was smoking crack right up until delivery. Jane Doe here is part of a tragic segment of our new generation, abused and abandoned."

"Is she going to be all right?"

"That depends on what you mean by all right. Is she going to live? Yes. Will she ever be a normal, healthy baby? Not a chance. Odds are she'll never surpass the intellectual level of a seven year old during her lifetime. Our job is to keep babies like Jane Doe alive, but at the risk of sounding cold, I sincerely wonder if we're doing anyone a favor. We've successfully delivered a deformed baby into the world with no one to care for her, love her or nurture her. Sometimes it seems almost cruel."

"What will happen to her?"

"After she makes it through the critical stage, she'll be assigned to a permanent orphanage. Eventually, she'll be placed in a foster home. With her physical and mental condition it will be next to impossible to find parents who would be willing to adopt her."

Tyler felt sick to his stomach. "This is so sad. I can't believe someone could possibly do something like this to a child!"

"It happens more often than you might think, Tyler. And I'll tell you one thing. No matter how many times you see a baby like this, no matter how often you're exposed to similar cases of human neglect, you never get used to it. As a doctor, you're trained to develop a thick skin and maintain an emotional distance from your patients. You have to, or the job will eat you up. But this is one part of my job I can't seem to shut out. I've been down here before and seen a baby like this and gone up to my office and cried. I'm talking uncontrollable, hysterical weeping. To me there's no greater crime on earth than the physical abuse of a newborn baby by its mother."

"Is that what got you involved in Fresh Start? Babies like this?"

"Yes it is. I probably don't fit the mold of someone you might expect to be involved in something like this. I'm a liberal Jewish doctor living in the South. But politics and ideology aside, someone has to do something about this problem before it's too late for the next Jane Doe."

Tyler stared at the baby through the plastic bubble. Her eyes seemed to meet his for a brief second. For a moment, he thought he recognized something in those eyes. He could have sworn it was a cry for help.

Darkness had fallen and Tyler was on his fifth Corona when his home phone rang at eight-thirty. "Hello, Tyler, it's Don Abbott."

"Hello, Don."

"I spoke to Sam Katz a little while ago. He said you stopped by to see him today."

"Yeah, he gave me the grand tour of the NICU. It was a bit unsettling."

"I'm sure it was. The mother of that poor infant you saw today, Tyler, that's the type of individual we want to target with our program."

"I thought you said you weren't targeting anyone?"

"Forgive me—that was a poor choice of words. That's the type of person we hope will be attracted to our program. The world would be a better place without irresponsible parents who can't or won't care for their own children. We're the only ones doing anything about it. So tell me, Tyler, are you close to making a decision?"

"I have given the matter a lot of thought."

"That's good. We want you to go into this with your eyes open. So, what do you think?"

"I'm ready to do it but only under one condition."

"And that is…?"

"I want final say over the applicants. I have the right to arbitrarily refuse to accept individuals into the program."

"Tyler, we can't agree to that. If we show favoritism in any way to any particular applicant, it could compromise the entire program. Surely you understand that."

"No, I'm not sure I do."

"The whole premise of this program is that it's available to everyone. We can't discriminate against the wishes of any one individual in any way. That would do nothing but bring us potential problems down the road."

"I understand, but I can't in good conscience agree to act as administrator if there are individuals who I believe are not qualified or adequately prepared for whatever reason."

"You're just making this more difficult on yourself, Tyler. The idea is that you're not making this decision for anyone. They're making the decision of their own free will. It's an individual's right to decide what they do with their own body, and it's not your place or anyone else's for that matter to make that decision for them. Despite what some people might say to the contrary, we aren't trying to play God here."

"Look, Don, I'm not talking about most people here. I'm just saying that in the event someone comes to me who has absolutely no business making a decision of this sort, I have the right to deny or possibly suspend their involvement in the program for some time period that would allow them to think through everything first. That's all I'm asking."

"I don't know, Tyler. I think we'd be setting a dangerous precedent."

"Those are my terms, Don. Take it or leave it."

"Why don't you take some time to think about it, and then…"

"I have thought about it. I feel very strongly about this."

"I have to talk to the other gentlemen first. Is there anything else?"

"There is one more thing. I'm going to need informational brochures on Planned Parenthood and video for the illiterate applicants. All applicants will be required to read or view this material thoroughly before the surgery can be performed. I don't want anyone making any uninformed decisions."

"That's a reasonable request. Sam and I can help you with the materials. The school system has a warehouse full of pamphlets, not that they seem to be doing anyone any good these days. I'm extremely happy that you're on board with us, Tyler. This is the start of something historic. I can feel it."

Tyler hung up the phone, feeling strangely unsettled. These were uncharted waters he was navigating, full of uncertainty and doubt. He was moving out of his comfort zone and taking a real risk, something that he found both exhilarating and terrifying. One thing he was certain of—no matter what happened, it wouldn't be boring.

CHAPTER FIVE

After hearing from Don Abbott that his terms were agreeable on a case-by-case basis, Tyler went about his work setting up the mechanics for the launch of Fresh Start. He created a disclosure and indemnification agreement for applicants to sign, acknowledging they were participating of their own free will and agreeing to hold the trust harmless for any possible future litigation as a result of the impending surgery. He also outlined a parental consent form for applicants under the legal age of eighteen and required a parent's signature to be notarized. He assembled a small library of information from Planned Parenthood and drew up an acknowledgement for applicants to sign stating that they had reviewed this information prior to their final decision to elect surgery. He drafted an approval letter confirming the applicant had been accepted into the program and instructed the care provider to bill the trust directly for the cost of the surgery. Three care providers, including Savannah Regional Hospital, had been preselected and agreed to the fee structure in advance. He prepared a form for the care providers to complete before they could be reimbursed, which included an attachment of the original approval letter. No reimbursements would be possible without that letter.

With the necessary approval and consent forms and the information packages printed, Tyler felt more comfortable that the appropriate checks and balances were in place to protect the marginal candidates, those that might be harboring second thoughts about their participation in the program.

In addition, Abbott presented him with a list of demographic and personal information he wanted captured: race, age, sex, national origin, marital status, income level, social security number and whether the applicant had existing children. This information was required for acceptance into the program.

One Tuesday morning, a week after Abbott called agreeing to his terms, Tyler paid a visit to First Bank of Savannah shortly after they opened for business. The receptionist, with a desk in the center of the bank lobby was Amanda Dennison, the daughter of one of the members at Tyler's country club. Six months removed from Stetson University, a private school twenty-five miles from Daytona Beach, Florida, she was sporting a rather prominent graduation present from her daddy—breast implants. She wore a particularly low-cut top that displayed them proudly. His mouth switched into operation without bothering to consult his brain first. "Amanda, my how you've...grown."

She barely even looked up at him from her desk. Ever since his thirtieth birthday, Tyler had a creeping concern that he was becoming invisible to women under the age of twenty-five. "Hey, Tyler," she said, chomping on a stick of gum.

"Is Chandler in?"

"He's in his office. Go on back."

Tyler found Chandler Porter, the vice-president of the bank and one of the more prominent members of the city's business community, current president of the Chamber of Commerce and past president of the local Rotary Club, in his office practicing his putting. Photos and trophies of various member-guest golf tournaments at the country club where both he and Tyler were members lined his bookshelves, which were completely devoid of books. He was rather portly with a round cherubic face and a sly grin permanently etched on it. His sense of humor and affable manner drew people to him like moths to a bright light. If anyone had a future in politics, Tyler thought, this was the guy.

"How's the game, Chandler?" Tyler asked.

"If I could putt worth a damn, I'd be on the pro tour instead of arguing CD rates with grown men wearing diapers."

"It can't be all that bad. I see you've added some window dressing in the lobby."

"Amanda? Believe it or not, she's dressed modestly today. The first day after she got those things she came to work wearing a tube top. You believe that? A tube top! At a bank! After the fourth old lady complained I sent her home to change. Her daddy—you know Richard—called me and told me he was going to pull his money out and open an account at Wells Fargo if I didn't let his daughter "express herself" is how I think he put it. He actually said that! Can you believe it? Anyway, what you saw is the result of our compromise."

"That's not much of a compromise. Looks like you came out on the short end of the stick."

"I don't really mind that much. I like titties as much as the next guy, but I'm the one who has to listen to those old hags complain all day long. Why they don't complain to Amanda instead of me, I couldn't tell you. Anyway, that's enough of my problems. What can I do you for this morning?"

"I need your help with a wire transfer for a client of mine. I'll be transferring funds from a Cayman bank account to First Bank of Savannah."

"We're grateful for the deposits as always. Offshore money huh? You must be moving up in the world. The last client of yours that came in here, cashed a certified check from an insurance settlement for ten thousand dollars and took the money in cash. Stuffed it all in one of those plastic Ziploc bags, wedged it into the front of his pants and walked right out of here. Seems he didn't even have a checking account to deposit the money."

"Yeah well, we all find work where we can these days, I suppose. I think you'll find this client a little more substantial."

Porter chuckled. "I'm just playing with you, Tyler. Someone has to give you a hard time every now and then to keep you on your toes. You should see some of the characters that walk into the bank every day. I swear, this place is starting to look like Wal-Mart." Porter sat down beside his desk and punched a few keys on his desktop computer. "Okay, where are we transferring the money from?"

Tyler pulled a slip of paper with the transfer information from his coat pocket. "It's the Royal Bank of Montreal, Cayman Islands branch."

"Okay," said Porter, eyes glued to the screen. "What's the account number?"

"233GRF4015."

"And the phone number?"

Tyler read the number slowly from the paper.

Porter dialed the number for the bank as he continued to peck away at his keyboard. I need your personal identification number now."

"37805-36."

"Yes, this is Chandler Porter with First Bank of Savannah in Savannah, Georgia," said the banker to his Cayman counterpart on the line. "I'd like to make a wire transfer of funds to our bank from one of your accounts please." He repeated the information

Tyler gave him. "They want to know what the balance amount is to be transferred," he said to Tyler.

"The entire balance." Tyler watched the banker's face for a reaction.

"The entire balance," Porter repeated into the phone. Suddenly, his eyes widened, and his mouth fell open. "Excuse me one moment while I consult with my client," he said, putting the phone on hold. "Tyler, do you have any idea how much money is in this account?"

"Not exactly, but I want to transfer the entire sum, Chandler."

"Yes, the entire sum," said Porter into the phone. "Thank you very much." He hung up the phone after confirming the information for the third time and giving the Cayman bank all of the necessary details to conclude the transfer. "Tyler, there's more than one hundred fifty million dollars in this account!"

"Damn! I left my Ziploc bag at home! Does this mean I get a lollipop, Chandler?"

"For one hundred fifty million dollars, you get a whole box of lollipops. You mind if I ask what this money is for?"

"I can assure you it's all on the up and up. I'd like to place it in an interest-bearing account under the name, 'Fresh Start Trust." I have the trust documents with me if you'd like to see them as well as evidence of my power of attorney."

"That would be great. We do have an interest bearing account we call our Priority Account. It allows unlimited checks and pays two percent interest providing you don't fall below the minimum balance."

"Somehow I don't think that will be a problem," said Tyler as both men erupted in laughter.

Tyler, as he had promised himself, became the first participant of the program. After scheduling an appointment with the doctor, he began to have second thoughts. What if he changed his mind about having children five years from now? What if he met someone special who wanted kids, and he was unable to accommodate her? Despite these questions, he was determined to go through with the surgery if for no other reason than he felt he needed to experience the personal doubts and misgivings for himself before he felt comfortable interviewing potential applicants. He wanted to experience firsthand the thoughts that went through someone's mind as they contemplated this life-changing decision.

On Thursday morning, Tyler walked the few short blocks from his office to the clinic for his appointment. He was nervous. The permanence of the procedure, the possible irreversibility of the surgery scared him. It reminded him of his ill-advised decision to get a tattoo in college—the Greek letters of his fraternity etched on his left ankle—but at least then he had the benefit of a full night of beer pong to fortify him. Now, unfortunately, he was sober.

The clinic was located on the first floor of a two-story brownstone, very tastefully decorated in thick, masculine colors with bucolic paintings of horses lining the forest green walls. *I wonder how many of those are geldings?* An attractive young woman greeted him inside, smiling back at him as if in silent celebration of his upcoming emancipation from a world of climax-controlled condoms and paternity suits.

"My name's Marshall," he smiled back, lost in her translucent green eyes. "I'm here about the Fresh Start program."

Her winning smile faded to consternation.

"Is there a problem?" he asked.

"No, there's not a problem. It's just that I haven't done one of these before."

"The procedure's the same I hope. Isn't it?" he asked a bit too cheerfully.

"Of course. It's just the paperwork. I'm not sure what I'm supposed to do."

She sounded frustrated. Tyler felt like someone presenting food stamps at the gourmet grocery down the street. "All you need is a consent form signed by Marshall & Marshall," he said, producing the document from his coat pocket. "Like this."

"I better check with the doctor," she replied, unconvinced. "Please take a seat. I'm sure he'll be with you shortly."

Tyler was already on his third magazine, each coincidentally containing articles about prostate cancer, when the doctor appeared a few minutes later. He was surprisingly young and handsome in a chiseled, movie star sort of way. Tyler would have figured him for a cosmetic surgeon instead of an urologist.

"Mr. Marshall, please come in," he smiled, revealing a mouthful of perfect teeth. "I apologize for the earlier confusion. Brittany isn't fully up to speed on the procedures you and I agreed to over the phone. I assure you she will be going forward."

"No problem. That's part of the reason I'm here—to anticipate and head off any potential problems we might have down the road."

"Come right this way," the doctor said, guiding Tyler to a small room with a single, adjustable table. "I understand you are here to have a vasectomy yourself?"

"Yes, I'm here as the first Fresh Start patient. Treat me like you would any other customer."

"Certainly. Are you familiar with the procedure?"

"Not completely."

"The surgery itself is relatively simple, and I'll perform it right here in this room as soon as you're ready. It doesn't involve a scalpel or a surgical knife. I'll start out by administering a local anesthetic to numb the scrotum. Then I'll locate the vas deferens—a spaghetti-like tube under the skin of the scrotum through which sperm travels—by hand and hold it in place with a clamp. I'll use small pointed forceps to separate the layers of tissue and tease a tiny opening in the skin that allows the vas deferens to be lifted out and cut or sealed off. After that, I'll seal the tiny hole with a small bandage, and you should be up and ready to go home within a half hour. Aside from some general tenderness and swelling, there should be a minimal amount of discomfort. There's no reason you couldn't go to work tomorrow."

"That sounds easy," Tyler said. "I do have one question, though. What if I change my mind later in life and decide I want kids?"

"One option would be to undergo a reversal procedure. Basically, the vas ends are surgically reconnected by stitching them back together with ultra fine sutures, allowing the sperm to be restored to the semen. The cost of the reversal could cost up to ten times the amount of the vasectomy itself."

"Another option would be to "bank" sperm prior to the surgery, which could be used later with in vitro fertilization procedures. The sperm banking costs typically include an up-front processing fee and an annual storage fee."

"What's the success rate for reversals?"

"The success rate of vasectomy reversals seems to correlate to the length of time elapsed since the original surgery. In men whose interval is less than three years, the success rate of sperm present in the semen can be as high as ninety-five percent with more than fifty percent resulting in successful pregnancies. For intervals longer than four years, the success rate tends to decline steadily."

"I think I'd like to make a deposit to the bank if that's okay with you. I could always use my Fresh Start stipend to pay for it. Can I do that here?"

"Of course you can. I'll bring you a storage container. Would you like a magazine?"

Tyler shrugged. "I've already seen all of your magazines in the lobby."

"I keep the other magazines here in the back," the doctor winked. "They're more interesting. They might help."

Two hours later, Tyler asked the receptionist to call a taxi, and he headed for home, a little tender but in excellent shape, all things considered. The next day following the procedure, he issued a check to the doctor from the Fresh Start account and one for fifteen thousand made payable directly to himself.

Satisfied that the procedure was safe and relatively painless, and he had answered all of his own questions about the process, Tyler placed a simple advertisement in the Savannah Daily Journal:

Vasectomy/Tubal Ligation
Surgery Free
Earn $15,000
Applicants 16-40 years old
319 Drayton Street
Monday-Friday 9:00 a.m.-5:00 p.m.
Call 912-555-0236

A client of his owned a pizza delivery chain in town, and Tyler persuaded him to make his drivers available to distribute flyers throughout the community. The flyers read exactly as the classified ad and were printed on orange paper to make them noticeable. He paid them each fifty cents per flyer, and after a week, there were over a thousand large flyers posted on telephone poles at prominent intersections in both city and suburban locations. He wasn't sure if anyone would respond to either the advertisement or the flyers, but he was satisfied that he had promoted the program to the best of his ability.

After the ad was placed and the flyers distributed, several days passed without any calls or inquiries. Tyler was actually relieved by the apparent lack of interest. Perhaps this really was a crazy idea after all. He felt foolish for worrying so much and blowing everything out of proportion. Until one day, without warning, it began.

"Tyler," said Darlene over the intercom in a slightly agitated voice. "There's someone here to see you."

"Who is it, Darlene?"

"I think you'd better come see for yourself."

"I'm in the middle of something right now Darlene. Give me a few minutes please."

"I think maybe you better come right now." Her voice was insistent, strained.

"I'll be right there." As he entered the reception area it was readily apparent to him why Darlene had insisted that he greet this visitor immediately. His first reaction to the man seated in the three thousand dollar french provincial bergère chair was not his shabby appearance, his dirty clothes or the toes protruding from the tips of his shoes. It was the smell. An overpowering stench pervaded every nook and cranny of the room. It was a mixture of body odor, vomit, alcohol and urine all intermingled into one sickening, noxious, gag-inducing, olfactive cocktail.

Darlene whispered to him under her breath, "I tried to get him to leave but he wouldn't. He kept saying he was here for the money, and then he handed me this flyer," she said holding the folded, crumpled and mutilated paper delicately by the tips of her fingers as if it were radioactive. "What's this about, Tyler?"

Tyler winced. After all of the careful plans and preparations he made to ensure the program ran smoothly, he neglected to inform Darlene probably because he knew she wouldn't like the idea one bit.

"Sorry Darlene but I haven't had a chance to discuss this with you. Maybe we can talk after I have a chance to meet with Mr....uh Mr....excuse me, sir, what is your name?"

"Tin Man," came the hoarse, gravelly response. When he spoke, Tyler was taken aback by the cavernous blackness of his mouth—most of the man's teeth were missing.

"Yes, Mr. Tin Man. Won't you join me in the conference room?" Tyler felt Darlene's glare, full of reproach. How could he possibly have stooped so low as to bring a man like this into the sanctified presence of Marshall and Marshall?

Tyler didn't offer the man a drink for fear he might feel too comfortable and not want to leave. His first thought was to get rid of him as soon as possible. The man was obviously a vagrant, probably homeless by the looks of him. He appeared to be in his fifties, but Tyler had a suspicion he was much younger. His years on earth had surely been hard ones. He wore an old army jacket, full of holes, maroon corduroy pants, last stylish sometime in the seventies and high-top canvas sneakers with a hole in each tip and a hole in the big toe of each sock providing natural ventilation.

"So, you're here about the flyer. Is that right?"

"Thas right. I'm here for the money," the Tin Man said with a vacant stare.

"We have a procedure to follow before we can give you any money."

"Sign didn't say nothin' bout no procedure."

"That may be true, but there is a procedure, and if you want the money, you'll need to follow it."

"What I gotta do?"

"First, I need to ask you some questions."

"So axe."

"How old are you?"

"Thirty nine. Forty maybe."

"Do you have a birth certificate or driver's license? social security number? The blank look in response provided the answer to those questions. "Guess not, huh? Okay. Let's try this one. What's your real name?"

"Robert. They call me the Tin Man 'cause I collect cans."

"Robert, do you have a last name?"

"Williams. Robert Williams."

"Great, now we're getting somewhere. Do you live here in Savannah, Robert?"

"I've been livin' here almost all my life. My folks moved here from Macon when I was kid."

"Where do you live now?"

"Right now, see, I'm on the street, but when I get me that money, I'm gonna get me a room."

"Do you have a job, Robert?"

"Nah. I work odd jobs sometimes."

"Do you have any history of medical problems or any major illnesses, things like that?"

"Nope."

"Do you understand there is a good chance the surgery cannot be reversed and sterility may very well end up being a permanent condition?"

"Yeah, I understand."

"Okay, well the first thing I'm going to do, Robert is give you some information on vasectomies, which I want you to take home...ah, wherever and read it over so you can make an informed decision."

"Say what? Vas what?"

"Vasectomy. Do you know what that is, Robert?"

"Nah, I don't think so."

As Tyler patiently described the procedure he noticed the glazed, faraway eyes suddenly become wider and more focused. "Damn!" said the Tin Man. "Does that I mean I can't...you know?"

"Can't what?"

"Fuck."

Tyler blushed. "Oh! Of course you can, Robert. A vasectomy doesn't affect your sex drive or your ability to have an erection or an orgasm. You just can't have children. Everything else works the same as it did before."

"Well, that's okay then. I don't need no kids slowin' me down noways, ya know what I'm sayin'?"

Tyler had no idea what could possibly slow down the Tin Man, but he was concerned the smell might be settling into the furniture permanently and was anxious for him to leave. "I know exactly what you're saying, Robert. Take this material with you and read it. If you still want to go through with it, I'll ask you to sign a few papers, and then I'll give you the contact information for a doctor who can perform the procedure for you. He'll bill us for the cost, and once the procedure is completed, we'll issue you a check for fifteen thousand dollars. It's very simple. I did it myself."

"Okay then, I'll see ya tomorrow. Thanks, man. I could really use the money."

"Sure thing, Robert. Good luck to you." Tyler escorted the man out the front door as Darlene held her nose, a look of utter disgust on her face. He was ashamed for her narrow and close-minded outlook. Despite his ragged appearance and rough demeanor, the Tin Man was a human being and one who was worthy of their compassion. He was obviously down and out, probably an alcoholic and quite possibly he suffered from some form of mental illness, but that didn't mean he wasn't worthy of help. He was obviously in need of money and a break like this could turn his life around. Now he could find a nice place to live, buy food and some clothes, maybe even find a full-time job. Tyler felt a giant burden lifted off his shoulders at the realization that he was helping a fellow man in need. His conscience eased, he felt better about Fresh Start, better about himself. He didn't stop to think that subconsciously he'd passed judgment on this man. R. Tyler Marshall IV had decided that society was better off without another Tin Man in the world.

After the Tin Man came the others. At first, it was just a trickle of people coming through the doors of the venerable law firm, mostly friends of the Tin Man, grizzled, homeless men and a few women. They were every bit as shabby and unkempt as their pioneering forbearer, and at times the office looked more like a homeless shelter than a law firm. Tyler waived the age requirement and social security identification for these individuals as practically none of them could verify their age or their citizenship, and they all seemed especially needy.

One afternoon, Tyler was escorting a client out of the building after a consultation in his office. As they approached the reception area, they were surprised to find a tall, rail-thin man with a thick white beard wearing a faded flannel shirt and white painter's pants standing on Darlene's desk. Annie was trying to talk him down while Darlene stared in horror.

"Have you seen them?" the man shouted. "They're coming to take us away! There's no use hiding. They can look straight through buildings. Did you hear that? It's them, I tell you! Save yourselves while you still can before it's too late. Whatever you do, don't make eye contact!"

Tyler was able to calm him down, but the client was more than a bit unnerved. Tyler muttered something about the lack of police protection in the neighborhood and deftly escorted him out the front door to his car. Annie and Darlene were waiting for him when he returned.

Darlene was shaken and was close to tears. "Tyler, I cannot continue to work in this environment with these...animals. You have got to do something right now!" she demanded.

"Darlene, this is just temporary. We're getting the bottom of the barrel right now. These people are...associates...of the Tin Man, I mean Robert Williams. There are only so many homeless people in Savannah."

"If word keeps spreading about the easy money, every homeless person in America is going to move to Savannah," said Annie. "It'll be like one giant homeless retirement community. Maybe we can paint shuffleboard courts on the streets and hold bingo nights. The winner gets a cheap bottle of vodka."

"Annie, normally I appreciate your sarcastic humor, but now is really not the time."

"Seriously, Tyler, you don't even know if most of these people live here or how old they are. They could be from anywhere."

"I'm sure they flew in yesterday after wintering in Palm Beach."

"Some of these people are mentally ill, Tyler. They're not capable of making a decision on their own like the one you're asking them to make."

"So what do you want me to do?"

"Stick to the rules. If they don't have valid identification and can't verify their age, they don't qualify for the program. Believe me, this is word of mouth that you do not want. Let's not run off the few paying clients we actually have."

"Okay, I will be more restrictive about enforcing the rules. And we need to figure out a way to separate the Fresh Start applicants from our regular clients."

"We could put a sign out front directing them to use the back entrance," Darlene offered. "We can send them straight to your office."

"I like that idea!" said Annie.

"I don't like that idea," mimicked Tyler. "Darlene, can you just escort them to the conference room and shut the door? Annie and I can use our offices to meet with clients. We'll tell them we're refinishing the conference table, so the room's not available."

Darlene hesitated before replying. She clearly didn't like the idea. "I suppose I could. This is not what I signed up for though, Tyler. Your father would never have asked me to do this."

"Do what, Darlene? What would my father not ask you to do?"

"What you're doing here. It's a sin against God. And these people—why, they're practically beasts!"

Darlene was a devout Catholic who attended church at least three times a week. Tyler learned long ago not to get into any religious discussions with her. "Darlene, you know I respect your religious beliefs...and the Catholic Church for that matter, but I'm pretty sure the Bible doesn't weigh in on birth control. And what about the part where it says to love thy neighbor?"

"These 'neighbors' as you call them are going against God's law, and they're likely going straight to hell. I have no intention of joining them on their journey."

"I appreciate your concerns. Just show them into the conference room, and shut the door behind them. I'll handle the interviews and the paperwork, so there's nothing for you to do that might make you uncomfortable in any way. I certainly won't ask you to show compassion for your fellow man if that conflicts with what your Church tells you."

Annie's eyes widened at the last comment. She clearly wasn't used to seeing that kind of fire in him—only smoldering ashes. He knew he'd gone too far as soon as the words left his mouth, but he didn't care. Darlene was silently seething in her chair. "Will that be acceptable to you, Darlene?"

"Yes."

"Fine. If you'll both excuse me, I have work to do."

Over the next several days, Fresh Start traffic increased to a steady stream, sometimes as many as ten to fifteen applicants per day and the demographic makeup of the visitors grew more diverse. They came from all walks of life including young married couples who already had children and didn't wish to have any more and divorced men and women who weren't interested in starting new families. Some were working class trying to keep their heads above water.

But the majority of the applicants were poor, if not homeless. Many lived in public-assisted housing projects in the city and reported income under twenty-five thousand dollars annually. When Tyler handed them a check for fifteen thousand dollars, he got the distinct feeling that this was the most money they had ever seen in their lives. Some were crack heads who would likely blow through the cash in a few months, but most had definite plans for their future. One woman was using the money for the down payment on a house for herself and her three kids. One man was going to buy a car, which would enable him to find a better paying job off the city bus route. One woman in her early twenties with two children already was planning to get her GED and enroll in the local community college.

The surgical procedures went smoothly without any real complications to speak of, and there were no more office incidents to scare away clients. Despite the welcome calm, Darlene didn't seem to be warming to the idea, staring disdainfully down her nose at the Fresh Start applicants whenever they walked into the office.

"This isn't right, Tyler," she said to him one evening as the day's last applicant left, and he locked the front door behind him. "I've talked to Father Kinahan, and he thinks I could be in some danger, spiritually speaking, by my involvement here. No job is worth eternal damnation."

"Eternal damnation? Darlene, it's birth control. That's all it is. Millions of people all over the world practice birth control every day."

"The Catholic Church is very specific on the issue. The Holy Father himself, declared it morally and intrinsically wrong."

"That doesn't mean you're going to hell. Maybe you could switch to a Protestant denomination?"

She glared at him.

That was a joke, Darlene," he said. "Has Father Kinahan said anything to you about demonstrating or taking any sort of public position against Fresh Start?"

"Bishop Andrews has restricted his diocese from officially participating in public demonstrations of any kind in response to the scandals."

"Scandals?"

She fidgeted in her chair, noticeably uncomfortable. "The thing with the children…"

"Oh, that scandal. How could they take the moral high ground on the birth-control issue when they have priests sexually abusing young boys?" He wished instantly that he'd kept his mouth shut.

"There are weak men and women at every level of our society. Don't you dare try to tarnish the reputation of those who follow God!" she said with cold eyes.

"I'm sorry, Darlene. That was incredibly insensitive of me. I apologize, but we live in modern times now, and we need to be a little more open to different schools of thought. That's all I'm saying. If you don't agree, if you feel that your participation in Fresh Start puts you in a difficult position, I will understand if you feel the need to resign your position, but I'd hate to see you go. You've been a loyal employee to this firm."

"I couldn't do that to your father. If he were here..."

"Yes, I know. If he were here we wouldn't be having this conversation, but he's not here. Things change, Darlene. Ultimately, it's your decision whether or not to change with them."

"I'll think about it," she said morosely, as she gathered her things to leave for the day.

Keeping up with the heavier workload was becoming a challenge for Tyler. One Tuesday night, after a particularly hectic day, Annie caught him in his office working on a brief for a client.

"I think I must be seeing things! That looks like Tyler Marshall in his office, but it's seven-thirty in the evening, so I know it can't be him. Maybe I should call the police..."

"Very funny, Annie. This Fresh Start thing is taking up more and more of my time during the day, and I'm falling behind on my normal caseload."

"Starting to have regrets, are you?"

"Not at all. The past couple of nights, I've gone home in a good mood. I know this sounds weird, but I feel like I'm helping these people."

"There's nothing weird about that at all. You *are* helping them. You're giving some a second chance to change and make their lives better. You're giving them hope for the future. You should be proud of that Tyler. I'm proud of you for it."

"Wow! Three weeks ago I was a lost soul and now you're proud of me. What have I done to deserve that?"

"Maybe you've found the real Tyler Marshall. Or at least you're looking for him. That's progress.

"Thanks, Annie. I appreciate the support. I'm not sure anyone else would agree with you though."

"Have you heard from your father?"

"Not since we rolled out the program. I'm sure he's just steaming. I imagine Darlene has been giving him regular updates and telling horror stories about the barbarians at our gate."

"I was impressed, by the way, when you told her off the other day. I didn't know you had it in you. Why do you keep her on anyway? She's a self-righteous, close-minded closet racist, and she's not even a very good receptionist. Do you see the way she treats people she thinks are beneath her?"

"I know, but she's been with the firm longer than either of us. I just can't do that to her or my father for that matter. You know my dad treasures loyalty above all else, and Darlene is loyal."

"She's loyal to your father—I'll give you that, but to you or me? She'd stick a knife in our backs faster than you can say Hail Mary."

"One fight at a time, Annie. I'm afraid I don't have the energy for that one."

"I understand. Well, I've got to run. Don't work too late. And Tyler, if you need any help with this Fresh Start stuff, meeting applicants or whatever, I'd be happy to help out. I believe in what you're doing."

"Thanks, Annie. That means a lot to me. I may take you up on that offer. Good night."

"Good night, Tyler."

Tyler arrived home that evening around nine o'clock. There was leftover meatloaf in the fridge. He warmed it up in the microwave as he poured a glass of Coca-Cola three-quarters of the way full. He uncapped a half-empty bottle of Captain Morgan's Spiced Rum and moved to fill the rest of the glass but stopped himself before the first drop ever left the bottle. He screwed the cap back on the bottle and poured the rest of the Coke into the glass. The Coke tasted a little too sweet with the meatloaf, but it was a start anyway. He'd have to let his taste buds re-acclimate to mixers without alcohol. Halfway through the meal, his phone rang. Caller ID read Don Abbott. Tyler noticed the school superintendent seemed to prefer contacting him at home rather than work after his initial call.

"Hello, Don."

"Tyler, I hope I'm not disturbing you, but we haven't talked in a few days, and I wanted to check in to see how things were going."

"They've been going well so far. No major problems to report. It's been relatively smooth at the office."

"I like the sound of that. Low key is the way we want to keep it. We don't want any publicity if we can help it. That would only complicate things for us, and we definitely don't need complications."

"Agreed. The only issue I've had so far has been dealing with some of my existing clients. There have been a few isolated incidents when an applicant got a little out of hand and upset a client. I'm sure I don't need to tell you that some of the people who come in here to apply for the program are not the most solid citizens you've ever seen."

"I can imagine. Are you sure you're not complicating matters by insisting on screening the applicants up front? You could let the clinics do that for you, and pay them a small fee. That way, the applicants would never have to come to your office at all."

"I still feel it's important to meet face to face with them. We've had a couple of individuals who lacked the mental capacity to understand their decision. And although we haven't seen any yet, I'm concerned about minor applicants. I want to make absolutely sure they and their parents understand the ramifications of their decision."

"Remember what I said about playing God, Tyler. You're taking a big risk by letting yourself get personally involved with these applicants, and that could make things harder on you in the long run. Besides, young people may very well be the ones who could benefit most from something like this. They're not carrying the same baggage that some of the adults are. It's not too late for them to set their lives on the right track."

"You may be right, but I still want to talk to them first in any case."

"It's your decision, Tyler. We've already agreed to let you handle this in your own manner, and we won't stand in your way now. I hope you know what you're doing."

"I do, Don, and believe me, everything is under control. I don't think we have anything to worry about."

"I hope you're right, Tyler. I really do."

CHAPTER SIX

Mara Dressler stared grimly at the pile of plain manila folders on her desk. She was the veteran at the Savannah branch of DFACS, with almost four years on the job, but in those four years, the feeling of hopelessness never escaped her. She was a member of the SIU, or Special Investigations Unit, one of twenty-nine agents in the state charged with investigating all child deaths and serious injuries. She typically handled forty cases at a time, an impossible number for any one person to do the job properly. For this thankless task, she was paid about $40,000 a year. From a monetary standpoint, the logical career path for her would have been Case Manager, then Case Management Support, essentially managing call centers for state public assistance programs such as Food Stamps, Medicaid, Child Care and TANF (Temporary Assistance for Needy Families). Had she followed that path, she would likely be a Social Service Administrator or Program Director by now making sixty grand a year or more. But she had a stubborn streak in her that wouldn't let her quit no matter how frustrated she might get at times. Plus, she really loved the job.

Due to the high caseload, there was enormous pressure to handle the cases quickly and efficiently. That often meant taking only a cursory look at the lower priority cases. The trick was in knowing the difference. The families she worked with lived constantly on the edge of catastrophe. Their lives lacked structure, authority, and sustenance and sometimes worst of all—hope. It was like a powder keg with all of the ingredients for a fiery explosion: guns, drugs, and alcohol waiting for the tiniest spark to set them ablaze. Mara's job was to observe and appraise the powder keg's ingredients for potency. Inevitably, the spark would follow.

She didn't need the training DFACS provided or the findings of the Fourth National Incidence Study of Child Abuse and Neglect (NIS-4) to help her identify the more serious cases of child abuse. There was no substitute for an impromptu home visit and one-on-one conversations with family members. But the numbers from the NIS-4 supported what she already knew from first-hand experience. Children in low socioeconomic households had significantly higher rates of maltreatment in all categories. They experienced some type of maltreatment at more than five times the rate of other children; they were more than three times as likely to be abused and about seven times as likely to be neglected.

While there was no single defined profile of a perpetrator of child abuse or neglect, the highest at-risk individual was a single parent with multiple children, living at or below the poverty level and abusing drugs or alcohol. And odds were they never graduated from high school. These were Mara's "clients." Low-income neighborhoods and housing projects were where she spent the majority of her time. It was a completely different world to Mara, a world that most people never glimpse except maybe on the evening news.

She was fascinated by this world, perhaps because it was so uniquely different from the one in which she was raised. The youngest of three daughters, she attended a prep school in Northern Virginia, and her two older sisters married and had children within a few years of graduating college. Her father was a professor at George Washington University, and her mother owned her own marketing consulting firm. The Dresslers were upper-middle class, educated, white, liberal, well adjusted, and, for the most part, happy. The greatest scandal in the family's history was when Mara broke off her engagement.

It was only then that she realized something very important about herself. She was addicted to chaos. She craved discord and unpredictability. It excited and moved her, and she was drawn to it instinctively like a pyromaniac to a flame. When she broke up with her fiancé, she gave up the sure thing, the comfortable life for an uncertain future, and she never felt more alive. She knew this was probably not a healthy attribute—perhaps it was even dangerous—but better than being bored to death, she convinced herself.

It was this strange fascination that attracted her to many of the child abuse case families at DFACS. At first she blamed the parents. At times it seemed like they were almost intentionally self-destructive. They made all the wrong decisions. Many of them had children out of wedlock at an early age, dropped out of school, struggled to hold jobs, abused drugs or alcohol, sold drugs, committed crimes and sometimes did time in prison. Then she realized they were just products of their environment. They were merely repeating the same behaviors as adults that they learned when they were children from their parents and other adults in their community. It was a vicious cycle, but a cycle nonetheless, with very distinct, recurring patterns and predictable results. The children learned from the elders in the community and passed those learned behaviors down to their children in a sort of perverse legacy. One aspect of this legacy particularly concerned Mara. Statistically, one third of child abusers were abused themselves as children.

Mara believed that the only way to break this cycle was to focus on the children. Experience taught her that it was too late to change the parents' behavior, but if she could get to the kids early enough, they had a chance. She believed the most effective way to protect them from the negative pressures of their environment was to remove them from that environment whenever possible. Usually, the first choice was to keep the family together and try to help them relocate to government-subsidized housing in more desirable and stable neighborhoods. In the event that the parent or parents were responsible for the abuse or allowed it to continue, however, she wouldn't hesitate to move the child to a foster home. That was her first priority under any circumstance—protect the child.

"What's the matter, Mara?" asked Quinnette Rose, passing by her cubicle. "You look a little overwhelmed." Quinnette was new to DFACS, an administrative assistant in her fourth month with the department and six months removed from high school in Savannah. She was young, naïve and full of energy, thrilled with her new job and excited about the idea of helping people. Mara hesitated to become too friendly with her—Quinnette's type rarely lasted very long at DFACS. They tended to have the life span of a goldfish in a tank of piranhas.

"Take a look at all of these files. There's no way I can get to them all, let alone actually help any of these people. Unfortunately we need two more of me, and that's definitely not in the budget."

"Anything I can help with?"

"Thanks but I'm afraid not. You're not certified to work on these files."

"Are they all child abuse cases?"

"Yep. This one here?" Mara said, holding up a very thin file. "Charles Tomkins, age three. His mother left him in the backseat of the car under the hot sun with the windows rolled up for four hours while she was at work. One of her co-workers spotted the child and called 911. Charles is over at Savannah Regional being treated for hypothermia right now. And here's another one. Chastity Powell, age seven. Her mother left her alone with her boyfriend after school every day. Turns out, he's been sodomizing the child for three months. Chastity's older sister caught them in the act, and guess what? The mother doesn't want to leave her boyfriend! And then there are the Thurman kids. Their father came home drunk like he always does and passed out on the couch with a cigarette in his mouth. Burned the house down and two of the kids are in the hospital with third degree burns."

"That's terrible! How can people be so irresponsible?"

Mara shrugged. "I don't know. They just are."

"They wouldn't be like that if they had Jesus in their lives."

"I beg your pardon?"

"Jesus," Quinnette said. "Someone who believes in Jesus and accepts him as their Savior couldn't do those things to a child. That's Satan's work."

"If that's true then how do you explain all of the pedophile priests?"

"The what?"

"Pedophiles. Catholic priests who have sex with children."

"I don't know nothin' 'bout the Catholic Church. That's the white man's church. I go to the Community Church of the South—the Reverend Thaddeus Johnson's church. Reverend Johnson is one righteous man, let me tell you. He's got the spirit of God in him. Reverend Johnson loves us all, and he helps us to express our love for Jesus. That man is practically a saint. I promise you there's none of that pedrophilia stuff going on in his house. That's the House of God! You should come with me for service on Sunday."

"But I'm white, Quinnette. I thought you said the Catholic Church was for white people," Mara teased.

"You ain't white. You're just light-skinned, that's all. You'd be welcome in my church any time. You never know, it might do you some good."

"Actually, I've been there once with a friend just to hear the choir. They've got one helluva…heckuva choir there, that's for sure."

"They do! My sister sings in the choir. She's going to be a famous recording star when she gets out of school. Ludacris heard her sing one time and said she had the sweetest voice he'd ever heard. I'm going to be her agent when she makes it big. So, you've been there once—come again. You can be my guest."

"Thanks, Quinnette. I really appreciate the offer. I may take you up on it one day."

"Anytime, you just let me know. And bring some of those deadbeat parents with you. I guarantee the Reverend Johnson will whip them into shape in no time and get them back on the right path, the Lord's path."

"I wish it were that simple, Quinnette. Right now, I can use all the help I can get."

Annie found Tyler in his office, eating a sandwich over a pile of legal briefs. "You've got a visitor, another applicant. Darlene's about to have a fit. I think you better get down there now."

Tyler made his way down the stairs to the reception area. Darlene glared at him and nodded in the direction of the conference room without saying a word. He assumed it was another homeless person. He could certainly take care of that. He entered the conference room and was surprised to find a young girl sitting across the table. She looked to be no more than fourteen years old. Her hair was braided in pigtails, and her eyes were wide and expressive, radiating innocence. She was small and frail, and her delicate features made her seem fragile, like a porcelain doll that might break at the slightest touch.

"Hi, I'm Tyler Marshall," he said, extending his hand.

She took his hand timidly in her own, limp and lifeless. As she extended her arm, Tyler noticed a deep bruise on her forearm. "I'm Jennifer Patterson," she squeaked, in a high-pitched, mousy voice.

"I assume you're here about the program?" The young girl nodded at him, avoiding eye contact. She seemed frightened by something. "Jennifer, may I ask how old you are?"

"I'm sixteen."

"Do you have any identification?"

Silently, she handed him a folded piece of paper, which proved to be a copy of a birth certificate. The certificate verified that she turned sixteen two days ago.

"Jennifer, do you know what a tubal ligation is?"

Again a silent nod. She wasn't much for conversation. "Do you know what it means to have an operation like that performed?" Tyler asked gently.

"It means you can't ever have any babies."

"That's right. Now why would someone as young as you want to do something like that?"

"I just do, that's all."

"Don't you ever want to have children when you're older?"

"No, I don't guess so."

"How about your parents? Do they know about this?

"Yes, sir," she managed.

"And what do they say?"

She reached in her pocket and handed him another piece of rumpled paper. It read simply:

To who it mae concern,
My dotter Jennifer has my permishun to have the operashun.
Sined,
Elvis Patterson

"I see," Tyler said, handing her back the wrinkled letter. "Tell me, Jennifer, what are you going to do with the money?"

"I don't know. Probably give it to my parents. Daddy's been out of work a long time, and I know he could use the money."

"Don't you think they might like to have grandchildren someday?"

"Daddy says I'll probably just get pregnant by some boy, and then he'll have to support me the rest of his life."

"And what does your mother say?"

"She don't say much of anything. Whatever Daddy says goes for me and her both."

"It sounds to me like this is more your daddy's idea than it is yours. Is that right?"

She remained silent, staring at the table in front of her. "Jennifer, how did you get that bruise on your arm?"

"I fell off my bike."

"Uh-huh. Look, Jennifer, I'm sorry but I just can't recommend you for the program. I think you'd be making a big mistake."

A look of complete panic swept over the young face. "You can't do that!" she screamed. "What am I gonna tell Daddy?"

"You just tell him that I wouldn't let you. If he has a problem with it, he can come to talk to me directly."

"You don't know what he's going to do to…" she caught herself in mid-sentence and fell silent.

"What he's going to do to who, Jennifer?"

She sat there staring at the table. Her entire body was trembling.

Tyler was pretty sure she wasn't afraid of what her father would do to him. "It will be okay, Jennifer. Just tell your dad that I wouldn't let you. He won't be mad at you for that. If he doesn't like it, you have him call me. Here's my number," he said, handing her a business card. "Just have him call me if he's mad. Okay?"

She nodded once again and rose to leave before he even had a chance to say anything else. In a moment she was gone, but before she got to the front door he was conscious of the doubt creeping back into his head.

Mara was one quarter of the way through her stack of case files when the phone rang. "Division of Family and Children Services, Mara Dressler speaking."

"Hi...Mara. It's Tyler Marshall. Annie's friend."

"Of course. How are you, Tyler?"

"I'm good, thanks. Um, I have something that I'd like to talk to you about, and I was wondering if maybe we could get together?"

She hesitated for a brief, awkward moment before replying. "Okay... is this personal or professional?"

"This is professional. I mean not that it couldn't be personal, but in this case, I mean...I need to talk to you about a girl."

"Tyler, I don't know what Annie told you about me, but I don't do relationship counseling."

"No! It's not that. It's a young girl. I think she may be a victim of child abuse. I'm not sure what I'm supposed to do. I thought maybe you could help me."

"That's different. That's in my wheelhouse. I'd be happy to help you."

"That would be great. Could we meet for coffee after work today?"

"Coffee? The last time I saw you, you were drinking tequila shots."

"I'm trying to clean my act up a bit. I'm taking your advice."

"I don't remember telling you that tequila was bad for you."

"No not that. You told me to find something I was passionate about. You also told me to do the opposite of what everyone expects me to do. I followed your advice, but I think it may be getting me in trouble."

"I love trouble! I can't wait to hear about it. How's seven o'clock at Starbucks sound to you?"

"The one on Bull Street? I'll see you then. Thanks, Mara."

Tyler ordered an espresso while he was waiting for Mara to arrive. He took a sip. *Not too bad, but a shot of Irish whiskey would really make this groove.* Mara walked in five minutes later. She was wearing a short skirt and heels revealing a pair of very shapely legs that were hidden under her long skirt the last time they'd met. She wore her dark hair long to her shoulders and a simple white blouse with the top three buttons unfastened. He thought her attractive when they first met, but she looked even better now.

"Hey, Mara," he said, rising to greet her. "Thanks for seeing me on such short notice. I'm new at this gourmet coffee stuff, I'm afraid. Can I get you something?"

"Sure, a decaf coffee with cream, please."

"Coming right up," he said, heading for the counter. He returned with her drink and sat down. "First, I want to apologize to you for leaving so abruptly the last time."

"You don't need to apologize. Annie and I were pretty hard on you. You probably felt like we were ganging up on you."

"Maybe a little," he grinned.

Mara found his smile winsome. He looked like a mischievous little boy too cute to punish. She also noticed an impish twinkle in his blue eyes that enhanced his youthful appearance. He really was nice looking.

"I have this unfortunate tendency to come across as pretty direct and intense sometimes," she admitted.

"That's okay. I like that in a woman."

"That's good because I don't see myself changing any time soon. So why didn't you call me?"

"I did call you. Today."

"I mean why didn't you call me after we met? Annie said you weren't interested."

"You really are direct! I don't know, maybe you intimidated me. Maybe you gave me some things I needed to think about first. I've also been sort of...pre-occupied lately."

"Doing what?"

Tyler told her the whole story about Fresh Start while Mara silently sipped her coffee. He told her about the offer, the advertisement and flyers, the information materials and disclosures, the Tin Man, the other applicants and the personal interviews. He left out the identity of his clients and his own personal visit to the doctor's office. When he finished, she was staring back at him quietly. "So what do you think?" he asked.

"I don't know what to think. I'm not sure I understand the point of it all."

"I can't speak for the people putting up the money because I don't know who they are. I can only guess they believe the money being offered is more enticing to poor people, which represents the demographic that puts the most strain on our social systems. I suppose if you think about it, fifteen thousand dollars isn't much to spend compared to a lifetime of potential public assistance costs."

"Is that what you're seeing? Are all the applicants poor?"

"It's too early to tell. I don't have a big enough sample to judge, but so far, I'd have to say there's been a broad mixture. If I had to guess, I'd say the majority of the applicants are poor, and some of them are homeless, but it's not the overwhelming majority I thought it might be. I had my doubts when I first heard the idea, but I've got to tell you, Mara, if you could see the look on some of these people's faces. Fifteen thousand dollars is a lot of money, and for many of them, it's a chance to improve their lives. I really feel like I'm helping, and that makes me feel good about myself. Is that so bad?"

"Maybe not. There are lots of people out there who just need a break to turn things around. Then there are people who have no business procreating in the first place. I've got a stack of files in my office of child abusers who definitely shouldn't be having children. Most of them would have been sorely tempted by the money."

"I have to admit, I know very little about child abuse. Is there a correlation between child abuse and income levels?"

"Yeah, a pretty strong one actually," Mara admitted. "Below fifteen thousand in household income, the odds of abusive incidents rise significantly."

"What does income have to do with it?"

"In some cases it's a primary determinant. Parents don't have money for day care or baby sitters, so they sometimes leave children unattended. They're forced to live in undesirable neighborhoods where crime and drug use is more prevalent. They can't pay for medical expenses or emergencies, or in some cases, provide proper nutrition for their children, that sort of thing. Then there are the secondary determinants. The mental stress of living in poverty contributes to alcohol or drug abuse. These are key predictors of child abuse. Sometimes that stress just causes people to snap and exhibit behaviors they might not otherwise."

"Could this program actually help curb child abuse if it targeted lower income people?"

"It depends on how you define help, I suppose. I doubt that the people putting up the money are doing so purely for altruistic reasons. I doubt they're doing this to 'help' anyone. If you ask me, it sounds more like class warfare."

"What do you mean?"

"There are plenty of ways of helping people better their lives through financial assistance, education, counseling, and so on. This program you're talking about seems a bit more sinister to me. It's like the upper class decides that the lower class is a burden to society, so their solution is to eliminate the lower class altogether by preventing them from reproducing."

"Does it occur to you that maybe the people who've put up the money have seen decades of financial assistance, education and counseling efforts fail?" Tyler asked. "Maybe a more radical solution is worth pursuing, but regardless, no one's talking about consciously eliminating an entire class of people."

"I'm not so sure they wouldn't if they could, but I don't think they'd accomplish that with this program of yours anyway. I just don't see it having a significant effect."

"That's what Annie said. So what's the harm then as long as the program is voluntary, and it helps people better their lives?"

"I guess the real question is whose standards are we using to determine whether their lives have improved or not? Yours? Mine? Some anonymous group of investors?"

"The only opinion that matters is the applicant's. I assume they believe they're making the right decision because it is, after all, their decision."

"Trust me. A lot of these people aren't capable of making their own decisions—good ones anyway," Mara said.

"And whose standard are we using now? Mara Dressler's?"

"Touché. Why don't we just agree to disagree on this one?"

"I'm okay with that. Can we still be friends?"

Mara reached over and took his hands in hers. "Maybe even more."

"You really are direct, aren't you?"

"Is that a problem?"

"Not with me," Tyler replied. "There was something I wanted to talk to you about though."

"Sorry, I thought we just had that conversation."

"There's something else. A complication. A young girl came to register for the program this morning. Barely sixteen years old, she brought a note from her father granting permission. I got the distinct impression that her coming to see me was his idea—not hers."

"What did you do?"

"I turned her down. I told her I thought she would be making a mistake."

"I think I like you better already," Mara said, smiling.

"That's not the problem. She had bruises on her arm and seemed deathly afraid of her father and his reaction when she had to tell him that I rejected her application. I think she could be a victim of abuse. I thought maybe you could help."

"What's her name?"

"Jennifer Patterson."

"Elvis' daughter." She didn't sound surprised.

"You know him?"

"Forget a vasectomy. He should have been castrated years ago. He's a nasty, low-life, drunk wife-beater. How's that for a reference? I've been to their home more than once. The wife and daughter are both scared shitless of him. I believe he got Jennifer pregnant a year ago, but I couldn't prove it, and she was too terrified to testify against him. Elvis knew once the baby was born, a DNA test would land him in prison for the rest of his life. The next thing I knew, Jennifer had an abortion. It seemed Elvis swept away all of the evidence."

"My God!"

"He's a monster. You did the right thing, Tyler. I'll stop by and check on her this week. In the meantime, let me know if you hear from her...or him...again."

"Will do."

"Now where were we?" she said running her finger down his arm seductively.

CHAPTER SEVEN

Tyler woke up with Mara's head on his chest. She was completely naked, her long hair flowing over her shoulders. *God, she's beautiful, a bit crazy maybe, but beautiful.* He'd never been with a woman so intent on getting what she wanted. No small talk, no games, she just came right out and said whatever was on her mind. He couldn't possibly think of anyone more opposite from Deborah, who never said what was on her mind. She just expected you to know what she was thinking, like you were a mind reader or something. Southern bred through and through, Tyler wasn't accustomed to women being so bold and forceful. It was intimidating and liberating at the same time—intimidating because it forced him outside of his comfort zone, liberating because it took the pressure off him to play the traditional suitor role, something he didn't enjoy, nor was he particularly adept at it. Coffee yesterday had turned into dinner, then her apartment. It was her idea, and she was the one to initiate physical contact. He was just along for the ride, which was fine by him. To top it off, it was the best sex he had since, well, ever.

He looked around Mara's bedroom, one of only three rooms in the tiny apartment, the other two being a bathroom and a living room/kitchen combo. It seemed even smaller in the daylight. There was a double bed, a creaky armoire made of cheap pine and two nightstands that looked to be made of particleboard covered by a small tablecloth. There was a Widespread Panic poster on one wall and an honest-to-God lava lamp on one nightstand. On the other nightstand was an alarm clock.

"Shit! It's eight thirty!" he said, jumping out of bed.

"What's the hurry, baby? Let's play hooky this morning. I'm working this Saturday anyway. Come back to bed."

"No can do. I've got client meetings all morning and who knows how many new applicants. I'm already past being late."

"But you're the boss, aren't you? Can't you make someone else do your dirty work for you?"

"You know Annie, right?"

"Sorry, bad idea."

"I've really got to go," he said, pulling his pants on two legs at a time. "I'll see you later. I mean, thanks for last night. I mean…oh hell, I'm not sure what I'm supposed to say. I'm a bit rusty at this sort of thing."

"If you're rusty, I'm looking forward to seeing you in action when you're a well-oiled machine."

"You're incorrigible."

"But you love it, don't you?"

"As a matter of fact, I do." He kissed her, long and lingering. "I'll call you later."

"Look forward to it," she said, escorting him to the door.

He didn't have time to change for his nine o'clock meeting, so he rinsed with some mouthwash in the car and splashed some of it under his arms while he was driving. He made it to the office with ten minutes to spare and sneaked in the back door. He grabbed a clean shirt and matching tie from his desk drawer, which he always kept on hand for just such emergencies. Unfortunately, neither shirt nor tie matched the suit he was wearing. *Too late to worry about that.* He hung the coat on a hook behind the door. *At least now it's only the pants that don't match.* The message light on his phone was blinking. "Good morning, Darlene. I have messages?"

She sounded annoyed. "There are four of those people in the conference room waiting."

He approached Annie in her office. "Annie, can you take the Fresh Start applicants this morning for me? There are four of them here already, and I've got a meeting in five minutes."

She visually inspected him, amused, taking special note of the brown checked shirt, beige tie and gray pants with black shoes. "Another rough night, Tyler?"

"What? I saw this in GQ. All the guys in Milan are wearing it." She looked skeptical. "It's not what you think, Annie. I've been behaving myself lately."

"So it's a woman then."

"Who are you—my mother?"

"I should be. I know when you're lying and when you're telling the truth. I know if you've been bad or good."

"That's Santa Claus—not a mother."

"Anyone I know?"

He hesitated just long enough for a broad smile to form on her face. "You were with Mara, weren't you? You were, and you know how I know you were? Because you're blushing!"

He didn't share her amusement. "Can we talk about this later? Cover for me?"

"I'll cover for you. And Tyler, we *will* talk about this later," she said, smiling.

As it turned out, there wasn't time to talk about anything that day. A record twenty-five applicants, "those people" as Darlene snidely referred to them, strolled through the doors between the hours of nine and five. Darlene had to lock the front door at five o'clock as there was still a steady stream of applicants wanting to enter. No doubt they'll be back the next day.

And they were back the next day, thirty-two applicants in all. There was no way he could keep up with the new pace, so he offered to pay Annie one hundred dollars per head for each interview she conducted. If she saw twenty applicants in a day, she'd make two thousand bucks—not bad money for one day's work. He also offered to pay Darlene ten dollars per applicant to take over more of the administrative duties, something she did begrudgingly.

The money was nice, but Tyler and Annie were both concerned about their regular clients. They knew this was a temporary situation and worried about the long-term effects it might have on the practice. They were responding to the needs of their existing clientele as much as possible and working overtime to accommodate them, but they couldn't even begin to think about soliciting new business. If this kept up much longer, the pipeline of regular business was going to be empty by the time Fresh Start ran its course.

Within a week, they were averaging forty to fifty applicants a day. Word was quickly spreading out in the community of the easy money to be found at Marshall & Marshall. Tyler noticed people staring at him whenever he went out in public. He had lived in Savannah his whole life and knew many of the people in town, but he had yet to see a single acquaintance of his apply to the program. Perhaps they were too embarrassed. Still, they seemed to know all about it and his affiliation with it, which made the continued silence from his father all the more puzzling. Tyler hadn't spoken to him since the night he'd sprung the idea on him over dinner. Surely his friends at the club were asking questions. He pictured his father shrugging his shoulders and feigning ignorance, citing another example of frustration with his son's disappointing career. In the meantime, the mortgage on the office building was current, and all outstanding creditors were paid.

Tyler met Chandler Porter from the bank for lunch at 17 Hundred 90. The restaurant was decorated in the old Southern tradition with brick floors and walls and was a favorite among the local business crowd. Porter was in the lounge waiting when he arrived. The hostess escorted them to their table in the rear corner of the large, open dining room. As they walked through the room, Tyler could hear the noise level fall and felt the eyes of the restaurant's patrons boring holes in him. It was a feeling he was growing used to, but it still made him uncomfortable. It wasn't his imagination. Porter noticed too.

"Does that happen to you often?" asked Porter, as he spread a napkin over his lap.

"Seems like it's happening more and more lately," Tyler said. "I can't say that you get used to it. I guess by now you've figured out what the one hundred fifty million dollars was for, Chandler."

"You'd have to be deaf, dumb and blind not to have heard about your little program by now. Everyone in town is talking about it. You've become quite the celebrity."

"That kind of notoriety I can do without. Savannah's still a relatively small town. People are going to talk. There's not much we can do about it."

"I suppose you're right, but doesn't it bother you what people are saying about you behind your back?"

"I don't care what they're saying." Tyler paused a moment for effect. "What *are* they saying, Chandler?"

The banker laughed so loud his belly shook. "I'd say that of the people I've talked to, your approval rating is running about one hundred percent. Everyone seems to think this is an idea whose time has come. They're fed up with all the crime and the drugs, and the schools here are for shit now. Hell they'd vote to castrate the sumbitches if they could."

"That's more than a little extreme, but it's nice to have folks on our side anyway."

"Maybe so. The problem with those folks is that they're in what you might call the silent majority. They might talk big at the bar in the men's locker room or the Garden Club meetings, but if there's even a hint of controversy, they'll be scurrying for cover like cockroaches when the kitchen light's turned on."

"What's that supposed to mean?"

"It means that should this program of yours become more public and let's say ...controversial, then you're going to be out there fighting a war all alone. A war you stand very little chance of winning."

"That seems a bit extreme. Do you really think it will come to that?"

"There's a damn good chance of it. Somebody out there is going to have an issue with this, and if it's somebody who screams loud enough, you better watch your ass. And it's not just your ass I'm worried about. I have concerns for the bank as well."

"Chandler, it's not like we're doing anything illegal."

"That's not what I'm worried about. If this becomes a public issue, the bank is open to a potential backlash through its association with the program. Remember, our name is on all of the checks. Like you said, that kind of notoriety we can do without."

"Exactly what kind of issue do you think we're going to run into? What are you afraid of?"

"I'm afraid you're going to make the African-American community very upset when it realizes you're sterilizing a sizeable portion of its population. That could be a very explosive issue. Surely you've thought about that possibility."

"Of course it's a concern, but this program is open to all applicants, regardless of race or sex. I haven't noticed an over-representation of African-Americans relative to the population. If there is any trend at all, it's more weighted to lower income individuals than anything."

"In the South, you can't talk about lower income citizens without meaning African-Americans. You know that."

"But they're not the same, Chandler. Believe me, there's plenty of low-income white people, Hispanics and Asians too. Just stop by my office some day, and you'll see."

"The difference is that poor white people aren't politically active. Frankly, no one gives a shit about them. Save me the lecture on your non-discrimination policies. If the heat gets turned up on this thing, I don't want my fat ass on the front burner when it happens."

"Don't worry. If something like you describe should happen, I won't say or do anything that might cause embarrassment to the bank. But I really don't think you've got anything to worry about. So far everything's going smoothly, and we haven't run into any major problems. I don't expect there are going to be any public relations issues."

"I hope you're right, Tyler, I really do. For both of our sakes.

Mara and Annie met for drinks at a small wine bar down by the river on Thursday after work. The front door was left open and a cool, easterly wind was blowing off the water as tourists strolled along the sidewalk in search of tacky t-shirts and cheap beer.

"I understand you and Tyler are together now," said Annie, with more than a hint of curiosity in her voice. "I want details. He won't tell me anything."

"I don't know if I'd go so far as to say we're together," said Mara. "Let's just say we hooked up."

"More than once?"

"Yes."

"More than twice?"

Mara hesitated for a brief second. "Actually, every day for the past five days."

"That definitely qualifies as together. When he spends the night, does he bring a change of clothes for work the next day?"

"After the first night, yes."

"Then it looks like you got yourself a boyfriend."

"I'm not into labels. How did you find out anyway? Did he tell you?"

"I saw him the morning after the first night. At least I think it was the first night. He was wearing a brown shirt and gray pants. The rest I pretty much figured out on my own. He always thinks he's sly, like he can fool me or something."

"Men are so predictable. I kind of like this one though. He seems a lot better adjusted than I expected after talking to you. I owe you for setting us up. Are you sure you're okay with it?"

"Of course I am. I told you, it's not like that with Tyler and me. We're just friends."

"I can tell by the way he talks about you there's more to it than that. I can't explain it though. The relationship between the two of you is just…weird. In the meantime, though, the sex is great!"

"It must be having an effect on him. He seems like a new man around the office. His attitude is better, he's got more energy, and he seems a lot more focused. I haven't heard him complain about his ex-wife for over a week now. He even told me he cut back on his drinking."

"I don't know if I can take credit for all of that. On our first date, or whatever it was, we met for coffee at Starbucks."

"You have got to be kidding me!"

"I'm serious. I think this Fresh Start thing has energized him more than anything I've done. That was the reason he asked to meet me for coffee—he wanted to ask my opinion on what to do about the sixteen year old Patterson girl applying for the program."

"Right. He told you about Fresh Start? What did he tell you?"

"As far as I know, pretty much everything. He told me you've been helping out as traffic picks up."

"What do you think?"

"I don't like it. It's a classic example of exploitation of the lower class by the upper class. It's positively Machiavellian. It screams, 'We can't fix the problems with the lower class, so we're just going to prevent them from breeding until they no longer exist.' It treats the people as the problem instead of them being a symptom of a much bigger societal problem that no one seems to want to address."

"If you have that big of a problem with it, then why are you seeing Tyler? Isn't that a little hypocritical?"

"First of all, if I had a rule that every time I disagreed with a man, I would have to break up with him, I'd be heading straight for Spinster City. I am a bit on the opinionated side if you haven't noticed." Annie smiled at the understatement. "And secondly, I don't think it will have much of an effect at the end of the day. You're never going to stop people from getting pregnant, even when pregnancy isn't in their best interest. I read the other day about a professional athlete who had to file bankruptcy due to child support he was forced to pay to five different mothers! Now how dumb is that? Neither education nor birth control has been effective at addressing the problems of the poor and uneducated, and this crazy scheme won't either. In my opinion, someone's wasting an awful lot of money."

"You're probably right, but it's the clients' money, so who are we to tell them how to spend it? I didn't think this thing would have legs when Tyler first told me about it, but I have to admit that it seems like it's really picking up steam here lately. Time will tell I suppose."

"Not to change the subject," said Mara, sipping her Sauvignon Blanc, "but rich, elitist plots to take over the world kind of bore me for some reason. A girl at work invited me to her church this Sunday. I was going to stop by and visit the Patterson girl and her low-life scum of a father after I receive divine inspiration. You want to come with? They've got a great choir."

"Sorry, Mara, I don't do church. You want to talk about exploitation? Organized religion today has less to do with spirituality and truth than it does with political opportunism and moral entitlement. The local church, synagogue or mosque wants to tell you how to live your life, who to vote for, who to love and who to hate, all based on some abstract interpretations they make from anonymous texts written thousands of years ago. And each of them is convinced that their beliefs are the only true ones, that their internal code is the only real path to salvation. And they spout these beliefs with such conviction like there's no way—not even a chance, that they might actually be mistaken. It's the purest form of arrogance in existence today."

"Uh-oh," said Mara, "it looks like I may have hit a nerve. Sorry I mentioned it. My friend, Quinnette, tells me the preacher at Community Church of the South, Reverend Johnson I think, is supposed to be a stand-up guy. I thought you might enjoy it."

"Take my word for it, the Reverend Thaddeus Johnson is the worst of the worst."

There followed an awkward moment of silence before Mara motioned to the bartender for another round as Annie seemed lost in her reverie. When their glasses were refilled, Mara decided to change the subject. "So, have you seen any good movies lately?"

Community Church of the South sat on the same site as another church constructed at the turn of the century, but it bore not even a remote likeness to its predecessor. The old church was a modest, clapboard structure painted white with a simple steeple rising up to the heavens with pine floors and pews, scuffed by years of revelry and penitence. With parishioners standing in the aisles, its maximum capacity was slightly over one hundred souls.

In its place stood a glass and concrete structure that seated over one thousand people and included three full-length basketball courts, an Olympic size swimming pool, a community center, administrative offices, an atrium, a cafeteria and a gift shop, which one had to pass through in order to reach the main worship area. The facility was specially equipped with television cameras and sound equipment so the sermons could be broadcast for local access television. The audience seating was tiered downwards toward the pulpit in three sections: balcony, loge and orchestra. Huge high-definition video screens were mounted on the walls for the benefit of those sitting in the back rows. At the orchestra level, the pulpit rose several feet above the seating, towering over the congregation and an orchestra pit, which housed a small band with electric guitar, keyboard, drums and Moog synthesizer. The pulpit itself was a vast stage, spanning the entire width of the auditorium. It contained a lectern, a small seating area with overstuffed leather couches for more informal conversations and tiered platforms at the rear center for the world famous Community Church of the South choir.

With Quinnette's guidance, Mara steered her car to the multistory parking deck next to the church. As they made their way to the main church building, Mara noticed a black Rolls Royce parked in a reserved section directly adjacent to the side entrance of the facility, which housed the administrative offices. "Nice car!" said Mara. "Whose is that?"

"That's Reverend Johnson's car," said Quinnette proudly. "The congregation all pitched in and bought it for him. The reverend let my sister ride in it the day they picked up Ludacris at the airport. Can you believe that?"

"I can't believe the congregation bought him a Rolls Royce! Aren't there better things to spend your money on, like feeding the hungry maybe?"

"The congregation wanted to buy him the car. He's so unselfish—he would have never bought anything like that for himself. That was just our way of showing our appreciation for all the wonderful things he does for us."

They made their way through the main entrance and found themselves in the gift shop. It was a fairly large room with a glass ceiling funneling beams of natural sunlight into the room below.

A large walkway led directly to the worship area and was flanked on both sides by two elongated rows of glass cases, which displayed spiritual books, CDs, DVDs and assorted religious pictures and trinkets. The cases opened from behind, where several attendants were standing by to assist customers. At the end of the wide aisle was a turnstile leading to the main entrance to the church, which tracked the number of visitors. Two very large men with earphones stood guard at the turnstile, scrutinizing every visitor. Each held a metal detecting wand, which they occasionally used on some teenage boys or other suspicious looking characters as they passed into the worship area.

Quinnette led Mara to their reserved seats, twenty rows back and left-center of the pulpit in the orchestra section. They had a great view of the pulpit and the band in the orchestra pit playing a lively, contemporary gospel tune as the choir sang from the enormous stage. The last time she attended this church, Mara came with a friend who attended only occasionally, and they had to sit in one of the back rows in the upper level. This was quite an improvement.

"These are great seats, Quinnette. How did you get them?"

"My sister got them. The reverend treats his people right, especially the stars of the choir," she said, with no small sense of pride. "That's her there in the center on the front row," Quinnette said, pointing to a beautiful young girl singing lead and flashing a toothy white smile that positively glistened under the bright stage lights. She was only fifteen years old, the youngest member of the choir. Her sweet and silky soprano voice wafted along columns of air, meandering its way into every nook and cranny of the great church like a furtive messenger on tip-toes. "She's going on a trip to Myrtle Beach next month with the choir to play the House of Blues Sunday Gospel Brunch."

The cathedral suddenly grew quiet as if on cue as a large screen descended behind the choir. The light dimmed as bright, white spotlights illuminated the choir. The band played a brief instrumental, sort of a jazzy riff, and then the choir broke into a gospel song, *Blessed*, all upbeat and high energy. The screen behind the choir flashed bright colors and designs that continually morphed into different shapes and colors. The screen reminded Mara of an old Grateful Dead concert, catered to a mellow crowd loaded up on hallucinogens, but this crowd was up on their feet dancing and clapping to the music. The vibe was infectious and Mara found herself standing and letting the music move her. She felt free and vibrant and marvelously uninhibited as the music flowed through her body and lifted her spirit to a level she'd never quite experienced before.

The music ended and before the crowd had a chance to be seated, the Reverend Thaddeus Johnson strode confidently to the pulpit. In his late-forties, with speckled gray hair, he appeared fit and trim and radiated energy. He was decked out in a white, double breasted suit with a lavender shirt and a deep purple tie with sparkling diamond cufflinks and a diamond-encrusted gold wedding ring that looked like it weighed at least a pound. He appeared not to be straining as he spoke, yet his voice carried through the church like a jet fighter taking off from a battleship, deep, resonant and booming.

"Praise Jesus!" he exclaimed.

"Praise Jesus!" came the resounding reply from his flock.

"Ladies and gentleman, please give it up for the greatest choir in the Kingdom of God, the sensational, world-famous, Community Church of the South Choir!" Quinnette rose to her feet, whooping and hollering for her baby sister as Mara quickly joined her. After the applause died down, the reverend took care of some housekeeping items, recognized some members of the congregation for outstanding achievements and announced that the church swim team finished in second place in the city championship meet.

As he started into his sermon, Mara was struck by the sheer force and range of his voice. It was like listening to a one-man symphony as he varied octave, pace, inflection and volume at precisely the right moments in order to keep his audience rapt and listening closely to his message. He was speaking of Judas' betrayal of Jesus in exchange for thirty pieces of silver by identifying him with a kiss to arresting soldiers of the high priest Caiaphas, who then turned Jesus over to Pontius Pilate's soldiers. "Now it has come to my attention," said the reverend, "that some members of our congregation are betraying their own people in exchange for silver pieces. Fifteen thousand dollars worth of silver to be exact." Mara stiffened in her seat at the words. *That number just has to be a coincidence, right?*

The reverend continued on. "I understand that in exchange for fifteen thousand dollars all one has to do is agree to be...sterilized." He spat out the word like it was vile and reprehensible, evil personified. "Is that all it takes for us to sell out, to sell our heritage, our culture, our dignity? Fifteen thousand dollars? If that's truly the price, then I'm ashamed for every brother and sister among us who may be tempted by this offer or even worse, has already accepted those silver pieces. We are God's children!" he bellowed and his voice filled the great hall. He paused for a moment as the room fell silent. In a low voice he said simply, "And our children are God's children until the day we take it upon ourselves to deny them their very existence. I wouldn't want to explain to God that I deprived him of his children in exchange for fifteen thousand dollars. Would you?"

He concluded the sermon, leaving no room for doubt where he stood on the subject. He was throwing down the gauntlet and daring anyone to cross it. To cross that gauntlet, to accept the money in exchange for the voluntary sterilization was to defy him, the Reverend Thaddeus Johnson, who clearly stood on God's side. The message was clear and unmistakable. Mara wasn't sure where this was going, but she knew one thing above all. As much as he might wish it were so, Tyler Marshall was no longer flying under the radar.

After the service Mara and Quinnette hung around as the crowd slowly filed out. Behind the stage was a gathering room where most of the choir members, musicians and church employees congregated after the service. Mara felt like she was backstage after a Broadway play as the cast and crew congratulated each other for a great show. And why not, for it certainly was quite a production. They found Quinnette's sister, Deondra, in the crowd holding a bouquet of flowers. Quinnette ran up and hugged her tightly, both girls squealing with pleasure.

"Mara, I'd like you to meet my sister, Deondra. Deondra, this is Mara Dressler. Mara and I work together at DFACS."

"Pleased to meet you, Deondra," Mara said shaking her hand. "Quinnette's told me so much about you. You have a magnificent voice."

"Thank you," replied the girl, softly.

Mara thought Deondra looked nothing at all like her sister. She had high cheekbones, a smooth complexion and mysterious dark eyes, while her sister had pockmarks on her face, the result of a long-running battle with acne, and a long, arching nose that dominated her other features. Deondra looked like a child next to her sister, a little over five feet tall and a bit gangly, like she hadn't quite grown into her body yet, but in a way her awkwardness made her more appealing as she was beginning to blossom.

"Those are beautiful flowers," said Mara admiring the bouquet. "I hope it was a boyfriend who gave you those!"

Mara noticed an ever so slight glimpse of alarm in the girl's eyes before she composed herself. She was sure Quinnette hadn't noticed.

"No boyfriend, I'm afraid," Deondra said shyly. "These are from Reverend Johnson."

"Isn't he sweet!" cackled Quinnette. "He knows who the star of his show is!"

As she spoke, a vacuum of sound and space filled the room as the Reverend Johnson walked in. All eyes were upon him and conversations were abruptly ended or redirected by his presence. He appeared smaller in person than he looked on stage. He was a slight man about five feet nine inches tall and maybe a hundred and sixty pounds, wiry and muscular like a bantam rooster. He wore a thin mustache, neat and groomed, and his eyes seemed to take in everything as he made his way through the crowd toward them.

"Hello, Deondra, great show tonight," he said, kissing the girl's hand and hugging her just a little too close with his hand just a little too low on her back, Mara noticed. "You like the flowers?" he asked, all teeth.

"I love them. They're beautiful, Reverend! Thank you so much!"

"You're very welcome. Make sure you hurry home, and put them in some water now, you hear?" Mara didn't like the way he was looking at her, like there wasn't anyone else in the room. *That wasn't how he looked two minutes ago.* Something just didn't seem right.

Quinnette seemed oblivious. It was obvious she worshipped the ground he walked on. "Hello, Reverend, you were just wonderful today! Really inspiring!" She threw her arms around him and squeezed him tightly, rumpling his suit.

"Thank you, Quinnette," he said, pulling away quickly. This was a different embrace than the one he gave Deondra to be sure. He spotted Mara and flashed another toothy grin. His eyes never moved from hers as he spoke. "And who might this be?"

"This is Mara Dressler," said Quinnette. "Mara and I work together at DFACS. She's my guest today."

The reverend grasped her hand in both of his and held them without breaking eye contact. "Welcome, Mara, to our humble house of worship."

Mara felt uncomfortable in his grasp and his stare. Experience had taught her that her first impression was very rarely wrong. *This guy's a player!* It took a surprising amount of force to remove her hand from his grip. "I don't know about the humble part, Reverend, but it sure is impressive. Thanks for having me today as a guest."

"No thanks needed. We love guests here at Community Church, don't we, ladies?" Without waiting for a reply, he grabbed her hand again. "It was nice meeting you, Ms. Dressler. Please come back again real soon." He released her hand and turned to leave. "Quinnette, you make sure to bring your friend back again now, you hear?"

"Yes, sir," said Quinnette, pleased that she had pleased him.

After saying goodbye to Deondra, Mara and Quinnette made their way to Jennifer Patterson's house. Quinnette seemed eager to tag along when Mara had told her a visit to the Pattersons' house was on her to do list for the day. Quinnette was still bubbling with enthusiasm over her new job and wanted to learn as much as she could. The house was located in an industrial area near the Port, just off the docks. It was a ramshackle house with front steps made of cinder blocks and an old Chevrolet Impala on blocks in the front yard. The paint on the side of the house was peeling badly, and insulation stuck out in a couple of areas where the wood had rotted.

Mara walked up to the front door with Quinnette in tow and rang the doorbell. A mangy mutt stared at them indifferently from his spot on the porch, making no attempt to protect the inhabitants of the house from possible intruders. *We'd probably be doing him a favor by taking Elvis away*, Mara thought. No one came to the door so Mara rang again. This time the door opened slightly, the chain still on its hook. It was dark inside the house but Mara recognized the tiny eyes staring back at her.

"Open the door, Jennifer. It's me, Mara, from the Division of Family and Children Services."

The door closed, and they heard the distinct sound of the chain sliding open before the door opened again. Mara could see instantly the bruise around the girl's left eye.

"That's a nasty shiner, Jennifer. How'd you get that?"

"I fell off my bike."

"That must have been some fall. What did you land on, a rock?"

"Somethin' like that."

"Yeah, sure. Somethin' like that. Jennifer, this is my friend Quinnette. She and I work together. We just came from church and thought we'd stop by. Do you ever go to church?"

"Daddy don't believe in God."

"Something tells me God doesn't believe in your daddy either. Is he home?"

"He's in back with Momma."

"I heard through the grapevine that you went over to that attorney's office to get your tubes tied. Is that true?"

"Maybe."

"Is that something your daddy put you up to?"

"We all thought it was a good idea—even Momma did, but that man, he wouldn't let me."

"What did your daddy say when you told him the man wouldn't let you have the operation?"

"He got real mad. He started yellin' and hollerin' and carryin' on."

"Did he hit you?"

The girl fell silent at the question. She'd learned from her mother and covered their terrible secrets for years. No matter what he did to them, no matter how hard he beat them, no matter what horrible things he did to her, she would protect him. "No ma'am."

"I don't believe you, Jennifer. I know you're lying to me. Just like I know you lied to me about your daddy getting you pregnant. All you have to do is say the word, and I can get you out of here. I can take you some place safe where he can never hurt you again. I can help you, Jennifer, if you'll just let me. But in order for me to help you, you've got to start telling me the truth."

The girl stared back at them, her entire body trembling. Mara could sense that she wanted to talk, but she was obviously paralyzed by fear. She felt encouraged by the girl's silence. She hadn't rejected the offer outright, which meant she was thinking about it. If she could just get her to talk…

"Well, look what we got here," said a voice from the darkness inside the house. "If it ain't Thelma and Louise!"

"Hello, Elvis," Mara said, knowing the moment had vanished. "Quinnette and I just stopped by to check on Jennifer to see how she was doing."

"Yeah, and what'd she tell ya?"

Mara looked at the bruise on the girl's face and saw the raw terror in her eyes. "She says she's fine."

"She says she's fine, huh? Well, don't that beat all! She's fine, is she? Seein' as everyone's all hunky-dory then, and you ain't got any pressing business with us, what do you say we end this nice little ole' social call right here, and you amscray? And take the nigger bitch with you!" he growled.

Mara felt the anger rise up inside of her. She knew he was baiting her but she didn't care. "We'll be moving on, Elvis, but I promise you, I'll be back, over and over and over again. I'm watching you, and I will nail your ass the first time you step out of line, do you understand me?"

He flashed a toothless grin and laughed out loud, the braying, harsh cry of a donkey. "I'm so skeered, I think I just pissed my pants."

"I'll be back, Elvis," Mara said, pointing at him. "You can count on it."

CHAPTER EIGHT

The Reverend Thaddeus P. Johnson was searching for his pewter cufflinks in the sock drawer of his bedroom armoire, the ones shaped like two balled fists, an expression of black power from days gone by, but they were missing from his valet. "Monique, have you seen my pewter cufflinks, the ones the NAACP gave me?" he asked his wife of seventeen years.

He stared at her reflection in the bathroom mirror as she squeezed into her exercise clothes for her daily morning workout ritual. She still had a fine body considering her age and the three kids she'd given him. He remembered the day he first set eyes on her like it was yesterday. She was sixteen, and he was one year removed from the seminary, assigned to this dusty, backwater Savannah church with fewer than one hundred members. She was mature for her age and smart, a little too smart for her own good he'd thought then. She was cocky, almost arrogant, the kind of sassiness you see in young women born into high stations in life. Her father was the president of the largest minority-owned insurance company in town.

She played hard to get, and eventually he saw her as a challenge, a conquest. He charmed her, pressed all the right buttons, and before too long he found what he was looking for in the narrow alley behind the old church. They'd done it standing, in a prone position against the rough-hewn siding, her dress hiked up above her waist, her fingernails digging into his back, drawing blood through his white robe. He had his prize after all. Now that he thought about it, he wasn't sure who had conquered whom. She was obviously used to getting what she wanted and, back then, she wanted him.

"You haven't worn those things in ages. Why do you need them?" she asked, admiring her athletic figure in the mirror.

Admiring her body—that was something they both still had in common after years of marriage. She was the love of his life, and no other woman could ever replace her. She was an inspiration to him as he grew his church from a tiny flock of hardy but depressed souls in a dilapidated old building into a mega-church with televised services on Sunday. Her daddy's money didn't hurt either. Still, she provided him with three healthy children: Thaddeus Jr. and the two girls, Abbie (Abdiel—servant of God) and Hana (Hanameel—gift of God). She was a loving mother to the children and was always there to support him. Members of the congregation absolutely adored her. She was their queen—beautiful, loving and kind. But more than anything, she understood him like no other woman possibly could. She understood his "special needs." She would never think to question him when he had to work late hours on unofficial church business or so much as raise an eyebrow when he needed to attend a last minute retreat at a resort in the Bahamas. It was his weakness, she knew, but what mortal man existed without a weakness? He didn't drink or smoke or gamble, but he simply couldn't resist the temptation of women, particularly young women. He felt certain that on Judgment Day the Lord would recognize his lifetime body of work as his loyal and dutiful servant and would surely understand the craving that stirred within him and gave him succor.

The pewter cufflinks were a gift from the NAACP and, to Thaddeus Johnson, represented political power. "I want the pewter cufflinks because I'm going downtown today. I've got a meeting with Quinton."

"Quinton Devereaux? The mayor? What are you meeting with him about?"

"I plan on putting a stop to this sterilization nonsense. Quinton owes me more than a couple of favors. I plan on collecting today."

Savannah's population was over fifty-five percent African-American, but during the last mayoral election there were two African-American candidates and one white candidate, all running on the democratic ticket. It appeared that the two African-American candidates might split the vote, thus surrendering the contest de facto to the white candidate, that is, until Thaddeus Johnson stepped in and threw his support to Quinton Devereaux. His primary rival subsequently withdrew from the contest, allowing Devereaux to win the primary and ultimately the election. Rumors of a back office deal persisted in the press for months, but nothing could ever be proven. Even if it could, what would be the point? That's what politics was all about anyway—power. In the old days that power was concentrated in the hands of a small number of white men. They held a party, and they made damn sure that African-Americans weren't invited. Today, that power and the votes that secured that power had simply shifted to the other side, the side that had been so sorely disenfranchised for over a century now, and they weren't about to give it back. Thaddeus Johnson saw Fresh Start as a transparent attempt by the old guard white elitists to take back the ground they had lost, and he wasn't about to let them get away with it.

Monique gave one last tug at the elastic band in her exercise shorts to smooth a wrinkle. "Don't you think you're making too

big of a deal over this thing, Thaddeus? What's the harm if someone decides they would rather have the money than children, or
more children for that matter? It's not like abortion. It's just a
method of birth control."

"It's just a method of *race* control is what it is. They're targeting
our people, Monique. Black people."

"You don't even know that! From what I understand, this offer
is good for any citizen, regardless of race."

"That's what they're saying, but you know there are more
black people taking them up on their 'generous' offer than white
people."

"I don't know any such thing, and I'd suggest you find out for
yourself before you go making any accusations. If I had to guess,
I'd say the numbers would be weighted to lower income people,
but I don't think that necessarily means black people. And besides,
I know more than a few lower income brothers and sisters who
shouldn't be having children."

"That's easy for you to say. Your daddy is one of the wealthiest
men in town. You were born with a silver spoon in your mouth. You
have no idea what it means to struggle in life, to put food on the
table for your kids…"

"Save it for your sermons, Thaddeus. Your daddy was a doctor
in Chicago, and you went to private school. We live in a fifteen
thousand square-foot house with a home theater in the basement.
You don't know anything more about being poor than I do, and
frankly, to insinuate that the majority of black people are poor
is not just a false statement, it's bordering on downright bigotry.
I thought you were above that sort of thing," she said, raising an
eyebrow.

"I never said that the majority of black people are poor. God
protects all of his creatures, rich and poor, black and white and, if
I'm to do His work, then it's my duty to fight for them as well. All
of them."

"That's all well and good, but they aren't asking you to fight for them. No one's putting a gun to their heads, and if the money helps them make something better of their lives, what's the harm?"

"Better their lives? That's certainly debatable. Half of them are probably out buying TVs or jewelry with their newfound riches. Anyway, this isn't about trying to stop some poor brother from getting his pecker clipped. This is all about the silent war that no one seems to want to talk about these days, a war between black and white, between rich and poor. This program is symbolic of that war. This is a plot by white elitists to undermine and eliminate all of the gains we've made over the past forty years. They've lost their political power and now they want it back. That's what this is all about."

"You don't even know who's behind this thing! How can you say it's some kind of white, elitist plot?"

"I know who's administering the fund—that blue blood law firm, Marshall and Marshall. And Tyler Marshall is the biggest, whitest, bluest-blooded, most elitist cracker of them all."

"Isn't he retired? I thought his son took over the practice."

"Doesn't matter. The apple doesn't fall too far from the tree."

"Doesn't Annie Burris work there? You know, Bittie's daughter."

The reverend flinched ever so slightly at the mention of Annie's name. In his mind, it just made it even worse that she worked there. It made it feel somehow more personal to him. "Look, I know that Marshall doesn't have the wherewithal to fund something like this, but I intend to find out who's providing the financing. And when I do, I intend to stop them. Watch me."

Monique Johnson was sure he meant it. He was like a pit bull. When he sunk his teeth into something, she couldn't remember a single time when he ever let go until his victim was bloodied and beaten.

Quinton Devereaux gazed out the window of his corner office in City Hall. The building sat on top of Yamacraw Bluff, where

General James Oglethorpe landed in 1733 with the first group of colonists who would establish the city of Savannah and the last of the thirteen colonies of England. The bluff afforded a scenic view of the Savannah River below, and he loved to watch the ships steam in and out of port. The foundation of his successful run for mayor rested on his economic development platform, encouraging trade and business investment by offering special tax incentives to businesses interested in locating facilities in the area. The port was a big selling point in attracting companies that relied heavily on the shipping of raw materials and finished goods throughout their distribution chain. This pro-business stance served him well as he worked to establish himself as a moderate candidate against his two democratic opponents who leaned far to the left of center. He also came out tough on crime, which was a real concern as the city had one of the highest per-capita crime rates in the country. Quinton believed that economic prosperity would help to reduce crime, but he wasn't counting on it alone. He also advocated expanding the police force and seeking tougher sentencing of criminals.

After ten years as a city alderman, Quinton saw these issues as important to the majority of Savannah's citizens, but perhaps more than that, he astutely recognized a change in the politics of the South. Like his father who served as a city alderman before him, Quinton was born into the Democratic Party. Ever since Reconstruction after the Civil War, Democrats, affectionately nicknamed 'Dixiecrats,' held the political power in the South. For years, the Democratic Party in the South consisted of an uneasy alliance between white conservatives and liberal African-Americans who shared power despite very diverse, almost opposite political leanings. Both sides stayed loyal to their party because it was the party of their fathers and grandfathers, but also because they were reluctant to give up their well-established base of power. Then, in 2002, Georgia elected its first Republican Governor since the

1870's. Immediately following that election, white state legislators switched parties en masse, giving Republicans control of both the state House and Senate chambers practically overnight. The end result was that conservative whites remained in power at least as far as state politics were concerned, while African-Americans, ever loyal to the Democratic party, were left on the outside looking in, completely disenfranchised. Local political power, primarily in the cities, remained vested in African-American hands as they had the population numbers to assure their on-going control, but that was small consolation. In essence, they'd won the battle but lost the war.

Some of Quinton's brethren were outraged, feeling like they were the victims of some terrible treachery, like a disconsolate bride jilted at the altar. Regardless of this new bleak reality, they would remain loyal to the cause and continue to fight for the rights of the poor and neglected. They would continue to support subsidies and other social programs as their fathers had before them. They would continue to fight for the rights of the "little man" over corporate America. They would remain loyal to the party that had always stood for these inviolable beliefs. They would cling to the past while the future passed them by.

Quinton saw things differently. Of course he cared about the poor and had a profound appreciation for the struggles that minorities and women faced to get ahead in society. But things were different now than they were in his father's day. The old prejudices and inequities were still there below the surface, but they were muted, less obvious. His father remembered segregation: schools, buses, water fountains, like it was yesterday, but to Quinton it seemed like ancient history. He went to an integrated school, had white friends, graduated from Wake Forest then went to law school at Michigan. He felt the same tug, the same calling to help the disadvantaged that his father did, but somehow it was fainter, dimmer. He began seeing political issues less and less as being African-American versus white as the distinction between the two diminished. The African-Americans he knew—his people—wanted jobs, opportunity, education and a safe crime-free environment to raise their kids, same as the whites he knew. His profession was politics, and his instincts told him that if he wanted to succeed, he would have to appeal to a broader audience without sacrificing his base. He would respect, even revere the efforts of the great civil rights pioneers who gave so much of themselves so people like him could enjoy the advantages of a free and democratic society. But he would not lose himself to the dogma of the past and its diminished relevance just to pay homage to these great leaders. This was a newer, more modern world. It was time for new leadership. It was time for change.

Quinton's assistant escorted the Reverend Johnson into the mayor's office. As Quinton rose to greet him, he could see the two hulking bodyguards over his shoulder, patiently waiting in the reception area.

"Quinton, I appreciate your taking time out of your busy schedule to see me today."

"Reverend, you know my door is open to you anytime," he said with a wide smile and a firm handshake. At six foot, four inches and two hundred and twenty pounds, he towered over the diminutive clergyman.

"We're all very proud of you, Quinton. You've accomplished so much during your brief tenure as mayor already. You've done well in the eyes of the Lord, and he is surely by your side."

"Thank you, Reverend. I need all the help I can get."

"And how are Johnetta and the kids?"

"They're all fine, thanks for asking. My oldest, Quinton Jr., is going to Duke next year. It seems like just yesterday he was running around the house in diapers."

"Duke! You must be very proud of him."

"I certainly am. My wife and I feel very fortunate to have raised two wonderful kids."

"Thank the Lord for the many blessings he's bestowed on you, Quinton. Only He can provide the love and happiness we all crave so insatiably."

"I thank Him every day, Reverend. Tell me, what can I do for you?"

"There's a situation that has come to our attention, and we could use your help with it. You know I wouldn't impose on you if it wasn't extremely important."

"Of course. Please sit down," he said motioning to the chair by his desk. "So tell me, what's this situation?"

"Surely you've heard of this outfit called Fresh Start? It's running out of Tyler Marshall's law practice. I think his son may be in charge, but I'm sure the daddy is behind it."

"I've heard of it. The sterilization thing, right?" The reverend nodded silently, a grim expression on his face. "I doubt the father has anything to do with it. This isn't his sort of thing. Too gritty. I did hear his son was having financial problems though. That might explain his involvement."

"In any case, we've got to put a stop to this."

"Put a stop to what?"

"To this entire charade!" the reverend's voice boomed like thunderclaps rolling over the marsh from the sea. "This vile, pernicious sin against God and his children!"

"I'm sorry, Reverend, but I'm not following you. To my knowledge, they're not doing anything illegal, are they?"

"That's not the point! The point is that this is a crime against God. The point is that this is something that has the capability of tearing the community apart. The members of my congregation are outraged by this profanity. I'm worried that things may get out of hand, possibly turn violent."

"Violent? How could this possibly lead to violence? I'm missing something here, Reverend."

"Quinton, who do you think it is lining up over there at Marshall and Marshall to collect their fifteen thousand dollars in exchange for a lifetime of infertility?"

"I don't know, Reverend. I would imagine lots of people for that kind of money."

"Lots of black folks, that's who. Poor people who think fifteen thousand dollars is all the money in the world, that's who. Poor, uneducated blacks, that's who. Don't you see what this is, Quinton? This is Tyler Marshall and his white, country club, elitist bunch trying to take back the territory they lost twenty years ago."

"You think this is some sort of racial thing?"

"Do I have to draw you a picture? Stay with me here. I hate to break this news to you, Quinton but you were elected mayor of this town not because of your good looks or your winning personality or your natural intelligence, but because there were more African-American voters than there were white ones. Period. What this program is doing is encouraging African-Americans not to have children—God's children. Fewer African-American children mean fewer African-American voters eighteen years from now. My father marched with Dr. King. I know racism when I see it, and this is the vilest form I've ever encountered!"

"Do you know for a fact that there are a disproportionate number of African-Americans signing up for the program?"

"I don't need to see a snarling dog's teeth to know it's going to bite me. Of course there is."

"Reverend, you know I'd like to help you any way I can, but I'm just not sure in this case what it is you expect me to do."

The reverend sat up in his seat and leaned toward the mayor. His balled fist matched his cufflinks as he pounded the desk firmly for emphasis. "I want to know who is behind this abomination, and I want it stopped! Now!"

Quinton had no idea what he could possibly do to help, but he understood clearly his assistance was expected. "I'll look into it right away. I can make some calls. I'll do the best I can, Reverend."

Reverend Johnson met his eyes with a steely glare. "I want them stopped, Quinton."

"I'll do what I can."

"If you can't, we'll just have to find another mayor who can. Good day." He rose from his chair and turned his back as he walked out of the office without so much as a handshake. Quinton watched him exit the reception area, flanked on either side by his two protectors, his head barely coming up to their shoulders. *That was definitely a threat,* he reflected. The reverend didn't make idle threats. He didn't have to.

Tyler looked out his office window as the shadows of night crept silently over the building. He was exhausted. Fifty applicants today. Annie took half of them, and he took the other half. That's in addition to an appearance in Probate Court, two paying client meetings, and he still had to prepare for a deposition tomorrow morning on a worker's comp claim. He glanced at his watch and felt a sharp pain in his stomach. *Seven-thirty and I haven't eaten a thing all day. Great diet, huh?* Annie and Darlene were both gone for the day leaving him alone in the office. He was supposed to meet Mara for dinner tonight, but there was no way that was happening now. He would have to call and cancel on her. His cell phone rang as he was dialing her number. He checked caller ID. *City Hall? On my cell phone? Wonder who that could be?*

"Hello, Tyler. It's Quinton Devereaux. I hope I'm not interrupting dinner."

Tyler knew Devereaux from his days as a trial lawyer just as he knew all of the city's attorneys, at least by reputation. He was a good lawyer, talented and smart as a whip. He was a plaintiff's attorney, typically suing corporations for negligence, personal injury and worker's compensation, and Tyler often found himself on the other side of the table representing the defendants. Devereaux was a formidable opponent.

"I should be so lucky. Actually, I'm still here at the office."

"Business must be good."

"Yes, it seems to be picking up. I'm afraid there's not enough time in the day. I'm sure you know the feeling."

"I'm afraid I do. Sometimes I miss the world of private practice. I envy you your independence."

It has its ups and downs, but I wouldn't trade places with you for anything. No offense."

"None taken. It was much easier when all I had to worry about were my clients. Now it seems I have the whole world to please. And that, as you know, is just not possible."

"No it's not. I'm sure it's a thankless task. You've done a great job so far. Keep up the good work."

"Thanks, Tyler. I appreciate the words of encouragement."

There followed an awkward pause. "Is there something I can do for you, Quinton?"

"Yes, actually there is. I'm hearing a few concerns being raised in the community about this program you've been running. The sterilization program."

"Fresh Start."

"Yes, I believe that's it. I understand this has been structured as a blind trust. I'd like to know who is funding the trust."

"I'm sorry, Quinton. That's privileged information."

"I thought you might say that. Tyler, I'm sure you'll agree with me that this program of yours is not something that's in the best interests of the city to continue."

"I'm sorry. I'm not sure I agree with you. We're not doing anything illegal, and so far I haven't heard any complaints." Mara had warned Tyler and Annie about the Reverend Johnson's sermon on Sunday. Annie completely dismissed him as a threat, but Tyler wasn't so sure. *Maybe the good reverend has friends in high places. He certainly didn't get where he is today by being a shrinking violet.*

"You may not have heard any complaints because you don't live in the same neighborhood where the complaining is coming from."

"And what neighborhood is that, Quinton?"

Quinton paused as he tried to get a measure of the man on the other line. *Is he baiting me or is he just naïve?*

"I'm talking about the African-American community. There are some…influential members of the community who view your program as targeting minorities for sterilization in an attempt to reduce their population."

"Do you believe that's true?"

"It doesn't matter what I believe. If my constituents believe it's a problem, then it becomes my problem."

"Are you sure we're not just talking about one constituent? One very influential and wealthy constituent?"

"Let's just say you have your financial backers, and I have mine and leave it at that. The question is, what are we going to do about it?"

"We're not targeting minorities and the program is strictly voluntary. I have no control over who chooses to participate."

"That's all well and good, Tyler, but if the majority of the applicants are minorities then your argument just doesn't hold water, at least in the court of public opinion."

"I've got numbers to back me up, Quinton. Forty-three percent of the applicants are African-Americans, a total of fifty percent counting all minorities. I believe that's consistent with the demographics of the community. Of course, you would be more familiar with those numbers than I would."

"Are we talking city of Savannah or all of Chatham County?"

"The program is open to all residents of the county."

"Those numbers sound close to the actual demographics of the county though they're weighted a little disproportionately to minorities. I'd have to see the breakdown of the city residents before I could comment."

"We don't have that, but we are capturing addresses whenever possible. I suppose I could get you that information if you wanted it. It would take me some time."

"I'd like to see all the data you've collected so far, if you don't mind. I appreciate your cooperation. I just don't get it, Tyler. Why would anyone in his or her right mind spend all of this money for no apparent reason? It seems like such a waste."

"I asked myself the same question. When you see the data though, one number really jumps out. There's one demographic that shows up disproportionately in our numbers, the same demographic that shows up disproportionately in crime statistics, government-subsidized social programs and domestic-abuse incidents."

"Oh, yeah? What's that?"

"Over thirty-five percent of the applicants to our program are poor, with household income of less than fifteen thousand dollars per year. They're the ones least able to care for their families, and they're the ones most in need of the money. I hate to disappoint you or your constituents, Quinton, but this really isn't a racial issue. If it's an issue at all, it's one of class, not race."

"Poor people vote too, Tyler. I'd like to take a look at those numbers, and I'll see what I can do to calm the waters a bit. I'm sure that you and your father would not welcome the kind of negative publicity this might bring."

"My father has nothing to do with this, but you're right in assuming we would like to avoid any undue publicity if possible. I'd appreciate any help you would be prepared to give us."

"I'm not making any promises, but I'll do my best. If my best isn't good enough, however, my advice to you is to shut it down.

The people whose feathers you've ruffled don't give up easily, and they don't fight fair. If it comes down to it, this is a fight you can't win. Believe me."

"Thanks for the advice."

"Don't take it as advice, Tyler. Take it as a warning."

Four days later, the mayor assembled his staff in the executive conference room of City Hall overlooking the river for a briefing on the Fresh Start statistics provided by Tyler Marshall. Carlton Glover, his chief-of-staff, Naomi Clark, general counsel and Regina Booker, his executive assistant smiled patiently back at him. At the far end of the table sat a wiry, bookish man, wearing a herringbone tweed jacket with elbow patches and wrinkled khaki pants.

"You've all had a day to review this information provided by the trustee of Fresh Start," said the mayor as he motioned toward the visitor at the end of the table. "I've asked Dr. Alan Joyner, Professor of Sociology at Savannah State University, to join us. Dr. Joyner has also had the opportunity to review the data, and I thought his insight would be helpful to us as we attempt to navigate through this issue. As you're all aware, Reverend Thaddeus Johnson, an influential member of our community and a strong supporter of this administration, has made certain accusations that this program is racially discriminatory in nature. I assured the reverend that we would look into his concerns and respond accordingly. That being said, I will turn the floor over to Dr. Joyner."

The professor rose and dimmed the lights. Using a laptop to project the charts, he began his presentation. "Thank you, Mayor. This first slide shows the 2013 U.S. Census Bureau population estimates for Chatham County. As you can see, the county is just under fifty-five percent white, forty percent African-American, slightly under six percent Hispanic and just under three percent Asian. Note that these numbers add to more than one-hundred percent because people may choose to report more than one race to indicate their racial mixture, such as Hispanic and White. This next slide illustrates the demographics of Fresh Start applicants, compared to the census data. There is very little difference between the two. African-American applicants are disproportionately higher by three percentage points, while the other three major demographic groups are either the same or slightly less than their representation of the overall population. Based upon this data, there does not appear to be a statistically significant racial correlation."

The chief-of-staff, Carlton Glover interrupted. "Professor, looking at the data, there seems to be a significant number of low-income applicants to the program."

"You are correct," Dr. Joyner commented, "which provides a segue to my next slide. This shows the percentage of Fresh Start applicants who report household income below fifteen thousand dollars to be thirty-five percent. I've compared that to the latest Small Area Income and Poverty Estimates (SAIPE) provided by the U.S. Census Bureau. This survey reports the percentage of Chatham County individuals living in poverty is twenty percent. The variance appears to be significant. Low-income citizens are applying to this program at one and a half times the rate of their demographic representation. However, keep in mind SAIPE defines poverty levels according to the number of adults and children in the household whereas Fresh Start simply defines it as under $15,000."

"I don't understand something professor," said Naomi Clark, the attorney. "How can lower-income citizens be disproportionately represented without the same being true for minorities?"

"I asked myself the same question," said the professor. "This next slide shows 2013 poverty estimates by race according to the American Community Survey. In Chatham County, the poverty rate for all blacks including African-Americans is twenty-six percent, and the rate for Hispanics and those of Latino origin is about thirty-two percent while the rate for whites is thirteen percent. If income was a factor, as it appears to be in the case of Fresh Start, you would expect minorities to be disproportionately represented. Statistics have shown that much of this difference is the result of family structure—minorities are much more likely to live in female-headed single families. For example, the gap between white and African-American poverty rates would be much less if married couple families were uniformly distributed across both groups."

"What does that have to do with anything?" asked Regina Booker.

"I'm not sure. Fresh Start data is skewed for other factors as well. For instance, males make up fifty-eight percent of the applicants but only forty-eight percent of the population. Unmarried individuals are over-represented. It could be that minorities are over-represented in the city but underrepresented in the county. I had to use different metrics in order to fashion a comparative analysis. In some cases we're comparing apples to oranges. Unfortunately we don't have enough data—or enough time for that matter—to answer all of these questions."

"Thank you, Dr. Joyner. I appreciate all you've done on such short notice." He escorted the professor out the door before he addressed his staff. "Anybody have any bright ideas?"

The following afternoon, Quinton Devereaux parked his car at the side of the church between a black Rolls Royce and a white stretch limousine. The reverend, it seemed, was in. He entered through the side door where the administrative offices were located and was promptly met by two burly security types, wearing tight-fitting black tee shirts and gigantic gold crosses dangling from their oversized necks. Quinton recognized them from the reverend's visit to City Hall a few days ago.

"I'm here to see Reverend Johnson," he said. "I believe he's expecting me."

The larger of the two men, his head shaved completely bald, revealing a nasty scar just above his ear, motioned him toward the door leading to the offices. As Quinton moved in the direction of the door, the shorter man stepped forward brandishing a metal detection wand. "Surely you're not going to use that on me," he said indignantly.

The man holding the wand looked inquisitively at his bald-headed counterpart, who nodded silently, occasioning him to step aside and clear a path for the mayor. "It's been a pleasure conversing with you gentlemen," he said as he made his way past them toward the reverend's office.

Quinton had visited the office several times during the campaign when things were ultimately decided. He was not a member of the congregation. He attended a smaller, quieter Presbyterian church on the other side of town, but he did attend occasionally as a guest of the reverend to show his support and his appreciation. It was an office in the sense that his Rolls Royce was a car—it was really much more than that. With over three thousand square feet including a sitting area with two large sofas, kitchenette, bedroom and full bathroom, complete with walk-in shower and Jacuzzi tub, it was bigger than many of his church members' homes. Quinton often wondered why the reverend needed a bedroom when his home was a ten-minute drive from the church, but he knew better than to ask. He found the reverend sitting at his desk, a monstrous piece of antique mahogany with intricate hand carvings depicting The Last Supper.

"Quinton, what a pleasure to see you again," he said rising to greet the mayor. "I hope you come bearing good tidings."

"I have done quite a bit of research since we last spoke, Reverend. I've had my entire staff working on this, including the city's legal council. Our conclusion is that there is nothing illegal about what they're doing. There are no grounds for the city to step in and stop them from continuing their enterprise."

"You didn't need to drive all the way over here from City Hall to tell me that, Quinton."

"I also talked to Tyler Marshall. The son, that is. I don't think the father has anything to do with any of this. I get the impression they don't see eye-to-eye on a lot of things. Anyway, he agreed to share with me the demographic breakdown of the program's applicants. We have breakdowns by sex, age, race and income. We found two statistically meaningful factors. Men are more likely than women to participate relative to their overall percentage of the population and lower income individuals are more likely to participate than higher income individuals, again relative to their overall percentage of the population. We did not see any indication that age or race is a factor. White people are just as likely to apply as African-Americans or Asians or Hispanics."

The reverend pressed the fingertips of both hands together, forming a steeple as he gazed at the ceiling. "I don't believe it."

"I've got the numbers right here. I'd be happy to share them with…"

"I don't need to see the numbers. I'm more concerned with the intent than with the results. And the intent, in this case, is pure evil."

"That may be so, but it doesn't give us any room to make allegations. We simply can't prove…"

"I don't need proof, Quinton!" the reverend's voice rose. "God doesn't need proof. Do you think Moses had to run the Ten Commandments by his attorney before he could present them to his people? I am not concerned with what the law says we can or cannot do."

"I'm sorry, but I just don't see how we have any alternatives here, Reverend."

The reverend eyed him coolly, and the mayor felt an icy tingle at the nape of his neck. "Frankly, I've got some alternatives of my own in mind, something more forceful than the power of the law."

"What's that, Reverend?"

"The power of God, my friend."

CHAPTER NINE

The buses rolled in with the fog on a humid and overcast Monday morning. Four buses, each carrying approximately forty members from Community Church of the South, pulled into the narrow side street adjacent to the law offices at 319 Drayton Street and parked. The church members filed off the buses in quiet, orderly fashion and began forming a perimeter around the brick building. They were mingling with their neighbors, talking in loud, boisterous voices as they shared their weekend activities with their compatriots. A visitor to the scene would have thought they had landed in the middle of a church social.

Fifteen minutes later, a late model, blue Cadillac Escalade pick-up truck pulled up in front of the building, and two burly men, the reverend's muscle, climbed out and began passing out cardboard signs, mounted on wooden posts with various slogans and messages, to the milling crowd. The two men immediately began issuing instructions over a wireless public-address system and quickly assumed control of the scene. The mood of the crowd was still light and playful, but they became more attentive and focused on the task at hand.

Another fifteen minutes after the arrival of the Escalade, a white, stretch limousine pulled up behind the truck. Out stepped the Reverend Thaddeus Johnson to the thundering applause of the crowd. He was wearing a double-breasted Brioni suit and Gucci shoes with a clerical collar for effect only - he rarely ever wore one in church. He grabbed the microphone from one of his security men and addressed the crowd. A sharp ray of sunshine pierced the dense fog and lit upon the crowd as he began to speak.

"Dear Lord, cast your light down upon your faithful children and obedient servants here today as we strive to do your work. Give us the strength to fight the forces of oppression that bear down upon us. Burn off the clouds and mist that blind us to injustice and show us the clear and brilliant path to enlightenment."

As he spoke, the warmth of the sun began to burn off the low-lying fog cover as if on signal from above. "Show us the way Lord, to stop the evil being done here today, stop this vile and pernicious attempt to cause the premature murder of your children. The very first command you gave us, Lord, was to be fruitful and multiply. It seems there are those among us today who would mock your command. We will defeat them with your help, Lord. Please give us strength to fight this good and righteous battle in your name. Amen."

The demonstration was officially under way. A line had been drawn in the sand, and there could be no doubt whose side God was on.

At nine o'clock, about fifteen minutes after the reverend's arrival, vans representing camera crews from two local television stations arrived just in time to beat the reporters from the Savannah Daily Journal. By now, the crowd was beginning to whip into a frenzy, loudly chanting slogans depicted on their hand held signs such as, "Stop Racism Now" and "Protect God's Children," for the benefit of the camera crews, who were obligingly recording the scene for display on newscasts later that day. The two men from the Escalade distributed flyers to the assembled members of the press, which contained talking points that espoused the position of the demonstrators as set forth by the Reverend Johnson. The great man himself was currently besieged by supporters and well-wishers anxious to shake his hand and communicate to him their fervent willingness to follow him eagerly wherever he chose to lead them. A speaker's podium was hastily erected out near the street and, before long, the reverend made his way through the throng of supporters to a place behind it. Looking intently into the cameras, he began to speak.

"We are here today to protest a grave injustice upon the African American people of this community. We have endured slavery. We have endured hatred. We have endured oppression, and we have endured repression. We have lived with the ugly face of racism staring at us every minute of every day of our lives, but in all of my life, I have never seen a more blatant attempt by certain members of white society to prevent black society from rising above these barriers. They thought they might appease us by giving us our freedom, but we demanded more! They thought they could appease us by giving us the right to vote, but we demanded more! They thought they might appease us by passing civil rights laws, but we demanded more! Now, because they cannot give us what we want, because they will not give us what we demand, because they cannot silence the deafening roar that is our united demand for equality—true equality, they have settled on a new, diabolic scheme."

"Who can cry out who has no voice? Who can march who has no legs? Who can demand change that does not exist? They sit in their ivy-covered mansions with their finely trimmed lawns surrounded by iron fences and say to themselves, 'How can we solve this black problem?' And the answer is as simple and clear to them as it is evil and poisonous to clear-thinking people around the world. If there are no blacks, then there is no problem."

The reverend stepped away from the microphone and removed a handkerchief from his coat pocket to wipe the sweat off his brow, while the crowd surrounding him let off a chorus of boos drowning out any competing noise within a mile of the speaker. They were spellbound, hanging onto his every word and shouting encouragement after every sentence. He was in complete command as they stood captive under his spell. After a moment's pause, he raised his hands for silence so that he might continue.

"They ask themselves, what do we have that they do not? What might we offer them to convince them not to bear children? Not to breed? What might we bribe them with to ensure their ultimate destruction? The answer is so simple—money. Cold hard cash. 'For we have so much and they have so little,' they say to themselves from their mansions and suburban palaces. But I ask each of you here today, are we prepared to sell our souls for a few gold coins?"

"No!" the crowd roared.

"Are the lives of our future sons and daughters so incidental that we would put a price tag on their very existence?"

"No!" came the deafening response.

"Are we prepared to mortgage our future for a few measly dollars today?"

"No!" they shouted.

"No, we are not! Because to put a price on something as valuable as a human life is to say that we have no worth at all. To put such a price on the lives of our children is to establish ourselves as a commodity, one that might be bought and sold, like a piece of meat. Do we wish to return to the days of slavery?"

"No!" emphatically.

"No, we do not! It says in the Bible, 'Bear fruit and multiply.' It is the word of the Lord passed directly down to us, and any alternate view that contradicts this word can only be the voice of Satan!

We are standing here in front of the house of Satan, and we shall not leave until we have thrust him out and put an end to his vile, despicable work here on Earth. Praise the Lord!"

"Praise the Lord," the crowd responded.

"We will remain here until the Fresh Start program, as its founders so innocently refer to it, is disbanded and abolished forever, and nothing, not the passage of time, not storms or inclement weather, not the Devil himself will prevent us from achieving our goal! We are God's messengers, his angels here on earth, and we will not shirk our responsibilities to Him. We seek no greater reward than the glory of God, and no one under any circumstances shall stop us from performing His work."

"Amen, Reverend!" shouted the crowd. As the dense fog continued to burn off, rays of bright sunlight cascaded down upon them, illuminating their faces in eerie, incandescent brilliance. They were here for him and prepared for battle, righteous soldiers in the army of the Lord. The television cameras obligingly captured the looks of steely resolve in their eyes for the benefit of the audience watching at home. Who could possibly doubt their fervent belief in the cause at hand?

Tyler rolled out of Mara's bed relatively early Monday morning and groggily headed for the shower. Sleeping at her tiny apartment had become a ritual and, as a matter of convenience, he would bring a change of clothes with him to save him the trip home to shower before work, not to mention the prying eyes of his nosy neighbor, Mrs. Moynihan, one of his mother's bridge partners at the club. He wasn't ready yet to introduce Mara to his parents. Her liberal leanings, abrupt and straightforward manner and intense dislike of anything capitalist would certainly alienate them. Perhaps, he reflected privately, that's why he liked her so much.

As he was shaving in the bathroom mirror, she crept up behind him and he felt her hand underneath his bath towel, caressing, exploring. That was another reason he liked her so much. He had never been with anyone that sexually uninhibited before, certainly not his ex-wife.

"Be careful down there," he admonished, "I'm shaving. You wouldn't want me to cut myself, would you?"

"I'm not nearly as concerned with that head as I am with this one," she said as her hand found its way to his quickly rising member. I think you might be late to work today."

"What makes you say that?"

"This," she said, undoing the sash on her robe and letting it fall to the floor, exposing her naked body.

"I'm sure Annie can handle whatever's going on at the office this morning," he said without a trace of concern, as his tongue gently explored her body, leaving tiny patches of shaving cream, like icebergs in its wake.

Annie pulled up to the office to find a line of protestors blocking her entrance to the parking area. Her first instinct was one of surprise. This was something she clearly did not expect. Then she saw the signs they were holding as she began to understand what was happening. She spotted the Reverend Johnson preening in front of the cameras and felt a raw, concentrated anger sweep through her body. She felt her jaws tighten as she hit the horn of her BMW and surged through the human picket line, sending bodies flying in both directions away from the accelerating car. The protestors barely had time to react to the approaching car, so no one got a good look at its occupant.

From somewhere toward the back a voice screamed, "It's Tyler Marshall!" and a dozen protestors descended on the parked car, primed for a confrontation.

They quickly took a step back when Annie stepped out of the car. They were expecting a white lawyer, not this angry black woman, glaring at them menacingly. She spoke loudly but in a firm and controlled voice.

"You all are on private property right now. If you're not off this property in less than ten seconds, I will have each and every one of you arrested for trespassing. Do I make myself clear?"

"That's Bittie's girl, Annie," someone back on the street shouted. Annie flashed her best fake smile. "Hello, Dorothy. I suggest you tell your friends here to heed my advice."

The small group confronting Annie turned to Dorothy in confusion. They were caught in limbo, publicly exposed and unable to decide for themselves whether or not they should back down to this woman. "Oh, you better listen to what she's saying," said Dorothy. "That girl would just as soon cut you to pieces as look at you!"

Immediately they all shot for the safe refuge of the street, where the others were assembled. All eyes shot to the reverend, the flock awaiting instructions.

What they saw next, shocked every last one of them. Annie purposefully strode directly up to him. He seemed to them to be caught off guard, a bit unsure of himself almost. "Hello, Reverend."

"Hello, Ms. Burriss."

"I would suggest that you instruct your sheep...I mean your flock here to stay off private property. That way we can avoid any potential problems. Understood?"

"Now you just see here. You can't go on..."

"I can and I will. You see, Reverend, I have the power of the law on my side. I suggest you obey it."

"The only law I answer to, young lady, is the law of God."

"The law of God? Why isn't that interesting!" she said smiling. "You mean the law of God excuses two-bit hypocrites like you? Taking advantage of young girls? You know, Reverend, I haven't been to church in some time, but it seems like I remember God not being too supportive of adultery, let alone from a member of the clergy."

"It's sad you have so much hate in your heart, Annie," he said quietly, with a nervous look toward the television cameras, which were still trained on the marchers by the road. "Trying to discredit someone by throwing out false and untrue allegations. Is that what they taught you in law school?"

"Just keep off private property, Reverend. This is my first and final warning. If you're looking for a fight, you picked the wrong girl."

As she turned and walked away in the direction of the building, she could hear his voice clearly behind her. "We'll see about that."

Tyler finally arrived at the office a half-hour behind Annie and saw the throng of protestors in all their glory, chanting and yelling in front of the television cameras. He could also see Annie's car parked in its usual spot directly in front of the building, remarkable in its solitary amid the chaos of the unfolding scene. As he approached the building, his senses were dulled by the unexpected shock of the crowd. Given so little time to react, he obeyed his first instinct—flight. His foot hit the accelerator as he sped past the building and the unruly mob outside. Two blocks down the road, out of sight of the protestors, he stopped the car and dialed Annie on his cell phone.

"Annie, what the hell is going on over there?"

"It seems the good Reverend Johnson has decided to ratchet up the intensity level of his opposition to Fresh Start from his Sunday sermons. It looks like we have a full-scale protest underway, complete with coverage by both television and print media."

"Shit! That's the last thing we need right now! How did you get through that mob? Did they attack you?"

"They thought about it, then thought better of it. We have an understanding right now with the reverend that they are not to encroach on private property. Don't worry, Tyler. You'll be safe."

"I wasn't worried about myself," he lied. "What about Darlene? I didn't see her car."

"She called and said she's not coming in to work as long as "those people" are outside the building. She said she feared for her safety."

"This is just great. How long do you think this will go on?"

"I'm not sure but knowing Thaddeus Johnson, I wouldn't count on him going away anytime soon."

"Wonderful. I'm on my way in. Watch for me out the window. If things look like they might get out of control, call the police."

"Roger that, White Buffalo. Black Bear standing by. Over."

"Very funny. Just keep watch at the window please."

He turned the car around and approached the crowd. They all seemed to be focused on the cameras and appeared not to notice him. As he slowly turned left into the parking lot he heard a voice cry out from behind.

"That's him! That's Tyler Marshall!"

Instantly, he heard hands beating the trunk and side windows of his car and could feel the vibrations reverberate through his body. Cries of "racist" and "Satan" stung as hard as the physical pounding on his vehicle. He was slowly making his way to the safety of the parking lot but froze when a face appeared staring at him through his front window. It was a man's face, etched and time worn, black as night, full of hate. His hesitancy allowed the laggards in the crowd time to catch up to him, and he soon found himself surrounded. The mob started rocking his car back and forth, and he felt sure they were going to tip him over. Panicked, he set the car in park and gunned the accelerator. The rev of the engine was enough to send the protestors in front of the car scurrying for cover, and as they did, he slipped the transmission into drive and headed for daylight. Human hands and feet continued to beat against the car until he cleared the street and entered the parking lot of the building, at which point all of the hammering abruptly stopped. It seemed they were honoring the property boundary after all. He parked his car next to Annie's and walked quickly toward the front door of the building. He could hear the taunts and catcalls of the crowd and could see one of the camera lenses trained on him out of the corner of his eye. He instinctively turned away from the camera, shielding his face as he fumbled for his keys to unlock the door. Before he had a chance to find them, the door swung open. He was greeted by the smiling face of Annie, who appeared completely calm, almost amused by the situation.

"Did you see that, Annie?" Tyler asked, his body trembling. "They could have killed me!"

"I doubt that seriously, Tyler. They were just trying to scare you a little, that's all."

"I'd say they succeeded in their mission then. How can you be so sure they weren't trying to kill me?"

"Because they're only here following Thaddeus Johnson's orders. If he wanted to kill you, he'd probably have it done in a subtler fashion."

"Thanks. That's very comforting to know. No offense, but I don't care what you say, I'm not taking any chances. I'm calling the police."

"Suit yourself, but be careful. A lot of them are on his side."

"Whose side? Johnson's?"

"No, haven't you heard? God's side."

Tyler found the number for the Savannah Police Department. As he dialed, he was acutely aware that his hands were shaking. As he looked out the window, he could see the crowd was honoring the demarcation line between public and private property and didn't seem to pose an immediate threat as long as he and Annie remained in the building. This provided little comfort to Tyler. At the moment, he was scared to death.

"Savannah Police Department."

"Charles Mosely, please."

"Chief Mosely is in a meeting right now. May I take a message?" droned the receptionist, oblivious to the urgency of the moment.

"Tell him it's Tyler Marshall, and it's an emergency."

"I'm sorry sir, but he asked not to be disturbed."

"You better disturb him, goddammit!" Tyler felt his voice rising, a catch in his throat. "I said it's an emergency!"

"Hold on sir," came the irritated reply. A full minute passed before the voice returned. "Hold on please, Mr. Marshall. I'm transferring you to his office."

Tyler heard the familiar voice of the Police Chief as he picked up the phone. "Hello, Tyler. Is there some sort of problem?"

"You're damn right there's some sort of problem! I've got about a hundred and fifty extremely angry people on the street outside my office building carrying signs and yelling all kinds of ugly things. They attacked me in my car as I was pulling into the driveway just a few minutes ago. I thought they were going to kill me!"

"I don't understand, Tyler. What are they doing there?"

"What the hell do you think they're doing here, Charles?"

"Okay, okay, calm down. Just tell me who they are."

"As far as I can tell, they're some kind of church group. Community Church, I think. Only they don't seem to be acting very...Christian-like, if you know what I mean."

"Thaddeus Johnson?"

"Yep. I can't tell if they're protesting religious or racial lines, but it appears that almost all of the protestors are African Americans. In fact, I don't see white faces at all...except for the reporters."

Tyler noticed an uncomfortable pause of silence on the line. "Reporters?"

"Yes, reporters. Two local TV stations have crews outside."

"Tyler, it's important that we keep publicity to a minimum. You understand that."

"It's a little late for that I'm afraid, Charles."

"Right. Well, in any case, it's critical that we protect the confidentiality of this…"

"Don't worry, Charles. I'm not talking to anybody. Unless of course it takes you more than five minutes to get an army of cops over here to get these people under control!"

"I'm right on it. Just try and stay calm, Tyler."

"That's easy for you to say."

Within minutes, five patrol cars appeared on the street facing the building and immediately began herding the crowd away from the entrance driveway to the building and onto the sidewalk by the street. Barricades were set up along the perimeter of the driveway allowing free ingress and egress to the building. From an upstairs window, Tyler could see a well-dressed man talking to the police. Despite his relatively small stature, he seemed to command the respect of the officers, who treated him deferentially. He could feel Annie's presence, gazing over his shoulder at the scene below.

"Is that your Reverend Johnson?" he asked without taking his eyes off the street.

"That's him, but he's not my Reverend."

"You don't seem to think much of him."

"Let's just say we have a history."

"You mind telling me about it?"

"I'd rather not. It was a long time ago."

"Look, Annie. That man is sitting out there with over a hundred protestors, and we're going to be featured on the six o'clock news and tomorrow's paper. He could ruin us. The firm's very existence could be at stake here. If there's something between the two of you, I need to know about it."

She looked at him pensively, doubt filling the lines in her face. "Him being here doesn't have anything to do with me. If anything, he's probably a bit afraid of me."

"Afraid of you? Why would he be afraid?"

She stood mute for a while. A phone rang in an adjacent room, breaking the silence, but neither one moved to answer it. Each ring reverberated in Tyler's head, an unwelcome intruder to their privacy, like the kicking and pounding at his car only minutes ago. He knew she was struggling with something, and he began to have second thoughts about pressing her, but before he could speak, Annie broke the silence.

"When I was fourteen years old, Thaddeus Johnson raped me."

Tyler shut his eyes. "No, Annie."

"We went to his church. Momma dragged all of us there every Sunday. I was in the choir, and one day on a school night he made us stay late for practice. After practice, everyone left, but he asked me to stay behind. He said he had something he wanted to talk to me about. Next thing I knew, I'm in his office with two thugs outside. He's telling me I'm at a pivotal point in my life, that I've got to decide whether I'm ready to give myself to God. The next thing I know he's got his hands on me, pressing himself up against me. I yelled out, but no one ever came. To this day, I can't remember if I resisted or not. I was so confused by what was happening, and, of course, I trusted him. At some point, I must have blacked out or my brain shut down, I really can't remember. At the end he's telling me we needed to keep this a secret, that whatever happened was between him and me and God. When I left the office, the two thugs wouldn't even look at me. I was so ashamed. I didn't tell anyone, not Momma, not a soul. After a while, I convinced myself that it never really happened. It wasn't really that hard to do. I mean, I couldn't remember a thing anyway. I quit going to church after that. Momma never even asked me any questions about it. She just accepted it like somehow she knew, but she couldn't have known, could she? About two months later, I found out about the baby. I went to him, and at first he denied being the father. I started shouting—I was hysterical, bawling like a baby, and he started shushing me. He told me he'd take care of me no matter what, that

I didn't need to worry about anything. Two days later, one of his goons picked me up on my way home from school and took me to an abortion clinic. I didn't even know where we were going until we got there. I had no time to think. I just went along with it. Two hours later, the problem was 'solved.' I never told anybody until today, and I've never stepped foot inside a church since then. Tell me, Tyler, what kind of man rages against birth control and abortion as sins against God, while he commits those very sins himself in order to clean up his inconvenient messes?"

"An extremely hypocritical one and probably a very dangerous one as well. Have you thought about going to the police?"

"For what? It happened years ago and I can't prove anything anyway. What happened to me is past history, and there's nothing I can do to change it. I'm more worried about the others. Mara thinks he's got a new one now. She met her at his church—the younger sister of one of her co-workers. Did she tell you about it?"

"Yes she did, but I thought she was exaggerating. Mara can be pretty dramatic sometimes. Now it doesn't seem like an exaggeration at all."

"No, I don't think so."

"Annie, I'm so sorry. I don't know what to say." Tyler studied her face and saw something he couldn't remember ever seeing before, something that unnerved him. Annie, the tough, cynical, battle-hardened defender of his youth was crying. He pulled her to him and held her tightly as his shoulder grew moist from the tears.

They spent the rest of the morning answering the telephone and keeping an eye on the crowd gathered on the sidewalk in front of the building. Tyler tried to bury himself in paperwork in an attempt to take his mind off the scene outside, but he couldn't resist peeking out the window occasionally. Each time, he held out some faint hope they would be gone, having grown tired or bored from their efforts, but they stubbornly remained, like kudzu clinging to a chain link fence. At eleven a.m., the camera crews departed, no doubt in a hurry to make their deadline for the twelve o'clock news. Tyler noticed the intensity level of the protestors dropped significantly in the absence of the media. Picket signs were rested on the sidewalk, donut boxes were passed around, and a queue for coffee was formed at a makeshift tent. Tyler looked on in wonder as the mood changed from violent anger to merriment, the demonstrators laughing and joking amongst themselves, seemingly without a care in the world. *I can't believe these are the same people who tried to kill me this morning.*

As Tyler viewed the lull in activity on the street, he spied a man, white, in his mid-twenties walk toward the building from the bus stop down the street. The man stopped at the barricade and appeared to be conversing with the police standing sentry by the front entrance. After a brief conversation, they waved him through in the direction of the building as the protestors crowded behind the police to view the solitary figure passing through their self-imposed gauntlet. They seemed confused by his presence, unsure how to act. All the fiery emotion and indignation of the morning seemed to have dissipated. It was almost as if they hadn't been briefed properly on their position of this eventuality. *Do I care if this happens to a white man? Is it the act itself or the subject of the act that should concern me?* An awkward silence settled in as they debated these questions in their minds.

Tyler greeted the man at the front door. He was wearing a three-day beard with a faded t-shirt and holes in his jeans. Tyler recognized the not-so-faint smell of marijuana cloaking the man like cheap cologne.

"I'm here about the ad in the paper," the man said. Tyler held out his hand in a greeting and immediately noticed the track marks on the inside of the man's right arm.

"Sure, come on in," he said. "Sorry for the mess out there. They showed up this morning unexpectedly."

"No worries, man. They were cool. The cops made me more nervous than the people they were supposed to be protecting me from. I don't like cops."

"If you had been here a couple of hours ago, you'd understand why the cops are outside. So I take it you're here about Fresh Start?" The man nodded, a bead of perspiration forming at his temple. "That crowd out there seems to think this is a bad idea," said Tyler. "Tell me. What do you think?"

"I think it's none of their business," said the man, "and I could sure use the money."

After that, Tyler kept an eye out the window for the rest of the day. He could see a pattern clearly forming. The picketers allowed white or Hispanic applicants to pass through unchallenged, with nary a word of reproach. Black applicants, on the other hand, were berated and verbally abused if they attempted to approach the street entrance to the building. Several lost their nerve and turned away to the jubilant cheers of the crowd. They seemed nervous and intimidated. This was something they were obviously not prepared for. Tyler didn't blame them one bit. Occasionally a brave soul passed through the gauntlet undaunted. Tyler witnessed one such exchange from his second story view.

"Don't do it, brother. Don't sell yourself to the white man," one of the demonstrators shouted at a thin, young black man.

"Who's going to put food on the table for my family? I've already got three kids!" the man snapped angrily at his accuser. "Are you?"

"God will provide for you if you have faith in Him," answered the protestor.

"I don't see God handing me no check for fifteen thousand dollars, do you brother?"

"God will forgive you for your sins. That's worth more than any amount of money."

"Don't preach to me unless you've walked in my shoes," the man said as he turned his back to the crowd and marched toward the building.

Tyler received calls from every single media outlet in the city requesting comment before they ran their stories but thought it best to withhold any statements until he had a chance to talk with his clients. They would be upset by this unwanted publicity—of that he was sure. His mind raced as he thought about what he could have done to avoid this mess. Mara had warned him about the reverend's sermon. Perhaps he should have taken the mayor's call more seriously. Still, he hadn't expected a reaction of this magnitude.

Fresh Start activity was down eighty percent that day. They'd been averaging thirty applicants a day. Today there were six: three whites, two African Americans and one Hispanic. The demonstration definitely had the effect its organizers were hoping for. Tyler couldn't help but wonder what other fall-out there might be to the law practice as a result.

At four o'clock, Tyler's cell phone rang. Mara. "Lucifer speaking," he said.

"I see you still have your sense of humor—that's good. It seems you're a celebrity here in town today. You should hear the radio talk shows."

"I'd rather not. Today has been pretty rough."

"I bet. You can't say I didn't warn you though."

"I'm sorry, I don't remember you telling me there was going to be a civil rights march on my front lawn, or I would be attacked and almost killed by an angry mob on my way to work."

"I told you I thought it was a bad idea."

"You told me to do the opposite of what everyone expects me to do! Don't play Monday morning quarterback with me. I had no idea things would get this out of hand."

"I'm coming over to see you."

"Mara, don't even think about it. It's way too dangerous…"

"Too late. I'm pulling into the driveway now."

"Mara!" he shouted as the signal died. He ran to the window in time to see her yellow Volkswagen Beetle pull up to the front entrance and stop. He felt his hands go clammy as she got out of the car and walked past the police guard directly into the mass of humanity. Within seconds she was hugging and greeting the demonstrators like long lost relatives at a family reunion. Someone handed her a bottle of water, and she accepted it gratefully, smiling and laughing conspiratorially. *She's acting like she's one of them!*

"Looks like your girlfriend's gone over to the dark side…literally," he heard Annie's voice behind him.

"I don't believe what I'm seeing," said Tyler, shocked.

"You shouldn't be so surprised. She's friends with a lot of those people out there. She identifies with them a whole lot better than we do, I'll promise you that."

"Still, it seems almost…"

"Traitorous? Most people see the world in absolute terms, good versus evil, us versus them, black versus white. Mara's not like that. She's comfortable standing on either side of a conflict…or both."

"Then why is she so damned opinionated all the time?"

"She's a debater. She'll take either side of an argument—she doesn't care. If you have a strong opinion about something, she'll take the other side just to force you to defend your position, test your convictions, find the truth. I've always told her she'd make a great lawyer."

"Maybe that's why I make such a shitty one," said Tyler. I don't have time for games like that."

"You have plenty of time," Annie said. "You just don't care. There's a difference."

They both watched as Mara approached the Reverend Johnson. He hugged her, a little too closely Tyler thought, with his hands extending oppositely around her back to the sides of her breasts. She broke the embrace firmly but politely, as they fell into a private discussion like two old friends catching up on recent events. Mara was doing most of the talking while the reverend's head bobbed in implicit agreement. Occasionally he laughed, like she'd just told him some deliciously funny joke, shared only by the two of them. Tyler had the sneaking suspicion that the joke involved him in some way, but he preferred not to think too hard about it.

After a brief while, the reverend clapped his hands and shouted something to the milling crowd, which began to move in the general direction of the waiting buses on the adjacent side street, Mara waved goodbye and hugged several of them as they left, as if she were sending them off on some great adventure. As the crowd filed onto the waiting buses, the two security men picked up the signs and placed them in the bed of the truck along with the speaker's podium. Their cargo fully loaded, the buses slowly pulled out with the Cadillac Escalade and white limo following closely behind. As quickly as they had arrived, they were gone, all of them, except for Mara and the police sentries, dutifully guarding the diminutive building from an invisible enemy.

CHAPTER TEN

After the schizophrenic mob departed, Tyler and Annie walked out of the building to survey the damage. Paper, aluminum cans, empty water bottles and assorted trash intermingled with chunks of Bermuda sod uprooted from the soil gave the manicured front sidewalk entrance the appearance of a fraternity house lawn the day after a band party. Tyler was struck, however, not so much by the leftover remnants of trash and debris but by the eerie silence that hung over the area. A gentle warm wind whistled by, and he thought he could hear in it the faint echoes of the departed protestors. The wind subsided, and the hushed stillness returned.

Tyler approached Mara stiffly, as if he was seeing her for the first time. Annie stood behind him, her arms crossed, eyes questioning. "Do you mind telling us what that was all about?" he asked.

"I thought you wanted to get rid of them?"

"I did, but what did you say to make them leave?"

"I told them I knew you and that I could talk some sense into you if they gave me a little space and time."

Tyler felt the blood rush to his face. "Talk some sense into me? Who appointed you chief negotiator?"

"No one. I just thought you'd appreciate a break to think about what you're doing here. I certainly didn't make any promises on your behalf."

"Think about what I'm doing here? I don't remember any huge protests from you when I told you about it the first time."

"That was before things escalated. I told you it was a bad idea— I just didn't think it would end up being such a big deal."

"What do you suggest I do, Mara?"

"Shut down the program. It's not worth it. Whatever money you make, you'll lose from the rest of your business. Your name and face are going to be plastered all over this town by tomorrow morning. Can your practice really afford that kind of publicity?"

He paused while he considered the implications of what Mara just said. He knew she was right. This would not be good for business, especially if it turned out to be a long, protracted battle. He needed a second opinion. "Annie, what do you think?" he asked.

"Mara's right about the publicity. It will make things more difficult for us in the short term. In the long term, it may actually bring more public awareness to the firm. Who knows? I don't like the idea of backing down to that self-righteous, hypocritical bully though. Sometimes you've got to stand up for what you believe in. You haven't done anything to be ashamed of Tyler."

"What if I do back down? Would you be ashamed of me if I did?"

"It's not my opinion you should be worried about," Annie replied. "That's up to the man in the mirror to decide."

"Be careful not to let your ego get in the way of your brain, Tyler," Mara cautioned. "This just isn't worth it. My advice is to quit while you're behind, and live to fight another day."

Tyler surprised himself with his own reaction. For reasons he couldn't quite understand, he didn't want to quit. "Maybe if

I could sit down and talk to this Johnson guy, we could work this out. I shared the applicant data with the mayor after he called. African Americans are not disproportionately represented compared to whites or Hispanics. It seems like this is all being blown out of proportion. If I could share the data with him, maybe he'd back down."

Annie shook her head. "If you gave the data to the mayor, you have to assume that Johnson has seen it. Who do you think got him elected?"

"But the mayor seemed satisfied with the results. He certainly didn't give me the impression that he felt there was any sort of racial injustice going on here."

"He might have been satisfied with the results, but that doesn't mean Thaddeus Johnson was. The mayor is an intelligent, rational man who takes the time to really understand both sides of an issue before he acts. Johnson is a grandstander. He's much more about imagery than facts. You've given him the opportunity to paint a picture of some nefarious plot, one of white versus black, rich versus poor, good versus evil. Like it or not, those kind of themes still resonate in our society, and as long as they do, men like Thaddeus Johnson will figure out a way to profit from them."

"I've said from the beginning that this doesn't have as much to do with race as it does class," Mara added. "This is a textbook case of class warfare."

"You're right to a point, Mara," said Annie, "but the piece you're missing is that in some segments of the black community, they're one and the same. White people came to America in ships originally from England, then the rest of Western Europe followed by Eastern Europe. The countries they came from all had well developed social caste systems in place: nobility, landowners, merchants and peasants. Their social standing defined who they were to the rest of the world until they came to America and found those barriers didn't exist to the same extent they were accustomed to back home. Black people, on the other hand, came to America on ships as slaves. They were all equal in their poverty, their bondage and their misery. It wasn't until after Reconstruction that blacks got even the most basic freedoms, and civil rights didn't come along for most until the sixties. The only way we could survive and thrive as a race was to stick together and fight for equality in a society that clearly wasn't willing to give it to us. We fought together, and we voted together because we all had the same issues and craved the same opportunities. Now, thanks to some great leaders like Martin Luther King Jr., we have many of those opportunities today, and we're beginning to understand what white people knew long ago—that not all men and women are created equal."

Mara interrupted. "Are you saying that just because white society uses social stratification as a means to oppress the permanent underclass that it's okay for African-Americans to do the same?"

"I'm saying that educated, successful black citizens today identify as much and often times more with their white counterparts as they do with their black brothers and sisters living in poverty. Those of us who've taken advantage of the opportunities available to us and made something of ourselves don't feel the same tug to the plight of the poor as we used to. Don't get me wrong—it's still there, it's just not as powerful as it once was. Now, in addition to seeing poor people as victims of an unfair system, we also see them as lazy, ignorant and unmotivated, labels whites have been comfortable using for centuries. There is class stratification in black society, which is a healthy sign of any developing culture. Sorry, Mara, but we're new to the game. There's the new school, like Mayor Devereaux and me, who accept it for what it is and play the game to win. Then there's the old school, men like Reverend Johnson, who are still clinging to the ideals of the past. They believe they're fighting a noble battle by being defenders of the poor, but they can't see how this sort of politics alienates a rapidly growing segment of their own support base. Every now and then you'll hear a black political leader accuse a successful black public figure of "acting white," like somehow by pursuing a successful career and trying to assimilate into society, they're turning their back on their own people. That kind of regressive thinking is getting us nowhere."

Mara was seething. "I don't care what the color of your skin is, turning your back on the plight of the poor is unconscionable. I admire Reverend Johnson for fighting the noble battle as you call it. If he doesn't, then who will?"

"Calm down, sister girl," said Annie. "I'm not advocating turning our backs on anyone. I'm just saying it's a wonderful thing that black people are succeeding in all walks of life today, and it should be noted their political beliefs and needs are changing and becoming more diverse as a result. As for the Reverend Johnson, feel free to think of him as some sort of protective angel if you'd like, but personally, I question his motives."

"This is all very interesting from a historical and sociological perspective," interrupted Tyler, "but I don't see how any of this brings us any closer to a plan. You say you think it's a waste of time to approach Reverend Johnson, so let's assume that's not an option. What about taking our case directly to the press?"

Annie shrugged. "You might be able to score some points on the race issue with your statistics, but they're hardly going to be sympathetic to your cause. And if you share the actual statistics with them, be prepared for a creative interpretation."

"I agree," echoed Mara. "A rich, white attorney paying poor minorities to undergo voluntary sterilization? That's like Christmas in May to them."

"It appears that my options are somewhat limited," he said.

"So what are you going to do?" Mara and Annie both asked at once.

Tyler experienced a familiar dull ache at the back of his head. He felt a little dizzy and fatigued, like his blood cells weren't getting enough oxygen to the rest of his body. His brain was shutting down, or at least going into some sort of temporary idle, while his thought processes systematically collapsed. He recognized the symptoms and knew this wasn't the time to be making difficult decisions. He needed to escape, just for a while, before he could begin to think clearly again. "I think I need to sleep on it. It's been a long day, ladies. What do you say we call it a day?"

Tyler was on his second Scotch by the time the six o'clock news began. He was sitting in his favorite recliner with a bottle of Glenfiddich and a bucket of ice at his side to save him the constant trips back and forth to the kitchen. Remote in hand, he surfed the local affiliates in an attempt to survey the damage. Two out of three channels led off with the day's protest as the lead story. The other network ran it as the second story behind a jailbreak at the county prison. There was footage of the marchers in addition to the reverend's speech as well as comments from Clarence Cooper, the director of the Savannah branch of the NAACP.

Cooper, when asked of the organization's response to the protest commented, "We vigorously support the Reverend Johnson in his opposition to the Fresh Start program. He has long been a leader in the civil rights movement in this country, and we will continue to support him in his fight against racism, which this program encourages."

A young, female announcer Tyler had never heard of stated that both he and Mayor Devereaux declined to comment. One of the segments ended with an interview of Reverend Johnson outside the front entrance to the offices of Marshall & Marshall, the brick monument sign looming prominently in the background.

When asked how long his group intended to remain protesting he replied ominously, "As long as it takes."

Tyler's cell phone rang at the end of the last news segment. It was Don Abbott. He pressed a button and sent him off to voice mail. Five minutes later it rang again. Mara. Once again he sent the call to voice mail. Annie called a little later, then Mara again. Don Abbott called twice more. He dropped the cell phone in the melted ice and drank the Scotch straight. By the fourth drink, the dull pain in his head had subsided along with the insistent ringing of the submerged phone. By the sixth drink, he found himself in a state of ephemeral bliss, safeguarded in his own private sanctuary from a demanding and unforgiving world.

Deondra Rose stayed late at the church after choir practice that night. No one seemed to take notice. It certainly wasn't the first time she remained behind as the rest of the choir members filed home to their loved ones. Deondra's true love was the church. Her sister, Quinnette, always teased her that she would scare the boys away with her piety, but Deondra didn't care. Besides, she wasn't much interested in boys her own age anyway, so immature and juvenile, all raw energy and testosterone, their brains developing at a snail's pace compared to their bodies. They were nothing like the Reverend Johnson. She couldn't imagine ever being lucky enough to meet a man so caring, so loving, so devout in his faith in God. He was such a charismatic leader. Deondra felt a prickly tingle of pride when she saw the way the women of the congregation stared longingly at him. She took pleasure in imagining the envious looks on their faces once they learned the real truth. She spent hours daydreaming of the time when their passion for each other would finally become public knowledge. The entire congregation treated Monique like royalty. How would they react when they learned that it was her, Deondra Rose, who was his only true love? She didn't feel any ill will toward Mrs. Johnson. Perhaps they might even be friends someday, comparing notes with each other over tea at the Desoto Hilton, on the awesome responsibility that comes with being married to such a visionary man.

She was nervous, agitated all day. She wasn't sure how he was going to take the news. Things were moving faster than even she anticipated. After all, she was only fifteen. Once she entered the church, however, she felt a strange calmness wrap itself around her like a warm blanket. *What happened was God's will,* she told herself. *He's sending a message to us that we're meant to be together for life. Surely Thaddeus will see it that way.*

She made her way upstairs to his office. The short, stocky one—James, was hovering outside the office door, looking bored. He nodded at her as she walked past him. Out of the corner of her eye, she saw him staring, leering really, at her ass. She was used to this sort of thing from the boys at school but for some reason, it always unnerved her coming from James. *It's just so disrespectful. I really need to bring it up with Thaddeus now that things have changed between us. Surely he wouldn't dare look at Monique that way!*

She found him at his desk with his reading glasses perched at the tip of his nose perusing a stack of papers. She loved the way his brown eyes peered over the top rim of the lenses. It made him look so mature, distinguished.

"Deondra," he said, looking up from his paperwork. "What a surprise. Not tonight baby, it's been a long day, and I've got a lot of catching up to do." His eyes broke contact with hers, went back to the paperwork.

"That's not why I'm here, Thaddeus. There's something I need to talk to you about."

Her tone caught his attention. She'd never called him by his first name before. "What is it, Deondra?"

"I'm pregnant."

"I see," he said pushing the stack of paper away from him and slumping back in his chair. He removed the reading glasses and stared intently at her. "Who's the father?"

"I haven't been with anyone else. You know that."

"No one truly knows anything in this life, except for God."

"It's your baby. Our baby."

"Well, well, our baby. And tell me, Deondra, what do you propose we do about it?"

"I…I thought you might be pleased. It's God's baby too."

"Yes, it most certainly is, but Deondra you must understand that this is most unsuitable for a man in my position."

"I understand your wife might be upset at first, but over time I think she'll come to accept it. Accept us."

"My wife? You don't think we would share this with her, do you? Deondra, surely you understand the situation. I'm afraid keeping the baby is just not an option."

"I don't understand. Are you suggesting that I have an abortion?"

"It's really for the best. For both of us."

"But I saw you on the news tonight. You said it was a sin against God to prevent one of his children being born. Isn't it even a bigger sin to take a baby's life once it's wiggling around in my tummy?"

"The Lord works in mysterious ways, child. God understands that my duty to my flock and to Him creates the need to make… exceptions from time to time. I'm a sinner like any other man— we're all sinners in God's eyes, but I have a greater responsibility than most ordinary men. God will forgive us for our past sins, but he will not forgive either of us if we shirk these responsibilities for our own selfish pleasures. I know this may be difficult for you to understand, but sometime God requires us to make great personal sacrifices in his name. I'm afraid this is one of those times."

Tears began to well in Deondra's eyes. This was not the conversation she envisioned in her mind. "Don't you love me?"

"Of course I love you, just like I love all my children and my family here at the church. God loves you too. Often times love, our love for each other and our love for God, requires us to make great sacrifices. Do you understand that?"

"I guess so," she whimpered.

"That's a good girl. Now don't you worry about a thing. I will personally take care of all of the arrangements. This will all be over before you know it, and we can put this unpleasant business behind us. In the meantime, it's extremely important that we keep this between the two of us. No one else needs to know about this, all right?"

Deondra felt like all of the air had been sucked out of her lungs. She couldn't breathe, couldn't talk. All she could manage was a tearful nod of submission. He was a wise man. Surely he knew what was best for her, didn't he?

He hugged her tightly against him, and her entire body trembled against his touch. Within moments she could feel his hard erection pressing against her body, and suddenly she felt cheap, dirty. She thought of James ogling her, leering at her, and the room started spinning. How could God do this? How could He betray her like this? She felt the blood drain from her face and her knees buckle as she hit the floor, and the room spun into darkness. Through the black void she thought she heard the voices of angels calling out to her, calling for her unborn baby.

Tyler woke up in bed alone the following morning, with a screaming headache. *Just like old times.* He downed three Tylenols and hit the shower. Beads of water pelted his scalp like tiny bolts of electric impulses. He'd been conscious of his sobriety over the past few weeks only to the extent that circumstances dictated that he engaged in activities other than drinking. There was no pledge of abstinence, no sacred promise to which he felt himself bound. It was as if an old friend left town for a few weeks on vacation and just got back. They had a little catching up to do, that's all it was. He felt no shame, no remorse and no sense of failure—just a damn headache.

Once dressed, he looked in the fridge for something to eat. He wasn't normally a breakfast eater, but it occurred to him that he drank dinner last night. He'd either been too upset or too drunk to eat, he really couldn't remember which. Sleeping over at Mara's had taken its toll on his food supply at home. There was some leftover pizza that looked like it was growing an additional ingredient and a half-empty carton of English muffins that had recently begun to petrify. He found two sausage biscuits in the freezer and cooked them in the microwave while he poured the remainder of the sour milk down the drain, the putrid smell causing him to gag, and grabbed a Coke from the refrigerator. He fetched the newspaper from the front yard and spread it in front of him on the table as he sat down to enjoy his gourmet breakfast.

On the front page was a photograph of the Reverend Johnson speaking behind a platform to a large, cheering crowd. Behind the speaker, clearly visible in the photograph, was the Marshall & Marshall brick monument sign. Above the photograph the headline blared:

AFRICAN-AMERICANS PROTEST LOCAL LAW FIRM
Sterilization Program Little More Than Induced Genocide Says Local Clergy

Tyler grimaced as he read the copy.

Racial tensions mounted in downtown Savannah yesterday as over one hundred and fifty predominantly African-American protestors held a peaceful but spirited demonstration at the law offices of Marshall & Marshall, located at 319 Drayton Street. One of the city's oldest and most prestigious law firms, Marshall & Marshall is acting as trustee for a philanthropic trust know as Fresh Start, which purports to pay applicants fifteen thousand dollars plus expenses to undergo sterilization operations. The program, funded by anonymous donors, offers to pay the generous stipend to any applicant between the ages of sixteen and forty regardless of race or sex, but critics contend the program targets minorities in a bold attempt to stifle and control the city's minority population.

The Reverend Thaddeus Johnson, leader of the vocal group and pastor of the Community Church of the South, lashed out at the controversial program in a fiery speech to cheering supporters yesterday and in a subsequent press conference with reporters covering the story. 'What we have here is an audacious attempt by the white power structure of Savannah to effect a slow but certain genocide on the minority population of this town,' said Reverend Johnson. 'This program claims to be offered to all people on an equal basis, but in reality the monetary inducement appeals disproportionately to the poor and underprivileged, many of whom are minorities. The supporters of this program would have us believe this is some noble civic project to promote responsible birth control, but this is really nothing but a wolf in sheep's clothing. This is something you would expect to see in Nazi Germany, not in the United States of America.'

Local civil right groups, including the local chapter of the National Association for the Advancement of Colored People (NAACP), have joined Johnson's call for a boycott of the program. Clarence Cooper, local director of the NAACP said in a prepared statement, 'We vigorously oppose both the means and the methods of the Fresh Start program, and decry the attempts of the program's founders to encourage African-Americans to participate. The NAACP wholeheartedly supports the Reverend Johnson in his call for a boycott of the program and has pledged its full resources to force abandonment of the program including the appointment of a legal team to investigate any and all legal actions which might be taken.' A spokesperson at Mayor Devereaux's office called the situation unfortunate and indicated that all possible steps were being taken to resolve the situation saying that the mayor was very sympathetic to the plight of the poor and was shocked by the methods being undertaken by the mysterious trust.

The identity of the benefactor or benefactors of the trust remains a well-guarded secret, despite rampant speculation. Tyler Marshall, managing partner of Marshall & Marshall and acting trustee of Fresh Start, declined comment and refused all interviews. Marshall, the son of the former congressman of the same name is said to be very well connected within the political and social circles of Savannah, fueling speculation that some of the city's social or political elite may be involved.

Meanwhile, applicants to the program continue to stream into the legal offices yesterday, undaunted by the ongoing demonstration. Several light skirmishes reportedly broke out between applicants and protestors, which were quelled by local police dispatched to the scene to restore order. More potential violence is feared as the protestors have vowed to remain until the program is disbanded. Police continue to maintain an uneasy vigilance, confronted with one of the city's most explosive issues in its long history, and local leaders continue to keep a watchful eye on the controversy, while they privately look for ways to ease the tensions, which appear to be escalating dramatically.

"Shit!" Tyler's head felt like it was going to explode with the pressure building up inside. He noticed the byline on the article—Gaines Shockley. Tyler knew or at least heard of most of the reporters at the paper, but this name was unfamiliar to him. The article was inflammatory, one-sided and played a little loose with the facts, he thought. He was definitely not off to a good start in the court of public opinion, but he was an attorney, not a public relations expert. He knew that it was his own fault that the article was one-sided. He should have talked to the press yesterday and told his side of the story. Too late for that now.

He drove to the office fantasizing that the crowd of demonstrators would somehow not be there. Surely they all had jobs to go to, obligations to meet. Perhaps they would honor Mara's request to give her some space to "talk some sense into him." He really could use a little time to think without all the yelling and shouting. The thought of spending the day in the solitude of his own office, catching up on old business, falling back into the steady, predictable rhythms of the workday gave him comfort and eased the tension in his head.

As he turned the corner onto Drayton Street, he was torn from his reverie like a hard slap in the face. They were back, as many as yesterday, possibly even more. He saw the motor coaches parked on the side street, adjacent to the television news vans. Someone had even taken the time to order portable toilets— Straight Flush, read the name on the front doors. There was a concession tent erected next to the buses complete with wide-screen TV and couches for lounging. It certainly looked like they intended to stay awhile.

His body tensed as he approached the front entrance. The police were already there and had set up an effective perimeter, keeping the crowd away from the driveway. Tyler drove through unscathed this time, though he could hear the taunts and jeers directed at him clearly as he passed. He spied Annie's car in the parking lot, solitary and isolated. Once again, she was waiting for him and unlocked the front door as he approached.

"I take it Darlene's not going to make it in again today?" he asked, irritated.

"Or any other day for that matter," said Annie. "She faxed her resignation letter over a couple of minutes ago. You look like shit. I tried to call you last night."

"My cell phone is on the fritz. I think I'm going to have to get a new one."

"Mara called me last night. She's worried about you. You should call her."

Tyler plucked at a stray thread in his lapel, avoiding eye contact. "Yeah, I'll call her this morning, thanks."

"So?"

Tyler's face was blank. Annie thought he seemed faraway, distant. She'd seen him this way before. "So what?" he asked.

"So, have you made any decisions? What are you going to do?"

"I haven't decided yet. I need some more time to think."

Annie knew better than to push him. He didn't respond well to pressure. "Will you promise me one thing, Tyler?"

"Sure, what is it?" he said, distracted.

"Will you promise to let me know what I can do to help?"

"There is one thing. We need to find a replacement for Darlene."

"Don't worry, I'll take care of it. Who knows, maybe we can find someone with some actual skills. Do you mind, while I'm at it, if I look into voice mail?"

"Yeah, sure. Whatever. Thanks, Annie."

Tyler's first call of the day was to Don Abbott. He needed to know what his clients were thinking before he made any final decisions. "Tyler, I tried calling you last night," said Abbott. He sounded irritated.

"Sorry about that, Don. Apparently my cell phone went on the blink, and I didn't notice until this morning."

"Yes well, it seems we have a rather unfortunate problem on our hands. I thought we made it clear to you, Tyler, that this was the kind of publicity we wanted to avoid."

"What? You think I somehow have something to do with this crap? And what is this 'we' business? I don't recall seeing a bunch of angry protestors marching outside of the school board's offices. Of course if you'd like, I can direct them over your way..."

"That won't be necessary, Tyler, and I didn't mean to imply this was somehow your fault. It's just that we have to do a better job of damage control. Reverend Johnson, it seems, is a worthy adversary. We have to find a way to neutralize him somehow."

"And how do you propose to do that?"

"We're not sure yet, but we're looking into a couple of avenues right now."

"So are you telling me you want to continue the program?"

"Of course we do. We can't let something like this stand in our way. I've spoken with our benefactors, and they are still very much supportive of our efforts."

"That's great that everyone is being so supportive, Don, but no offense, it's my ass on the firing line right now. This is the sort of thing that could ruin my practice. I don't know if I'm going to be able to continue to act as your agent."

"Tyler, hold on here! Let me ask you a question. Before yesterday, were you satisfied with the direction the program was going?"

"Yes, but things have changed now, Don."

"I understand, but do me a favor. Give us two weeks to work things out with Reverend Johnson. I'm sure he's a reasonable man, and we have the facts on our side."

"From what I hear about him, he's not the kind of man who lets facts get in the way."

"That may be so, but he's obviously a smart man and a successful businessman. There must be something he wants that we can give him, maybe a generous donation to his church?"

"What are you suggesting?"

"I'd like for you to meet with him in private, off the record. Find out what it will take to make him go away."

"I suppose I can do that. What about the press?"

"Talk to them, but be very careful about what you say. Tell them our side of the story. Tyler, I'm sure I don't need to remind you, but it's critical that you protect the identity of your clients."

"Yes, Don, you've made that very clear. Don't worry, I'm not talking about that subject to anyone."

"That's great, Tyler. You've done an excellent job so far. We're all very appreciative of your efforts. Someday you'll look back on this experience with a profound sense of accomplishment."

"I hope so, Don."

"Are you with us? Will you give it two more weeks?"

"Two weeks. I won't promise anything past that."

"Fair enough. Keep me informed of your progress with the good reverend, will you?"

Tyler hung up the phone. Following a pattern weaved throughout his entire life, he had let a moment of decision lapse into indecision. Two more weeks. That couldn't be so bad, could it?

After speaking with Don Abbott, Tyler checked his calendar for the day. He had a court appearance at eleven o'clock and a deposition at an attorney's office across town at two o'clock. As much as he hated being cooped up in the office, with the chants of the crowd outside ringing in his ears, he was unnerved by the idea of driving out through the line of protestors. What if a few of them decided to follow him? At the moment, the office felt like a fortress, protecting him from the angry mob outside his door. He knew it wasn't a rational thought. If anyone wanted to attack him, they could just follow him home. For that matter, his home address was easily obtainable on the Internet. He needed one more day to pull himself together. After today, he would be fine. He called and canceled the court appearance. The deposition was for a worker's compensation claim filed against a client, Savannah Power, one of the largest employers in the area. It was a minor matter, but it was the second time he postponed, so he felt a call to his client was in order. He quickly dialed Anne Kefauver, the Human Resources coordinator for the company.

"Hello, Anne, it's Tyler Marshall. I wanted to brief you on the Rodriguez deposition. We rescheduled for today, but I'm afraid I've got some pressing matters I really need to deal with so I'm going to have to reschedule again."

"Yes, I read the papers this morning."

"Oh, right, well it's nothing I can't handle. I'll try and reschedule for next week. Things should be back in order by then."

"Tyler, I was going to talk to you about that today. I hope you can understand our position, but we felt in light of the…the recent publicity that, well frankly, we can't take the chance of having our name connected in any way."

"Your name connected to what?"

"You know, all that stuff in the papers. We just feel there's too much controversy surrounding your firm at the moment."

"Anne, your case has nothing to do with any of this nonsense you might have read in the papers. They are two distinctly separate events."

"I understand that, believe me, I do. It's just that having you represent Savannah Power at this time might send the wrong message."

"Might send the wrong message to whom?"

"Tyler, you've always done a good job for us, and I'm sure we'll continue to use your services in the future, but right now you're just too hot of a news item. Surely you understand our position?"

"Sure, Anne, I understand. I'll talk to you soon."

He paused for a second until he heard the click on the other line and slammed the receiver on its hook with full force. He looked up from his desk and saw Annie standing silently in the doorway. "Are you okay?" she asked.

"Yeah, I'm fine. I just lost a client over this crap, that's all."

"Have you figured out what you're going to do?"

"It doesn't look like I have a whole lot of choice at the moment. I'm going to fight back."

Annie brightened instantly as a wide grin broke out across her face. "That's my boy! Show 'em who's boss around here!"

"Isn't that what they said to Custer right before Little Big Horn?"

"At least you'd be going down fighting."

"Once I feel the arrow in my back, I doubt that would provide me much solace."

"Hang in there, soldier," said Annie. "There's still time for the cavalry to ride in and save the day."

Annie excused herself to begin the search for Darlene's replacement before Tyler had the chance to ask where the cavalry might be hiding. He dialed Mara's cell phone. She picked up on the first ring.

"You didn't call me back last night," were the first words out of her mouth.

"My cell phone's not working. I didn't realize it until this morning."

"You're a terrible liar."

"All right, I had a lot on my mind last night. I needed some time to think."

"You got drunk, didn't you?"

"Why do all of the women in my life feel the need to play the role of my mother?"

"Look, I don't care what you do. Just don't lie to me."

"Okay, yes I was drinking last night."

"Fine."

The inflection in her voice sounded doubting, judgmental. She had never used that tone before. It seemed presumptuous that she would talk to him like that. There was no stated or implied "understanding" between them. He hadn't broken any commitments or promises to her. She didn't own him. What gave her the right to talk to him that way?

"Fine," was all he could manage as he privately seethed.

"You called me?"

"I need your help. I was hoping you could set up a meeting between your boyfriend, the good reverend, and me."

"Why are you talking to me like this? He's not my boyfriend."

"You two looked pretty close hugging each other out on the picket line yesterday."

"Oh, grow up Tyler. What do you think I am, your fucking cheerleader? If you want a nice girl who agrees with everything you say and do, then I'm afraid you've got the wrong girl."

"Just a little support every now and then might be nice."

"I am supporting you. I called you last night because I was worried about you. I missed you in my bed. What else do you want from me?"

"Will you do it or not?"

"I'll do it. What are you going to talk to him about?"

"I want to see if we can come to some sort of agreement."

"I doubt he'll agree to anything except for you shutting down the program, but it's your call. Whatever happens, Tyler, I hope you don't let this drag on too long. I'm worried someone will get hurt."

"Don't worry, everything's under control. Thanks, Mara. I'll call you later."

As he hung up the phone, he had to laugh at his own words. *Everything's under control.* That, he knew, couldn't be farther from the truth.

CHAPTER ELEVEN

Gaines Shockley couldn't believe his luck. Two years removed from the University of North Carolina's School of Journalism, where he majored in Electronic Communication, he'd been exiled to this sleepy coastal town at a starting salary of six hundred and seventy-three dollars a week. The plan was to get some valuable experience in the field, then find a higher profile position with one of the New York papers or possibly a television news gig in one of the major market cities. He had the looks and voice for TV. He just needed the newspaper reporter experience to build his resume and position himself as a serious journalist. It was a good plan, but the problem was there was very little "newsworthy" to cover in this town. His body of work consisted of handling the occasional murder or domestic violence story or reporting about the city's budgetary struggles or failed crime prevention plans. So far, there was nothing he could really sink his teeth into, something that would get him noticed up the food chain. Until now.

It was blind luck. He was hanging out in his editor's office when the call came in with a tip an hour in advance of the scheduled protest outside the law offices of Marshall & Marshall. The senior reporter was at the dentist's office, and the next-in-line reporter was at his daughter's school for Parents' Day. Shockley practically sprinted out the door when the editor handed him the assignment. This wasn't just a great local story, it was a story of national interest. Rumor had it that the big boys, the major networks, were putting their people on it this afternoon. Shockley found himself riding the biggest story of the year, and he intended to leverage it for all it was worth. At this point, he would do just about anything to get out of this town.

His editor, George Hawthorne, congratulated him in the office the day the story broke. "Good work on that Fresh Start piece, Gaines."

"Thanks," Gaines said. "I think it's got legs. I've just got to figure out how to position it properly."

"What do you mean?"

"I've interviewed several of the protestors, but they seem more interested in socializing with their neighbors and eating donuts than battling injustice. There wasn't a lot of fire or emotion out there yesterday except when Thaddeus Johnson got them riled up."

"I couldn't guess that from your story. You painted a beautiful, contentious portrait. That's what sells newspapers."

Gaines allowed the complement to settle, gently caressing his ego. "It just feels like there's something missing."

"You need a victim," Hawthorne said.

"Huh?"

"A victim. Right now, the story is the white establishment's oppression of minorities, but that's too esoteric for the average reader, and the connection is tenuous at best. You need to humanize the story, break it down to the most basic level of human understanding. You need a victim, preferably African-American, if you want this story to really resonate."

"Where do I find one?"

"That's what separates the stars from the also-rans in our business. You want to be a star, Gaines? Go find yourself a victim."

One hour later he was out on the front lawn of Marshall & Marshall, looking for an edge. Several of the protestors from the prior day were absent, replaced by people who seemed to be primarily attracted to the free coffee and donuts. More than a few of them appeared to be homeless or at least have some sort of mental problems that would prevent them from working in any kind of structured environment. He was successful in speaking with a couple of the applicants, but they wouldn't go on record with anything meaningful, and they certainly didn't view themselves as being victimized. They didn't experience any regret or remorse over their decision, and they actually seemed excited at the prospect of being fifteen thousand dollars richer.

He was mingling among the picketers, speaking with a woman who claimed her grandfather marched with Dr. King, when his cell phone rang.

"Hello, Gaines. This is Tyler Marshall. I hope you don't mind me calling you on your cell phone, but I got the number from your voice mail at work. We haven't had the chance to meet yet, but I read your story in this morning's paper."

"Oh yeah? What did you think?"

"It was pretty one-sided and missing a few facts, but I understand I'm partly to blame."

"I left a message on your voice mail."

"I know. I was a little pre-occupied yesterday. I hope it's not too late for me to tell my side of the story?"

"Of course not. I'd love to sit down and talk with you."

"I'd like that very much. When would be a good time?" Tyler asked.

"Anytime. I'm outside your office, as we speak."

"I suppose now is as good a time as any. The police will stop you at the entrance. I'll come down to the front door and wave you in. See you in a minute."

Tyler descended the stairs from his office and made his way to the front door of the building, which was locked, as it had been over the past two days. Tyler opened the door and saw a man talking to two policemen and gesturing toward the building. He stood out in stark contrast to the crowd around him. White and preppy with a blue blazer, khaki pants and a maroon striped tie, he looked like he just walked out of a fraternity social. He appeared young enough to still be in a frat, with dark brown curly hair roughly combed down over his eyes and smooth, tanned skin stretched taut across his angular face. Tyler motioned to the police to let him pass and watched him walk toward the building, tall and erect with a boyish gait, his long arms swinging from side to side.

"You must be Gaines."

"Mr. Marshall," he said, extending his hand.

Tyler felt his grip, firm and strong, like a young buck trying to assert his dominance over the aging stag. *Jesus, he's just a kid.*

"Please don't take this the wrong way, Gaines, but do you mind telling me how old you are?"

A look of annoyance swept over the young man's face for a flicker of a second and then quickly returned to its placid simplicity. "I'm twenty-four, but everyone tells me I look young for my age."

"Twenty-four *is* young, Gaines. Sorry for asking. Come on in."

Tyler ushered him inside and locked the door behind them. He led him into the conference room and winked at Annie, who was coming down the stairs to monitor potential visitors at the front door. So far today, there had been very few.

Shockley took a seat and pulled a tape recorder out of his coat pocket. "Do you mind?" he asked.

"Of course not," said Tyler finding a seat opposite him and pulling a recorder out of his own jacket. "I don't mind if you don't, that is."

Shockley nodded, a wry smile crossing his face. "Why don't you go first," he said. "You wanted to tell your side of the story."

"Thank you. It just seems to me that this whole thing is being blown way out of proportion. I read your article this morning, and it was very…racially focused, which I don't completely understand. This program is open to all Chatham County citizens: white, African-American, Hispanic, Asian, men, women, rich and poor. There is absolutely no discrimination involved in the application process."

"Isn't it true that the majority of the applicants are African-American?"

"No it's not. So far, the percentage of African-American applicants is around forty-three percent. African-American citizens are not disproportionately represented in this program compared to their representation of the general population, in a statistically meaningful manner."

"I assume you have numbers to back up this statement?"

"Yes, I do. I will be happy to share them with you off the record."

"Why off the record?"

"I don't have the permission of my clients to share this information. It also changes daily as new applicants enter the program. It's a bit of a moving target, I'm afraid."

"If you're not willing to go on record with the numbers, then I don't need to see them."

"They'll show you that these allegations of targeting minorities are unfounded. The program does not discriminate in any manner among potential applicants, and the data shows that the end results are consistent with the demographics of the population from a racial perspective."

"If there is no target audience, then what's the point? Why spend all of this money?"

"It's not my money, so I can only speculate as to my client's motives. I believe they feel there are too many people bringing children into this world without thinking about all of the responsibilities that parenthood entails. Many of them are not prepared to adequately care for a child, which is unfair to the child who has no say in choosing his or her parents. All this program is doing is raising the public's awareness of birth control and hopefully making people think first before deciding to have children. What's wrong with that?"

"I guess I never saw it that way, but if this is just some sort of public service then why offer the money? Why not just pay for the operation?"

"We currently have several methods of birth control at our disposal, which are being offered in many cases at no cost to the intended users. Condoms and birth control pills are distributed for free at some of the local health clinics, but in many cases, these items are going unused. The decision to use or not use condoms and birth control pills comes up almost every day in a person's life. The decision to have a vasectomy or tubal ligation is only made once. The money is offered to get people's attention and ensure that everyone gives serious thought to the subject of birth control. I can't think of a subject that deserves more attention. The future of our children is at stake."

"That all sounds very noble, but don't you think by offering this money that poor people would be more likely to apply than wealthy?"

"That's something that our numbers reflect. While we aren't seeing race as a significant factor, household income is. Over thirty-five percent of our applicants report household income of less than fifteen thousand dollars per year, which is demographically disproportionate."

"That's a huge percentage. Doesn't that concern you?"

Tyler shrugged. "I guess it depends on how you look at it. These are the people who are most in need of the money. That's obvious. I've seen some folks who were really down on their luck walk out of this office with a very realistic hope for a better future. I truly believe this program is making a positive impact on people's lives."

"Interesting." Shockley made some notes in a spiral notebook he was carrying before he continued. "You mentioned this program was not your idea but a client of yours. Can you be more specific as to the identity of your client? There is a lot of speculation going on right now."

"I'm afraid I'm not at liberty to divulge the identity of my client or clients."

"There has been some speculation that your father is involved. Can you comment on that?"

Tyler felt the least he could do was to go on record to protect his father, who was against the idea from the beginning. "My father is not in any way involved in this, nor did I consult with him before taking on this client."

"What effect is the public reaction having on you? Are you considering demands that you terminate the program?"

"By 'the public,' I assume you're speaking of the Reverend Johnson and his followers? We haven't received any complaints or heard of any issues from anyone before yesterday."

Shockley raised an eyebrow in mock disbelief but didn't answer the question.

"I'd be lying if I said it wasn't a strain. I was physically attacked in my car yesterday morning by an out-of-control mob. In addition to that, it's had an effect on my practice. Our regular clients are somewhat uncomfortable with the sudden publicity. Are we thinking of shutting the program down? No."

"Both the mayor's office as well as the NAACP vowed to explore all legal avenues to force you to shut down the program. Can you comment on that?"

"They can talk all they want to about their legal options, but the facts are that we're not in any manner engaging in illegal activities. They can talk all they want to about this program targeting minorities but again, the facts say otherwise. Before the reverend and his demonstrators showed up yesterday, we had not received a single complaint. I believe if we just focused a little more on the facts, we could all see clearly that most of this...sensationalism is undeserved."

"Thanks, Mr. Marshall, I don't have any more questions. I'd like to call you from time to time in the future as events progress, if that's all right with you."

"My pleasure, Gaines. And please, call me Tyler. I'm not old enough to be Mr. Marshall yet," he said with a smile that seemed a bit too forced, even to him.

Quinnette Rose felt the warm sunshine hit her face as she exited the DFACS building exactly one minute past five o'clock. She was slightly out of breath, having descended six flights of stairs in the drab, ten-story government building. She learned months ago it just wasn't worth it to fight the stampede for the five o'clock elevator. It was almost always full by the time it got to her floor anyway. She had just enough time for the short walk to the bus stop at Oglethorpe and Montgomery to catch the five-twenty, which took her to Liberty Parkway and Gallard Avenue. From there, she had a fifteen minute walk to her mother's house off Ogeechee, a small two- bedroom house half covered with kudzu without central heating or air. She was living at home still, trying to save enough out of her meager paychecks to afford the down payment for a car. The bus wasn't so bad, except for rainy days, when she'd come home soaking wet, caked in red Georgia mud up to her ankles. There were no sidewalks on her part of town.

She got off at her stop at five thirty-eight, right on schedule. She stepped out onto the curb and spied her younger sister, waiting with a pained expression on her face. "Deondra, what are you doing here? Don't you have choir practice?"

Quinnette was consciously aware of a slight tremor coursing through her sister's body as if she'd caught a fever. "I need to talk to you, Quin. I'm in trouble."

"What's the matter, baby?" Quinnette said, embracing her. Her skin felt cold and clammy to the touch.

"I'm pregnant," said the young girl, bursting into tears.

"Pregnant? Deondra, how can that be?"

"How do you think?" she said, sniffling, her lower lip quivering.

"That's not what I meant. It's just I never see you around any boys. You never seem very…interested. Who's the daddy?"

"I can't tell you. I promised to keep it a secret."

"A secret? You can tell me. I'm your sister, Deondra!"

"I can't tell anyone. Please don't ask me. You've got to promise me you won't say anything to Momma, Quin!"

"I won't say a word if you don't want me to. What are you gonna do, baby?"

"I…I don't know. He wants me to have an abortion."

"He does, does he? I don't suppose he's willing to pay for it is he?" Deondra nodded her head silently in affirmation. "Now what boy do you know that's got money for an abortion? Is he dealing drugs?"

"No, nothing like that. He's…older."

"How much older?"

"Older. He's got a job. And a wife."

"Oh, my Lord! You tell me who it is, and I'll have his sorry ass in jail by nightfall! Deondra, you're only fifteen years old!"

"It's not what you think, Quin. I knew what I was doing. I wanted it. I love him…or at least I think I do. And he loves me."

Quinnette could feel the anger rising inside of her. No man was going to do this to her baby sister and get away with it. "Apparently he doesn't love you enough to leave his wife and own up to his responsibilities."

"It's not that way, Quin. You wouldn't understand. It's… complicated."

"Things are gonna get real complicated for him when I…." Quinnette could see the hurt and anguish etched on her sister's face like a permanent scar. Pity for her sister washed the anger away. "Oh baby, I'm so sorry. What do you want to do?"

"I know I'm young. I know I'm not ready to take care of a child. I may not graduate like you did, and it probably is gonna mess up any singing career I might have had. But I can't kill it, Quin. I can't murder my own baby. I just can't do it."

Quinnette held Deondra tightly, as if she might somehow transfer her own strength to her baby sister through the force of their embrace. "Whatever you decide to do, I'll be right here supporting you all the way. We're in this together."

Tyler checked his watch—the dial read five-thirty—and couldn't believe how fast the afternoon had blown by after the interview with Shockley. At the time of the interview, they had received only a few visitors, but after Shockley left, it was like the floodgates opened. All told, twenty-two applicants came and applied to the program that day. Tyler had expected traffic to slow to a crawl assuming most people would be intimidated by the demonstrators outside, but just the opposite was occurring. It must be the extra publicity. Word was really spreading around town after the newspaper article and television exposure. Even two of the demonstrators came in to apply, though they both appeared to be among the small cadre of mercenaries the reverend enlisted for the cause. Neither one had a drivers license or a mailing address.

The sudden rush of applicants used almost all of their time during the day. Both Tyler and Annie were surprised by how much they missed Darlene, who was nothing if not organized, but they made do as best they could. Annie wanted to take her time finding the right full-time assistant to replace Darlene but requested the employment agency send over a temp in the meantime. The temp had shown up around one-thirty: dirty brown hair with purple highlights, a black skirt above the knees exposing her leggings and black commando boots laced up the front. She wore purple mascara and had four earrings in each ear and, of course, a nose stud. In contrast to her dark appearance, she carried a bright fuchsia canvas tote bag, bearing a large, yellow smiley face, which contained a few personal cosmetic items, a dog-eared copy of *Foucault's Pendulum* by Umberto Eco and two twelve-ounce cans of Monster Energy drink. Her name was Geena something or other, and she was pretty much the anti-Darlene. What she lacked in fashion sense, she made up for in attitude. She didn't seem to have any reservations at all about the protestors. The employment agency explained to Annie that their first three choices all refused the assignment. In fact, Geena seemed to rather enjoy the excitement. And she had a calming, tranquilizing effect on the applicants, who were unnerved by the frenzied clamor outside. Her demeanor relaxed everyone in the middle of a chaotic situation. Tyler couldn't help but chuckle at the thought of his father walking in on them at one particularly hectic point in the day when there were six poorly-dressed applicants waiting in the reception area, attended to by this goth receptionist. Surely his grandfather would be rolling over in his grave.

It was the first time Tyler had laughed, or even experienced a light moment, in the past two days. It wasn't a healthy, sidesplitting, belly laugh, more of an obligatory release in reaction to a ridiculously absurd situation. He was trying his best to be optimistic. If Gaines Shockley wrote a favorable article in tomorrow's paper, if he could work out something with the reverend, perhaps things might return to normal. *Normal! That's ironic, isn't it?* It was normal that led to his divorce, normal that made him loathe his job, normal that led him to drink in order to escape the boredom, the spectacular dullness of everyday life.

For the first time in his life, he had stepped into the unconscious beyond, to the other side, a place bold and fresh, bursting with light and energy and excitement and yet, at the same time, dark, cold and frighteningly unfamiliar to him. An inner vertigo, dizzying, sickened him as he attempted futilely to balance himself with a foot in both worlds: the old one safe and comfortable, the new one unpredictable and potentially dangerous. He thought of Annie and Mara, both so comfortable in their own skin as he could never be, and he felt ashamed of his own cowardice and stifling diffidence.

Mara. There was so much he wanted to tell her. How it felt like the windows suddenly burst open, and a breeze filled the room whenever she entered. How he loved the way her bottom lip turned up, like that of a small child pouting, whenever someone or something disappointed her. The invigorating self-awareness he felt when she challenged him intellectually, and the paralyzing fear that sprang from the realization he might fail to meet her expectations. But he wouldn't tell her any of this. He wasn't ready. Mara represented that new world he had yet to come to grips with, the one that terrified him so much at the moment.

On impulse, he picked up the phone and dialed her number. "Hey, it's me," he said.

"Hey. How was your day?"

"Busy. Crazy. Insane. I'm sorry I snapped at you earlier today."

"That's okay. I know you're under a lot of stress right now."

"My cell phone was working fine last night when you called. That is, until I dumped it in the ice bucket. I got roaring drunk right after that."

"I know."

"I miss you."

"I miss you too. Am I going to see you tonight?"

"I can't."

"Have I done something wrong? Are you mad at me for some reason?"

"It's not you. It's me. God, I can't believe I just said that! I can't explain it Mara—I don't really understand it myself, but I just need a little time to think. I'm a bit confused right now. Just a couple of days at most, I promise. Then I'll be back as good as new."

"I like you just fine the way you are now, but I understand. Call me when you're ready. By the way, Thaddeus Johnson will be at to your office to meet with you tomorrow at ten o'clock. I hope that's okay."

"That's great. Thanks, Mara."

"No problem. Call me?"

"I will, I promise. Soon." He heard the line go dead from her end. "I love you, Mara," he said to the dial tone.

Elvis Patterson was slumped on the couch, a can of beer in his hand, watching *Nightly News*. His wife and daughter were in the room, though not paying attention to the television. They were accustomed to his obscenity-laden tirades anytime he saw something happening in some remote corner of the world that he didn't particularly agree with. They both knew to keep a low profile when he was in one of those moods and let him rant. Twenty minutes into the broadcast, they were all surprised to hear their hometown mentioned.

"And in Savannah, Georgia, local civil rights activists are protesting a privately-funded program that is offering fifteen thousand dollars to any citizen of Chatham County between the ages of sixteen and forty years old who voluntarily agrees to undergo sterilization procedures. Critics contend the program specifically targets minorities in what appears to be a racially charged issue. News correspondent Caroline McCoy is in Savannah for a full report. Caroline."

Elvis was glued to the set as the cameras fixed on the news reporter with what appeared to be hundreds of protestors in the background, almost all African-Americans. "Look at all them niggers," he said in disgust as his daughter and wife watched silently. They learned long ago not to do or say anything to provoke him when he was drinking, which was pretty much all day these days since he'd lost his job down at the loading docks. "Ain't that the place that turned you away, Jen?" he said to his daughter.

"Yes, Daddy, but the man said I wasn't eligible," replied Jennifer Patterson.

"Tell me, Sissy," he said to his wife, a meek, terrified, mouse of a woman who learned long ago the futility of opposing her husband on any matter, "what could we do with fifteen thousand dollars?"

Sissy was knitting a potholder, appearing to be concentrating intently on her handiwork, while actually dreaming of a place and a life, far, far away from Elvis Patterson. "I don't know. Lots of things, I guess."

"You bet lots of things. We could get that old car outside fixed, patch the roof, replace the air-conditioner, maybe even buy a new TV."

Jennifer knew he was talking about her. Both her parents were over forty and not eligible for the program. She was the only one in the family of qualifying age. "But, Daddy, I tried already. They wouldn't let me."

Elvis leaned back in the couch and let out a loud belch. The stench of stale beer permeated every corner of the tiny room. "We'll see about that now, won't we?"

CHAPTER TWELVE

The headline in the morning paper, under Gaines Shockley's byline, read:

RACIAL STANDOFF REACHES THIRD DAY
Local Attorney Vows to Fight to the End

"Despite being violently attacked by an unruly mob of demonstrators and receiving threats on his life, R. Tyler Marshall IV, son of former Congressman R. Tyler Marshall III, vowed to continue his fight to sterilize a significant portion of Chatham County's citizens through the Fresh Start program, of which he is serving as trustee. In an exclusive interview with this reporter, Mr. Marshall claimed the program does not target minorities, though when pressed for details, he declined to share actual data. Critics, led by the Reverend Thaddeus Johnson, claim the program targets poor minorities by offering a monetary inducement of fifteen thousand dollars per person. 'Over thirty-five percent of the program's applicants report household income of less than fifteen thousand dollars per year,' Marshall freely admitted. Mr. Marshall further stated that he is acting on behalf of a client or clients who wish to remain anonymous. He could only speculate as to their motives. 'I believe they feel there are too many people bringing children into this world without thinking about all the responsibilities that parenthood entails. What's so wrong with that?'

Reverend Johnson, when apprised of Mr. Marshall's comments, responded angrily. 'Who are they to tell African-Americans we're not prepared to raise our children properly? They think just because they're rich and powerful, their money gives them the right to pass judgment on us? I don't think so. We will continue to fight for our cause because it is a just cause. Nothing less than the future of our race is at stake here.'

Tensions continue to mount as the stalemate between the attorney and the scores of vocal and determined protestors enters its third day. Mayor Devereaux has vowed to do everything in his power to settle the issue, which is dividing the city like no other event in its history and is beginning to receive national attention. Some civil rights' activists from outside the area have indicated they are monitoring the situation closely and may join the protest in the near future as a show of support. Meanwhile, applicants to the program, many of them poor minorities, continue to stream in at a torrid pace despite the presence of the demonstrators, causing several skirmishes along the picket lines. Police on the scene fear further violence as they struggle to maintain control over the volatile situation. Reports from Atlanta indicate the Governor may soon become involved in an attempt to find a peaceful solution. In the interim, Savannahians wait and watch in fear that the controversy will leave visible scars for years to come."

Annie was at her desk when the buses rolled in that morning at eight-thirty. Johnson didn't usually arrive until at least a half hour later and then only to mug for the cameras before he was off, leaving his subjects to do his dirty work for him. She knew he and Tyler were meeting at ten o'clock and thought this might be a good opportunity to do a little reconnaissance work of the enemy's troops in advance. Before the demonstrators filed off the buses, Annie was ready to do battle armed with boxes of Krispy Kreme donuts and cups of Starbucks coffee, both significant improvements from their grocery store inspired fare of the past two days. She saw their eyes light up as soon as they spotted the treats laid out for them. She took a quick look around. The two bodyguards in the Escalade pick-up truck were nowhere to be found.

As the demonstrators fought for position at the refreshment table, she scanned the line looking for familiar faces. To her surprise, there were very few she recognized. Stranger still, they didn't seem to have any idea who she was. They must have thought she worked for the catering company even though she was wearing a business suit. Finally, she spotted a woman she knew, Dorothy, the one who warned the others about messing with her on the first day of the protest. Dorothy worked for the church full-time as an administrative assistant.

"Hello, Dorothy. Welcome back," she said with the biggest smile she could make.

Dorothy's face was full of distrust. "You're feeding us?"

"Why not? We're all Christians here, aren't we?"

"I suppose so."

"There you go. I'm a little surprised though. I thought I'd see Mrs. Conklin here. And Jackie Thurmond, Mr. Davies, Helen Lawrence. What happened to them?"

"I guess they got other things to do. It does get kind of old after a while, walking around in this hot sun."

"I'm sure it does. It takes a special person to stick to their conviction, like you I guess." *And I'm sure you'd be out of here too if you weren't getting paid to be here!* "So, who are all of these people? I've lived in Savannah my whole life, and I hardly recognize anyone here."

"A bunch of them came down from Atlanta last night. The NAACP's regional office in Atlanta sent them. They're not so bad. Better than those bums they brought in yesterday. One of them smelled so bad, I had to take two showers and spray myself with lemon juice just to wash the stink off my body!"

"It's good talking to you, Dorothy. I guess I better get back to work. Enjoy the donuts."

"Are we going to see you back in church anytime soon?"

"Don't count on it," Annie said under her breath as she walked away.

Like any good theatrical production, the movements of cast and crew were synchronized to perfection. The demonstrators were on site and waiting when the signs arrived at eight-fifty via Cadillac Escalade. Local, regional and national television crews converged there at ten after nine and the stars of the show, Reverend Johnson and Clarence Ferguson, head of the Savannah chapter of the NAACP, arrived by white limousine at nine twenty for their nine-thirty curtain call. At precisely nine-thirty, Clarence Ferguson took the podium.

A tall, slender, soft-spoken man in his late fifties, Ferguson appeared professorial with a frosty, closely cropped haircut and bifocals hanging precariously at the tip of his long, tapered nose. He wore a tweed sports coat, slightly frayed at the collar with a muted striped tie, and he spoke slowly and deliberately to his audience.

"I am here before you today to tell you a story about a young boy born into poverty. He was born and raised in Newark, New Jersey, the son of an uneducated construction worker doing his best to support a family of six, working two jobs to make ends meet. One night, driving home from his second job, exhausted from fifteen hours of hard labor, the boy's father fell asleep behind the wheel of the car and crashed into a telephone pole on the side of the road. He died en route to the hospital that night, leaving behind a widow and four young children. The boy's mother did the best she could, but she had no marketable job skills, and there was no one she could turn to for help. She was forced to go on welfare and moved her family into a housing project, like any other housing project you're ever seen: dull, graffiti-laden walls, boarded up windows, playgrounds of asphalt and broken glass that would cut you like a knife. She was a proud woman, and it killed her to take handouts from anyone, but she did what she had to do to support her family. She found work as a maid, making forty dollars a day and with the little money she received from the government, her family managed to survive. She taught her children there was more to life than what she was able to give them, and with hard work, perseverance, discipline and faith in God, they could achieve anything once they set their minds to it. Her lessons were well heeded as all four children studied hard in school, made good grades and attended college on various scholarships and entitlement programs. The boy I spoke of went on from his undergraduate studies at Rutgers University to obtain a Masters Degree and subsequently a Doctorate Degree at Columbia University. He is no longer a boy but rather an old man, but nonetheless, he is here speaking to you today."

The audience broke out in cheers as the speaker paused for effect. Mara was in the fourth row, applauding loudly. Behind Ferguson, Thaddeus Johnson stood smiling. He winked at her in a sort of leering manner that suggested more than casual acquaintance.

"We are gathered here today to voice our opposition to a program known as Fresh Start, which is designed to stem the birth of poor African-Americans in our community. This program would diminish success stories such as mine because people like me would not be here to tell future generations their own stories of overcoming adversity. I believe my own mother would have been too proud to accept money in exchange for having fewer children, but I cannot say this with certainty. It's possible I would have never known the love of a younger sister or brother. It's possible I wouldn't be here myself, before you today."

Ferguson took off his glasses and wiped his eyes with a handkerchief, tears flowing freely down his cheeks. A hush fell over the crowd as he composed himself. Gaines Shockley glanced up at the second story window to see if Tyler was watching, but there was no one there. After a brief interval, Ferguson continued, a lump rising in his throat, his voice cracking with emotion.

"As bad as things may get, as severe as our problems may seem to us sometimes, we must never give up hope because hope is what sustains us. Our youth is looking to us for support, and we cannot afford to turn our backs on them now. Sometimes it seems that guiding them properly is an impossible task. We turn to quick, expedient solutions we hope will make our problems go away. But we must never shirk our responsibilities to our young people. We must never turn away from them because helping them is too hard. All they need is for someone to give them a chance and perhaps a guiding hand, and they too can achieve great things in this world. We must never turn our backs on these children for they are our future, and without them we have no future. I stand here today, living, breathing proof that a young man or woman from the projects can succeed. I think it's time we give them the opportunity they are so desperately seeking, rather than removing from them any chance at all as some have proposed. Our society cannot and will not survive the decline of its youth. It's time we do something about it. It's time we sent a message to our young people that we are here to help them—not to prevent their very existence! It's time we let them know we have not given up hope for their future, for that is the only hope they have."

"Fresh Start sends the wrong message to our youth, a message that we've given up hope, that we're abandoning our effort to make a better future for them. We must not allow this message to be delivered. We stand here today to protest a grave injustice on our youth and on our future. We must never let the forces behind this movement succeed, for if we do, we lose everything we've fought so hard for in our lifetime. I ask you today for your support, for your prayers and for your voice. United, we can accomplish anything we set out to do. I ask that you all stay with us for as long as it takes to accomplish our goal, and I can assure you the world will be a better place for your efforts. Thank you."

Tyler, Annie and Geena were watching the speech live on CNN on the television in the break room. As the camera panned the cheering crowd, Tyler saw Mara four rows back, applauding. He caught Annie watching him out of the corner of her eye and knew she saw her too. It seemed surreal to him that she was this close, right outside in his front yard, yet he was watching her on television.

"That was one helluva speech, I've got to admit," he said. "After the hatchet job Gaines Shockley pulled on us in this morning's paper, it seems the reverend will be negotiating from a position of strength when he stops in for a visit this morning."

"Don't be so sure," said Annie. "I popped outside for a little recon visit on the picket line this morning. The majority of that cheering throng you're watching right now was bused in from Atlanta last night. It seems most of the locals, the ones who attacked you that first day, have already grown tired of the cause."

"What difference does that make? There are still a couple hundred angry protestors out there. No one watching that speech is going to care where those people come from. And no one reading the article in this morning's paper is going to care if that punk kid completely distorted the story to his own sensationalist viewpoint. Johnson's got the media on his side, and there's not much I can do about it. He wins. That's all there is to it."

"The media that you seem so afraid of has the attention span of a six year old child. Next week you'll be yesterday's news to them, and there won't be any protestors left. You don't have to beat the media, Tyler. Your opponent is out there wearing diamond cuff-links and a custom suit. You're smarter than he is, and you have more integrity than he does. And you have the power of law on your side. It's you who should be negotiating from strength—not him. Time is on your side, Tyler. You can beat him. It would be a mistake to give in now."

"Maybe I should let you handle the negotiations?"

"I'd be happy to, but you might have to find a new associate after they arrest me for assault and battery."

"I can just picture that in tomorrow's headlines, 'Civil Rights Advocate and Man of God Beaten Senseless by Angry Lawyer.' Thanks for the offer, Annie, but I can handle it," Tyler said, without a hint of conviction.

Tyler sat at the large conference table in a chair directly opposite Reverend Johnson. He didn't notice a thing about the man except his eyes, the intensity of their gaze, unblinking, focused, staring. Like the white blinding light of the sun, they forced him to look away, to seek a shady respite from the withering glare. *It's just a cheap trick. He's trying to establish dominance over me. He wants me to know he's the alpha dog. We'll see about that.*

Tyler held up a manila folder full of paper. "This is data on the demographics of the program's applicants through last Friday. They will show that minority representation in the Fresh Start program is consistent with their general representation in the overall population. Would you care to review this information while you're here?"

Tyler noticed the eyes remained fixed on his, ignoring the folder. "I don't think there will be any need for that," answered Johnson.

"I had a feeling you might say that. Tell me, Reverend, why are you making such a big deal about this program targeting minorities when the facts and statistics prove otherwise?"

"Humans are emotional creatures. They're not impressed with facts and figures and statistics. Love, hate, fear, anger, sorrow, greed—these are the feelings that rule our lives. They dictate our world view, they form our prejudices. That's what I do for a living. I appeal to those emotions. I connect with people's souls. People like you, automatons with your ridiculous statistics, you don't get it. You think what you do for a living has meaning, but it doesn't. If you quit tomorrow and walked away, nothing would be required to fill the void you left behind."

The words caught Tyler off guard, stung. He was petrified the reverend might see it in his eyes. "I appreciate the philosophy lesson, Reverend. It was actually very helpful. In any case, I think I understand where you're coming from. I've been instructed by my clients to approach you about a settlement."

"What is it you propose?"

"I was hoping you could help me out with that. Is there anything my clients might do for you in return for putting this all behind us?"

"Certainly there is. You can shut down the program."

"I'm afraid that's not something I'm at liberty to offer at this point. I was hoping that perhaps there might be something else."

"Something that would allow you to continue the program, in other words." Tyler nodded silently and felt his body relax as Johnson's intense gaze shifted to a spot on the ceiling. "I suppose if we were to receive funds for the purpose of educating our people, perhaps we could justify a cessation of activity."

"We're already providing education to our applicants. I'd be happy to show you some of the informational packets we're providing now."

"That's not the type of education I mean," said Johnson. "I was thinking more along the lines of family counseling with an emphasis on personal finance."

"Of course. I could see how that might be beneficial. We would be very open to helping to put a program like that together."

"Ten million."

"I'm sorry?"

"Ten million dollars. That should be enough to put such a program together."

"Reverend, I don't think we're in the same ballpark here. I'm certain my clients wouldn't entertain anything that exorbitant. Perhaps if you threw out a lower number, we'd have a better starting point from which to negotiate."

"I didn't throw that number out as a prelude to negotiating. There will be no negotiations. You can tell your clients that is a take it or leave it offer. I haven't even begun to put the kind of pressure on your little operation here that I intend to bring in the near future. This is just a sampling of what I can do. You and your clients would be wise to cut your losses early."

"Look, let's be practical here. This pressure you speak of has mainly been on me and my practice—not my clients. If I decide to withdraw my representation, they'll just find someone else to replace me. Then you're right back where you started. Try to think about it from their perspective. If they make a deal with you, there's no guarantee they still won't face opposition from other... civic-minded groups such as yours. I think I can help you Reverend if you're just willing to be more reasonable."

Johnson rose abruptly from his chair. "Reasonability is something we must not demand from God. He decides in His own divine judgment what is and isn't reasonable. I trust you'll communicate my offer to your clients, Mr. Marshall, and I hope you understand that regardless of the outcome, I win. My side always does, you see. Good day, sir."

Tyler watched him turn and walk away without even offering a handshake. In a moment, he was gone. Tyler also had a pretty clear view of the hole he was standing in at the moment. It seemed plenty deep enough to bury him.

Elvis Patterson arrived at the offices of Marshall & Marshall shortly after Clarence Cooper's speech. The television crews and reporters were mostly gone by then, off to file their stories for the day. He dressed up for the occasion, wearing his best flannel shirt over a t-shirt bearing the number of his favorite race-car driver. He had a tire gauge clipped to his front shirt pocket even though it had been months since the last time his car was actually operable. He wore blue cotton uniform pants and Husky work boots with a tobacco stain on the left toe. A string of keys jangled loosely from the belt loop at his side, and he carried his daughter's school notebook made of thick paper, with *English* scrawled in black magic marker across the front. Approaching from the south on foot, the milling protestors blocked his view of the police barricade on the other side at the building's front entrance, so he worked his way directly through the center of the crowd instead of going around it. One of the African-American demonstrators spotted him immediately. "Hey brother, pick up a sign, and join the cause," he said to Elvis.

"It ain't my cause, and you ain't my brother," he said, letting fly a string of tobacco juice at the man's feet.

"You mean you're not here to join the demonstration?"

"I'm here 'cause I got business in that there building over yonder," Elvis sneered, pointing to the law office behind them. "You got a problem with that, jigaboo?"

The man stepped back, startled before he regained his composure. "I guess I don't. In fact, if you've got friends or family members that have business in there too, I'm sure I could arrange for transportation for them," he said as laughter erupted from a few of the picketers behind him. "Make way for our little cracker brother here folks," he shouted as the crowd parted, letting him pass. "This is what I'd definitely call responsible parenting. Maybe this Fresh Start thing isn't such a bad idea after all!"

Elvis kept his head down as he made his way through the crowd to the front entrance, hearing them snickering and laughing behind his back. *Niggers.* He hated them all. Hated the poor ones always crying about being discriminated against, using that as an excuse for everything gone wrong in their miserable lives, always looking for a hand-out. Nobody ever gave him a damn thing in his entire life! What did they know about struggling? What did they know about being out there on your own with no one to turn to for help? Yes, he hated the poor ones, but he hated the affluent ones even more, always looking down on him like that asshole back there, like he was better somehow, superior. *He looks down at me, but he calls the sorriest excuse for a nigger next to him brother!* He missed the old days, his daddy and granddaddy's generation, when even a white man down on his luck was still looked at by society better than the most uppity colored person there was. The world was going to hell in a hand basket, and he'd be damned if he was going to let his daughter bring a child into it.

The front door of the building was locked, but before he could even knock, a black man about his size, wearing a fancy suit and diamond cufflinks shot out the door like the building was on fire, nearly knocking him over. "Hey, watch where you're going, asshole!" he shouted, but the man kept on walking like he wasn't even there. Yes, he especially hated the uppity ones.

He walked in the door, and was met by a girl who looked like she just walked off a horror movie set, *Night of the Living Dead* or something like that. Zombified, all the way. "Can I help you, sir?" offered the girl, a pale smile cached on an ashen face.

Well at least she has manners. "I'm here about the program I saw on TV."

"Of course, I have an application package right here," she said, reaching for the top folder in a large pile resting on a filing cabinet behind her desk. I just need to ask you a few basic questions before we get started. If everything checks out, you can fill out this application. It shouldn't take more than twenty minutes to complete. After that, you'll meet briefly with one of our associates for a face-to-face interview.

"That sounds great. Do you think I could get a glass of water? Those nig…those people out there kind of freaked me out a little bit, if you know what I mean."

"I understand. Sorry about that, but it is a free country I guess. I'll be right back with your water."

Elvis watched her walk around the corner into what appeared to be the break room. There wasn't anyone else around that he could see. He reached behind the desk and grabbed one of the application packages, emptied its contents into his daughter's English notebook and slipped the empty folder in a crack between the filing cabinet and the wall. He also spied a document on the receptionist desk with a signature on it. The signature was practically illegible, but he could read the typed name beneath it clearly—R. Tyler Marshall IV. He grabbed it and stuck it in his notebook as well.

"Here's your water," she said, returning with a styrofoam cup. "Now I just have a few short questions for you," she said, as she opened the application form at her desk. "First, I'll need your address."

"620 Henderson Road, Savannah."

"Okay, and your birth date?"

"The seventh of November, nineteen seventy-three."

"Great. Wait a minute. So you're over forty years old?"

"That's right."

"I'm sorry, sir, but this program is only available to applicants between the ages of sixteen and forty. I'm afraid you don't qualify."

"But I walked all the way across town."

"I'm sorry. We can't make any exceptions."

"Thanks for the water anyways. See you around." He winked at her in a way that made her uneasy as he turned to leave. There was something almost sinister about him, evil. That angry, soulless stare left a lasting impression on her.

Annie and Mara met for drinks right after work at a quiet, dim bar downtown located in the basement of a small, nondescript commercial building. Though they were the only customers in the bar, the bartender, clad all in black, seemed preoccupied and disinterested in serving them. A television hanging from the ceiling was tuned to CNN, playing a replay of Ferguson's speech that morning. It had played on a continuous loop once per hour all day long.

"Excuse me," said Mara to the bartender, in a voice too loud for the environs, "can we order a drink please?" After the bartender reluctantly took their order and casually made his way back to the bar Mara said, "Jesus, Annie, what made you pick this place?"

"Our new temp recommended it. Apparently the crowd doesn't start to arrive until at least eleven o'clock. I get the feeling she comes here a lot. She drinks at least two of those energy drinks every day at work. I'm starting to think she's addicted to them."

"I saw her this morning. The goth girl. Not exactly the kind of receptionist you'd pick for a stodgy, southern law firm."

Annie shrugged. "We'll take what we can get these days. Apparently the labor pool for administrative assistants willing to cross a picket line of religious zealots and rabid civil rights activists is somewhat limited, and besides, she graduated with honors from Boston University."

"I'm impressed. So how's our boy holding up?"

"You tell me."

"I wouldn't know. We haven't seen much of each other lately. He says he needs some time to think things through. He seems… distracted."

"You mean he's drinking again?" They fell silent, as both knew the answer to the question. "He is under a lot of stress right now."

"I told him he should walk away from this stupid program. It's not worth it."

"The irony of the situation is that he wouldn't be involved in the program if it weren't for you. Tyler's always taken the path most traveled, always done what's expected of him and never made waves, never did anything or said anything to stand out from the crowd. I've noticed the change in him since he met you. He's in uncharted waters and frankly, he's scared shitless."

"What do you think he should do?"

"It's not for me to give him advice," Annie replied. "He doesn't listen to me anyway. He's a grown man. He needs to make his own decisions. Whatever does happen, I'll be there to pick up the pieces."

"Does that include me?"

"We'll see about that. For now, all you can do is give him a little space and some time and see how it goes."

"You're wrong, you know," said Mara. "He does listen to you. He'd quit if you told him to quit."

"He'd quit because it's in his nature to quit. I'm not going to be the one to give him an excuse. He'll have to do that on his own."

"I still don't get you two. I used to think there was something going on between you, but in the time I've spent with him, I don't see it from his side. You on the other hand, you seem like you have certain expectations of him, like you have some kind of claim on him, and he always seems to fail you. I know he feels that from you, that disappointment. Like he can't ever please you, but he still wants to in some strange way. It's the same with his father. The man sounds like an absolute monster."

"He's not so bad. Has it ever occurred to you that Tyler projects the disappointment he feels about himself to those closest to him? That we're just a manifestation of his internal struggles? It's much easier to face an antagonist you can see and touch than it is doing battle with the demons inside your own head."

"None of this can possibly be helping. This is more than anyone could possibly be expected to manage. Forget all of that macho bullshit about him standing up for himself. The sooner this is over the better for everybody. Speaking of which, how did things go with Thaddeus Johnson today?"

"Not well. He demanded ten million dollars to go away. Can you believe the nerve of that man?"

"You don't like Reverend Johnson very much do you, Annie? You want to talk about it?"

"I'd rather not. Let's just say calling him a snake would be an affront to snakes everywhere."

"While we're on the subject, do you remember that time I went to his church with a co-worker? I told you I met her little sister—she sings in the choir and looks like she's maybe in her early teens—along with Reverend Johnson. I got this weird vibe between the two of them. And then he started kind of hitting on me, or at least I thought he was. The whole thing was very unsettling. Anyway, my co-worker comes up to me today, very upset and tells me her little sister is pregnant. She won't tell Quinnette—that's the girl I work with—who the father is, but she did tell her it was on older man, a married man. I started thinking about the way she acted around Thaddeus Johnson, and ...I mean he wouldn't...would he?" Annie fell eerily silent as she closed her eyes. Mara detected the slightest tremor that seemed to undulate through Annie's entire body in successive waves. "Annie, what's wrong?"

"Mara, you've got to talk to this girl. It's not just a possibility that Thaddeus Johnson is the father. At this point, you should consider it a probability."

"You're serious, aren't you?"

"Dead serious. You've got to talk to her."

"What is it you're not telling me, Annie?"

"Mara!"

"Fine, I'll talk to her."

Annie was distracted the rest of the evening and found it hard to concentrate on the conversation. She kept hearing a voice other than Mara's. It was the voice of a fourteen-year-old girl, a girl she had mentally locked away in a closet so many years ago. The girl had seen things, knew things that Annie preferred to forget, but no matter how hard Annie tried to block her out of her memory, no matter how hard she tried to forget, she still heard the sound of the girl's voice through that closet door, crying for help.

CHAPTER THIRTEEN

The afternoon of his impromptu visit to Marshall & Marshall, Elvis Patterson sat mystified by the Fresh Start application at his kitchen table, a folding card table with a vinyl tablecloth haphazardly draped over it. It might as well have been written in Greek. He never made it past the sixth grade, and he was two years behind when he dropped out. What was the use of school, really? He had more common sense than any of those wannabe assholes sitting at the front of the class taking notes anyway. They made fun of him behind his back, called him names like "retard" and "LD," short for learning disabled. He knew what they were saying. Never to his face though. They were too chicken shit for that. They knew he would thrash them within an inch of their lives if they did. Sometimes he'd do it anyway, just for kicks. No doubt, they had it coming. They might have been smarter than him, but he was older, tougher, meaner, and in the sixth grade that's all that counted. One time he roughed up a kid a little too much after school. The boy had laughed out loud in class when Elvis couldn't spell fermentation or some stupid word like that. The school expelled him.

His daddy didn't care. He put him to work at the garage where he worked. He wasn't much for school either, and look how he ended up. Nice uniform, steady paying job. Four bucks an hour back then was a lot of money. Who needed school?

The truth was he never could see the letters the way the other kids did. He always confused b and d or p and q, or he'd try to spell the words the way they sounded instead of the way they were actually spelled. He knew there was something wrong with him, even then, something that could have been fixed if someone would have taken the time, but no one cared, especially about him. Things might have turned out differently for him, but what was the use of looking back? Shoulda, coulda, woulda. That wasn't going to put food on the table or beer in the fridge. He'd get by like he always had—on his wits.

"Jennifer!" he barked.

"Yes, Daddy," said the girl, emerging from her bedroom. Her eyes were fixed on the floor, never making contact with his, just like her mother. That was good. It was a sign of respect. Or fear. It didn't matter either way. To Elvis Patterson, they were one and the same.

"Help me out with these damn forms."

The girl glanced through them, and a look of consternation spread across her face. "Daddy, I've already been to this place. They told me I couldn't…"

"Shut your trap! I went over there this morning and sorted everything out. They told me all we had to do was fill out a little paperwork, and we were good to go."

"But…"

"Don't interrupt me again, or you're gonna get a beating like you've never had before. Just tell me what these forms are goddammit!"

Her hands trembled as she leafed through the forms. "This is the application. It says for internal use only. This one says in-dem-ni-fi-cation agreement. It says for internal use only too. This form is for the parent's consent. It's supposed to be signed by a parent and notarized and given to the care provider. And this one is the approval form. It says it has to be signed by the trustee and presented to the care provider. The signature line for the trustee says R. Tyler Marshall IV. That's the man who told me he wouldn't approve me for the program."

"So we just need to sign these two forms then, right?" he said holding up the parental consent and program approval forms.

"I think so. This one has to be notarized, but you don't have a signed approval form."

"They probably just forgot to sign it. I'll go back there in the morning. I'm gonna pull you out of school tomorrow, and we'll get this taken care of right quick."

"But Daddy..."

"You hush your mouth, and go on back there to your room while I'm still in a good mood, you hear? You don't want me in a bad mood when I tuck you in tonight, do you?"

She smelled the stale mixture of cigarettes and beer on his breath, the pervading scent of her youth. "No, sir," she said meekly.

Elvis stopped by the bank the following morning and had his signature notarized authorizing parental consent to the operation. It was just a matter of tracing Tyler's signature from the document he stole from the office onto the approval form, and he was good to go. He walked the three blocks to Jennifer's school and signed her out for a doctor's appointment. One of the three care providers listed on the approval document was a health clinic not too far from the school. Father and daughter walked in silence, each lost in their own private thoughts of the future, his full of tantalizing visions of sudden wealth, hers full of remorse for hope's last breath.

The front-desk clerk at the clinic took the forms from Jennifer's hands indifferently, like a librarian checking out the umpteenth book of the day. Her eyes barely scanned the signatures before the forms were placed in a manila file to be stacked, processed and stored with hundreds of other manila files indistinct from each other.

Jennifer noticed only a small trace of recognition in the woman's eyes before her banal words pierced the air.

"Please have a seat. The doctor will see you shortly."

To Jennifer, the wait seemed interminable. She was sixteen years old with her entire life ahead of her, but she couldn't quite see it that way. Time held no significance to a child without a childhood. He'd stolen that from her. The thought of a normal life—marriage, children—seemed so distant, so far away as to not even be real to her. And besides, who could ever possibly want her as a wife? She was damaged goods, fractured and broken. No amount of tape or glue could ever make her whole again. Daddy said it was their little secret, that no one would ever have to know, but that case worker who kept coming around the house, she knew. Momma knew even though she turned a blind eye and was too scared of Daddy to do anything about it anyway. Worst of all, she knew herself, and the lie was written all over her face like an advertisement on a billboard for everyone to see. Who did she think she was fooling? Maybe the operation was for the best after all. She'd been pregnant once before, and if there was one thing she knew for sure it's that she never wanted to go through that again, not ever. When they took that living, breathing, being inside her, a part of her died. What remained, well, was just waiting around for the same inevitable result.

A nurse ushered her into a room full of equipment while her father waited outside in the reception area. In the center of the room sat a self-adjusting gynecological table with stirrups and a fold-down cushion at the end, covered with a white sanitary mattress.

"Have a seat on the table," the nurse said as she adjusted it to an upright position.

As Jennifer sat back she could see two large lights suspended overhead, hung from the ceiling. The room was cold and sterile, and she felt a chill raising goose bumps on her flesh. Within minutes the doctor walked in, an Indian man in his forties, who spoke English fluently with just a trace of an accent. She noticed his skin—it was the color of the coffee her mother drank every morning, loaded with milk.

"How old are you, Jennifer?" he asked. He seemed uncomfortable and ill at ease, and this made her nervous.

She stared up at the ceiling, evading his eyes. "Sixteen."

"Do you understand the surgery you are about to undergo?"

"Yes sir."

"You're very young for this type of procedure. Are you sure you want to do this?"

She noticed the paint was peeling slightly in the upper right corner of the room. "Yes sir."

He stared at her for several moments before speaking like he was grappling with some internal conflict in his head. "I am going to tell you how the surgery works. First, I will apply a general anesthesia, so you won't feel any pain. Then, I will make one or two small cuts in your stomach, near your belly button. Next, I will insert a narrow tube with a camera on the end—that is called a laparoscope. Finally, I will use an instrument that I will insert through the laparoscope that will cauterize, or burn, your fallopian tubes shut. This will prevent your eggs from moving from your ovary to your uterus so you can never get pregnant. You should be able to go home in a couple of hours, after the anesthesia wears off. Do you understand this?"

Jennifer just wanted it all to be over, to put this cold, sterile room and this man with the strange accent far behind her. "Yes sir, I understand."

"I'm going to ask you once again, Jennifer. Are you sure you want to do this?"

She thought she was going to cry, not from pain or sadness but because she felt so out of control, like her life was unfolding in front of her, and she was nothing but a startled spectator. She blinked back a tear, still refusing eye contact with the doctor.

"Yes sir. Please can we get this over with?"

She felt the slight prick of a needle and then a vague numbness gradually crept over her body. It comforted her to think about a place where you didn't feel anything. Maybe that's what heaven was like. Daddy didn't believe in heaven.

Her last conscious thought was of the case worker saying, "Maybe God doesn't believe in your daddy," and she laughed to herself deep down inside where no one could see or hear it right before the darkness descended, and her world faded to black.

Tyler's nerves were frayed. True to his word, the reverend had busloads of marchers outside at their regularly appointed time and more television cameras and members of the media than ever. It was clearly evident he was going to keep the pressure on. Tyler spoke with Don Abbott who let him know that a ten million dollar payment to Johnson's "educational fund" was out of the question and not to even bother responding to it. He did hint of another plan to reach a compromise with Johnson but was vague when Tyler pushed him for more details, only reiterating his request for a little more time to work things out. The two weeks Tyler had agreed to seemed an eternity to him right now.

By noon, Geena had fielded phone calls from CBS, ABC, NBC, FOX, CNN and MSNBC requesting personal interviews with him, all following up on CNN's footage from the day before. Representatives from the Associated Press called, as did *USA Today*, *The Wall Street Journal* and *The Huffington Post*. He wasn't granting interviews, but he did prepare a statement for Geena to fax or e-mail, which rebutted many of Reverend Johnson's accusations.

His mother called at lunchtime to tell him that *The View* covered the story as one of their topics—they were all against the program. She also let him know that his father was very upset, which was her polite Southern way of telling him she agreed with the four opinionated women on television.

During the course of the day, thirty applicants came knocking hesitantly at the door, continuing to establish a pattern that Tyler found interesting. Since the first day of picketing, Fresh Start applicants were increasingly low-income residents. Tyler could only speculate why. Perhaps middle to high-income applicants were frightened off by the marchers or didn't want to risk being seen by friends and relatives on television. Perhaps the extra publicity reached the low-income people in ways the traditional newspaper advertising and flyers failed. In either case, Tyler found it ironic that the reverend's attempts to shut down the program were actually *helping* his clients accomplish their intended objective.

He opened his desk drawer, pulled out a miniature bottle of Dewar's Scotch—the kind they serve on airplanes and poured it into his can of Coke. *Four o'clock.* It was a little early for a cocktail and one of the few times he could actually remember drinking at the office during regular business hours. His father certainly wouldn't approve, but then again, these were unusual times, and he needed a drink.

Mara had little trouble convincing Quinnette to let her talk to Deondra. She was a professional, she did this kind of thing for a living, and the girl needed to confide in someone, faced with such an important decision. Mara would not betray the girl's trust, but she would encourage her to speak openly with her older sister who was eager to help. To make things seem more natural, Mara gave

Quinnette a ride home from work that afternoon knowing that Deondra would likely be home.

They found her in her room doing homework. "Hey, Deondra, you remember my friend Mara, don't you?" asked Quinnette. "You met her at church."

"Oh, yeah. Hey."

"Hi, Deondra. How's choir?"

"Okay I guess."

"Mara, I totally forgot something," said Quinnette. "I'm supposed to call Claire at work and go over that spreadsheet with her. Her report is due in the morning, you know. It shouldn't take more than fifteen minutes. Do you mind waiting for me? Deondra will keep you company, won't you baby?" The girl shrugged without looking up from her work. "Great, well I'll come back for you soon."

Mara stepped into the room and looked at the trophies, ribbons and plaques displayed on her dresser—basketball, gymnastics, soccer, choir, school attendance, honor roll. She walked to the bed where Deondra was splayed diagonally and motioned at an unoccupied corner.

"Mind if I sit down?"

Deondra cleared a few papers to make room for her. "Your sister says you've been going through kind of a tough time lately," Mara said. "I'm a pretty good listener. You want to talk about it?"

"Not really."

"Sometimes when we have a problem, it's good to talk about it with someone else. A lot of times it's easier to talk about it with someone we don't know very well. That way, whatever we say isn't as likely to come back to us. I work with young girls like you all the time, Deondra. That's my job. I can promise you that anything you say to me won't go further than the two of us unless you tell me otherwise. You have my word on that."

"I don't know…"

"Why don't you just give it a try? As long as I don't tell anybody, you don't have anything to lose."

The girl spoke softly, her voice barely a whisper. "I'm pregnant."

Mara's tone was calm and soothing. "I see. Deondra, that happens to girls your age all the time. I know this is tough for you to deal with right now, but lots of other girls just like you have gone through the same thing. It's nothing you should feel ashamed about. Have you thought about what you're going to do?"

"A little, but I don't know what to do."

"What's the father say?"

"He wants me to have an abortion."

"Listen to me. There is one very important thing for you to understand, Deondra. This is your decision. No one can make this decision for you, including the baby's daddy. I'm assuming, because he's suggesting that you have an abortion, he doesn't intend to provide for the child. There are legal options that might require him to help you out financially. I can help explain those to you if you'd like. But if you intend to have the baby, you need to understand you're likely going to be the sole provider for that child, certainly emotionally and possibly financially. That's a big responsibility for someone as young as you are, and it's not something you should take lightly."

"I know."

"You want to tell me who the father is? Is it a boy in school?"

"No."

"Is it someone older?"

"I can't tell you."

"Can't or won't? Look, it makes a big difference if you're thinking of keeping the baby. If it's someone who can help out financially, it might influence your decision."

"He has money. He's married."

"It's important that you don't confuse his problems with yours, Deondra. You need to think about yourself first. How old are you?"

"Fifteen."

"In the state of Georgia, it's illegal to have sexual intercourse with someone under the age of sixteen. It's called statutory rape. If the person convicted is over the age of twenty-one, he's looking at a minimum of ten years in prison."

"I don't want him to go to jail! I love him!"

"That's okay, calm down. It's your decision whether to press charges or not. You're calling the shots here remember? It just means that maybe you have more options, that's all. Deondra, who's the father?"

"I can't. Please don't ask me that."

Mara saw fear in the young girl's eyes. She heard Annie's words ring in her head. *The girl could be in real danger.* There was no other option. It had to be done.

"You don't have to tell me, but I'm going to throw out a man's name. All you have to do is nod, okay?" Mara thought she saw the girl's head bob in agreement, but she couldn't be sure. "Deondra, is it Reverend Johnson?"

The girl didn't speak, didn't nod. She didn't have to. Mara could see the look in her eyes, a look bordering almost on relief—relief at not having to carry such a terrible secret all alone. It was like a burden had been lifted from her shoulders. They were in this together now, co-conspirators for better or worse. Mara was used to becoming involved in her wards' issues, many times too involved for her own good, but this felt different, murkier. There were too many personal connections at play—Quinnette, Annie and Tyler, not to mention Thaddeus Johnson, all potentially had some stake in the final outcome. Despite this, Mara knew the only result that mattered was Deondra's, and she would have to protect the girl above all else. *This was going to get interesting.*

Annie stepped into Tyler's office, a concerned expression on her face. "We have a problem."

"What a surprise," said Tyler. "Things have been going so smoothly. What is it now?"

"You remember Jennifer Patterson?"

"Sure. I rejected her application. Mara knows her."

"Her father's downstairs. He's pretty belligerent. He says he wants his money. According to him, his daughter had her tubes tied this morning at one of our approved clinics."

"But that's not possible. They wouldn't operate without an approval form signed by me."

"I called the clinic, and they confirmed that they have an approval with your signature on it. Geena says he was in here the other day. He came in to apply himself, but she told him he was too old for the program, and he left without an argument."

"If someone signed an approval form, I can assure you it wasn't me. I would have recognized her name."

"The only other possibility I can think of is someone got their hands on a blank form and signed your name. The clinic said Mr. Patterson expected them to cut the check after the surgery. They explained to him that all checks must come from our office, so he's here to collect."

"Surely he doesn't expect us to pay him after we rejected the application!"

"He definitely expects us to pay him. I think you better come downstairs and talk to him. This situation has the potential to become…volatile."

Tyler followed Annie downstairs and found Elvis Patterson sitting in the reception area, ignoring Geena's glare. She looked like she wanted to kill him. "Mr. Patterson, Tyler Marshall," he said extending his hand. "My associate here just filled me in on some of the details of your situation."

"There ain't no situation. I come for my money. Real simple like."

"Mr. Patterson, where did you get the approval form with my signature on it?"

"My daughter brought it back with her after she come down here to apply. I didn't ask no questions."

"That's not possible. Your daughter left here with a very clear understanding that she would not be approved for this program, and I definitely did not sign any document authorizing surgery. I'm afraid we're going to have to obtain the original signature from the clinic to verify its accuracy before we can proceed. If need be, we'll conduct a handwriting analysis, which could take some time."

"Judgin' from that angry mob of jungle bunnies out there, I'd say you were in a world of trouble already. You don't need no more trouble from me now, do you?"

"Mr. Patterson, if that's some sort of veiled threat, I should remind you that forgery is a felony crime here in Georgia. First degree forgery carries a penalty of one to ten years in prison."

"Forgery? Now who's threatenin' who? If my daughter's done somethin' illegal, I suppose she'll have to face the music on that. Like I said, she gave me the signed form. I thought she was tellin' me the truth when she said she got it from you, but you know how kids are these days. You can't trust a thing they say, but I still expect to git my money. It ain't gonna look good when those reporters out there find out how you're goin' back on your word, especially after the poor girl had the surgery. Makes you look a might small and petty, don't ya think?"

Tyler felt like he might explode and drew a deep breath, searching for control. "I want to see the original approval before we have any conversation about money. After that, I will respond to you appropriately. Now if you would kindly get the hell out of my office..."

Elvis rose from his chair with a sly grin on his face that only fed Tyler's frustration. "I'll look forward to hearin' from you, counselor."

Tyler made plans with Mara that night to order in Chinese food at her apartment. It had been several days since they'd been together, and he missed her—needed her. Plus, he knew Mara was involved with the Patterson girl, and he needed advice on how to handle the situation.

He knocked on her door at seven-thirty, and in the instant he saw her face through the slight crack behind the chain lock, his emotions took hold of him. She unlocked the door, and he hugged her tightly, taking in her familiar scent, letting her hair tickle his hands as it fell carelessly off her shoulders.

"I missed you," she said.

"I missed you too."

An awkward silence fell between them, the first they had ever experienced together. They had a lot of catching up to do, and neither one knew where to start. Tyler heard a clock ticking on the kitchen wall—he had never noticed it before. "So what do you want to do?" asked Mara, breaking the silence. "Talk, fuck, eat?"

Tyler blushed. "You always get right to the point, don't you? How about all of the above?"

"Did you have any particular order in mind?"

"As a matter of fact, I do," he said, leading her into the bedroom.

Once there, she assumed complete control, undressing him, pushing him back on the bed climbing on top and straddling his body, undulating, rocking, slowly at first, then gradually faster into an insistent rhythm. Her eyes were closed, and she seemed in a world of her own. He watched her intently, like a passive bystander, a furtive voyeur hiding in the closet, achingly conscious of his submission to her. He was merely an object of her desire, existing only to please, and he found it strangely fulfilling, purposeful, in ways he couldn't pretend to understand. He felt his body strain and grow tense as her movements quickened, then an uncontrollable release as she cried out, leaving him spent and ineffectual. Mara rolled off him and walked to the bathroom to freshen up without saying a word. Tyler stared at the ceiling feeling necessary and useless at the same time.

Mara ordered the Chinese food and uncorked a bottle of cheap Chardonnay while Tyler lounged on the sofa. "Sorry if I was a little self-absorbed there baby," said Mara, "but it's been a while."

Tyler shrugged. "It's okay by me. You seemed like you were enjoying yourself."

"Oh, believe me, I was. Don't worry. Later on, after we've finished with the talking and eating, you can be the boss. I'm going to pour myself a glass of wine if you don't mind. I need it after a day like today. Would you care to join me?"

It was the first time she'd offered him any alcohol at her apartment since they'd been seeing one another. What that signified had gone unspoken between them. "Sure, I'll take a glass," he said. "I bet my day beats your day. Why don't you go first?"

She poured a second glass for him and sat at the opposite end of the couch in a shabby cotton bathrobe, her right foot, resplendent with purple toenails, resting on his crotch. "Before I start, you have to swear to keep this to yourself. It's about Reverend Johnson. I know he's the enemy as far as you're concerned but there's someone else, someone innocent, who could get hurt if word were to get out."

"Sounds scandalous," Tyler remarked, grinning.

Mara increased the pressure of her foot against his crotch. "Swear!"

"That hurts! Okay, I swear!"

Mara related the entire story to him. Tyler listened patiently without interruption until she finished. "Have you told Annie?" he asked.

"Not yet. She hates him for some reason. Do you know why?"

He shrugged, feigning ignorance. "You'd have to ask her."

"Deondra wouldn't even let me tell her sister. She won't press charges against him and doesn't want him to get into any trouble with his wife or the church for that matter. After what he's done to her, her first instinct is to protect him. I probably shouldn't have told you, but I thought you should know the kind of man you're up against. He inspires blind loyalty from his followers and he doesn't play fair."

"What's she going to do about the baby?"

"She's not sure at this point. He's encouraging her to have an abortion."

"How convenient for him. You've got to appreciate the raw irony here. He's protesting outside my office, screaming about protecting God's children, and at the same time, trying to coerce a fifteen year-old girl to abort his own child. It seems the Lord really does work in mysterious ways."

"You can't use this information Tyler. Promise."

"What good would it do me? That would be like attacking a bear with a BB gun. He's already got me beat, and he knows it. He's not going to let up, no matter what I say or do at this point. I feel sorry for the girl, though. She's learning a hard lesson about life at an early age."

"Do you still think your day was worse than mine?"

"I'll let you judge for yourself." Tyler told her about the office visit by Elvis, the possible forgery and his threat to go public. He saw the knuckles of her fingers turn white around the wine glass.

"That fucking bastard!" Mara cried. "I'll kill him myself!"

"Now that would be really helpful. I was hoping you'd think of something a little more civilized."

"You don't understand. This guy's a monster. Civilization would be better off without him. He raped his own daughter for Chrissakes!" Tyler watched her patiently, smiling, waiting for her temper to subside. "Baby, don't you see?" Mara said. "Everything's gone too far. It's just not worth it anymore. You've got to shut the program down. Nothing good can possibly come from all of this."

"I promised my clients I'd give it two weeks."

"So, shut it down in two weeks. It's time you cut your losses."

"What about Elvis?"

"Pay him. It's not your money anyway."

"What about principles?"

"What about them?"

"On one hand I've got Reverend Johnson calling me a baby killer when he's about to order the abortion of his own child, and on the other hand I've got Elvis Patterson, who has knowingly committed fraud in order to circumvent the rules of the program. If I let them both win, where does that leave me?"

"In exactly the same place you were before this whole mess started. What's wrong with that?"

Tyler sat up straight in his seat and placed his wine glass on the table next to the couch. "I don't want to go back to that place, Mara. Maybe I can't go back."

Mara scooted over to his side of the couch and wrapped an arm around him. "It's one thing to stand up for what you believe in, Tyler. That's heroic. It's quite another thing to let it destroy you. That's suicidal."

"Sometimes, it seems, they're one and the same," he said, kissing her gently on the cheek.

After dinner, Tyler stepped out on Mara's balcony and dialed the number he had for Elvis Patterson on his cell phone. He heard the distinctive voice on the other end. Patterson sounded drunk.

"Mr. Patterson, this is Tyler Marshall. I had a courier deliver the approval form you presented at the clinic this afternoon, and I was able to verify that it was indeed forged. I am submitting it to a professional handwriting analyst for official confirmation, but there's no doubt in my mind the signature is a forgery. As a result, my decision is final. You will not be receiving any funds from Fresh Start, and I will leave it up to the clinic as to whether they want to attempt to collect the cost of the operation from you. I will consider, however, reimbursing your daughter for the cost of reversal surgery if she is interested in going that route. There's no guarantee that surgery would be successful, but at her age there is a good chance it would be."

"She don't need no more surgery. You gonna pay me what's mine and that's that," Elvis slurred.

"No sir, I'm not going to pay you anything because nothing is owed to you. And if you persist in pursuing this matter, I plan on going to the authorities with forgery charges against you."

"I already tole you my daughter did that."

"We'll let the police and the courts decide that for themselves. Either way, you'd be smart to let this drop."

"You think you can intimidate me? You have no idea who you're messing with mister. I'm gonna git you and git you good. You'll be beggin' for mercy before I'm done with you. That's a promise."

"We'll see about that, Mr. Patterson. Good night, sir." Tyler's hand trembled as he turned off his phone. It was an emotion he hadn't felt in a long time. Rage.

CHAPTER FOURTEEN

The call Tyler had been expecting came shortly after lunchtime the following day. "Hello, Gaines. What can I do for you?"

"I spoke with Elvis Patterson a while ago. He is making some rather serious accusations about your program not living up to its obligations."

"Believe me, you haven't heard the entire story. I assume that's why you're calling?"

"Of course."

"I appreciate the opportunity to tell my side of the story. Jennifer Patterson came in to my office several weeks ago to apply for the program. After discussing with her the levity of the decision, I was under the distinct impression she was having second thoughts. In fact, it seemed obvious to me she wasn't really interested at all, that her father had put her up to it. As a result, I rejected her application and sent her home. I let her know that her father was welcome to contact me directly if he had any questions or issues he wanted to discuss. I never heard from either of them, so I assumed the matter was closed, at least until Mr. Patterson showed up in my office yesterday demanding payment based on a forged approval form."

"Mr. Patterson said that his daughter forged the form—not him."

"I'd bet my last dollar he signed the form. If it comes to it, I'll submit it to a handwriting expert for confirmation."

"I've taken the liberty of contacting one already," Shockley said. "He told me it was unlikely to get a confirmation as this signature was probably traced, not written in free form. It proves that the signature isn't yours, but it can't be determined who actually forged it. Mr. Patterson said the girl will go on record admitting to it. I'm supposed to meet him and his daughter this afternoon for a formal interview."

"Regardless of who forged the document, I don't see this as much of a story. We followed proper procedure and didn't do anything wrong. If there was any illegal activity, it was on the part of the Pattersons. For the record, I have offered Mr. Patterson to reimburse him for the cost of reversal surgery if they elect to go that route in order to repair the damage from his…their poor judgment."

"Will you pay Mr. Patterson the fifteen thousand dollar stipend that normally goes to program applicants?"

"Under the circumstances, we do not intend to reimburse them any other monies."

"I think that about does it for me. Is there anything else you'd like to add?"

"I think that covers it." Tyler paused for a second, not wanting to appear anxious. "So are you going to run the story?"

"I'm not sure yet. I'd like to speak with the daughter first. Get her side of things."

"Of course. I would appreciate a heads up if you decide to go with it."

"I'll see what I can do," Shockley said, noncommittally.

Deondra was walking home from school when she spotted the blue Cadillac Escalade pick-up truck approaching on her side of the road.

The truck came to a stop next to her as the driver, Rodney, the taller one, motioned for her to get inside. He wasn't much for small talk. "Reverend Johnson wants us to take you to see the doctor. Get in."

"I'm not going anywhere with either of you two thugs. And I don't have any doctor's appointment."

"You do today," said Rodney. "The appointment was made for you. Now get your ass in the truck before I throw you in."

"You tell the reverend he can talk to me directly if he wants, but I'm not going to any doctor's appointment with you, ever. You got that?"

Before she knew it, James, the stocky one, bounced out the door and grabbed her forcibly by the arm. She let out a scream, and her books went flying as she struggled against her attacker who had almost two hundred pounds on her. James picked her up sideways with one arm, while he tried to corral the books strewn all over the grass with the other.

The school crossing guard spotted them. "Just what do you think you're doing? You put that girl down right now before I call the police!"

James shot a quick glance at Rodney as the girl kicked and flailed at him from her prone position under his arm. "Leave the girl, and get in the car," Rodney said to James, as he abruptly dropped her face first on the ground. "We'll be back for you later," he sneered at Deondra. As James climbed in, he turned the car around in the middle of the road and gunned the accelerator. As he looked in the rear view mirror, he had a clear view of the diminishing form of the crossing guard, standing in the middle of the street and writing his license plate number down on a small note pad.

"Are you okay, sweetheart?" the guard asked, stuffing the license number in her front pocket.

"I'm fine," Deondra said, collecting her books. A small group of kids stood staring at her, mouths agape. As she made her way home, the humiliation stung her like a swarm of angry mosquitoes from the soggy marsh. To be grabbed by two thugs on the side of the road in front of her schoolmates and delivered to some waiting doctor like she didn't have any choice in the matter was outrageous. Humiliation quickly turned to anger, as the realization set in that Thaddeus probably didn't love her at all. She was just an amusement to him, one easily discarded once he had tired of her. Strangely, this acknowledgment built a resolve in her she didn't know existed before. She would have this baby. As soon as she got home, she would share the news with Quinnette and Mara. They would know what to do next.

Gaines Shockley left the Patterson home feeling like he had kissed his sister. He'd been looking for an angle in this Fresh Start thing for days, and after speaking with Elvis on the phone, he thought he had it, but there were too many missing ingredients to make this a real story, the kind that would get him noticed nationally, outside of this frontier outpost. He found his victim, but Elvis Patterson just didn't quite measure up. To begin with, he was white and a racist to boot. The Fresh Start story was clearly about minorities being exploited by whites. This theme just wouldn't resonate through Elvis Patterson. Aside from that, the man was just creepy. He half-believed the daughter when she told him she forged the signature, but she seemed overly frightened and intimidated by her father. Maybe it was just her age, but she definitely kowtowed to him. She would make a more sympathetic victim, but she lost credibility with the reader if she had, in fact, forged the documents. It wasn't what he was hoping for, but it was a start. He just needed to massage things a little. There was a story in there somewhere, and he'd find it, wherever it was.

The next morning's headline of the Savannah Daily Journal, under Gaines Shockley's byline read:

Shoddy Procedures at Fresh Start Puts Children at Risk

"Like most parents, Elvis Patterson dreamed of his daughter experiencing a happy, fulfilling life and the joy of starting her own family someday. Those dreams were brutally crushed recently when she applied to the Fresh Start program and, through a myriad of procedural breakdowns, underwent sterilization procedures without the consent of her father.

'She didn't know what she was doing,' lamented Patterson. 'She's only sixteen years old. She thought she was helping her mother and me out financially, since I've been out of work lately.'

According to the Pattersons, their daughter bypassed the formal approval process of the controversial sterilization program and presented two simple forms to a local clinic. The personnel at the clinic did not bother to verify the accuracy of the information.

'She presented the forms Fresh Start requires us to collect in order to proceed with the surgery,' said a spokesperson for the clinic. 'We assumed the information was accurate.'

Tyler Marshall, Trustee for Fresh Start, said, 'We followed proper procedures and didn't do anything wrong.' Marshall added that an offer had been made to reimburse the Pattersons for the cost of undergoing a reversal procedure but would not pay them the fifteen thousand dollar stipend awarded to regular participants.

'They want my daughter to have a dangerous operation to undo what they did to her in the first place without my permission,' said Mr. Patterson. 'What kind of people are they that would take advantage of a poor little sixteen year old girl like this?'

Critics assert that the program takes advantage of poor, uneducated people—notably minorities—and preys on their desperation to induce them into undergoing sterilization procedures. 'We're just poor, hard-working folks trying to get by,' said Patterson. 'My daughter is too young to make this kind of a decision on her own and now it'll haunt her for the rest of her life.'

Reverend Thaddeus Johnson, one of the most outspoken critics of the program, issued this statement. 'We continue to oppose the Fresh Start program, which victimizes minorities and others who struggle every day just to survive. What message do we send our children, children like this young girl, when we abandon them in their time of need? This program must be stopped, and I call on the mayor and the governor to step in and do something about it's before it's too late.'

Thaddeus Johnson smiled as he read his quote in the paper at the family breakfast table. The chef had prepared blueberry waffles, his favorite. *This should turn up the heat a few notches on Tyler Marshall.* Overall, he had to be satisfied with the way things were going. The local protestors picketing the law office were down to a few church employees—that was a concern. The original group had melted back into their everyday lives as the initial thrill of the movement waned for them. The professional picketers sent down from Atlanta were costing him three thousand dollars a day, money that was coming straight out of the church coffers. The homeless picketers were cheaper. All he had to do was give them something to eat and enough money to buy a cheap bottle of booze at the end of the day, but they showed up stoned drunk and offended the others, so he had no choice but to let them go. He was still working on getting some of the national civil rights groups on board, but so far the only support they pledged was moral support. He needed money...and bodies. He knew it was only a matter of time before Marshall caved. He could see it in his eyes during their face-to-face meeting. The man simply didn't have it in him. With the heat turned up, he would fold. It was simply a matter of when.

The phone rang, and he heard the housekeeper answer it in the adjoining room. It was a little early for anyone to be calling. "Reverend, it's for you," said the housekeeper. "It's Deondra Rose. I told her you were eating breakfast, but she says it's an emergency."

All eyes at the breakfast table met his inquisitively except for his wife's. Monique never looked up from the plate in front of her.

"What's she calling for, Daddy?" asked Abbie, his middle child.

"I can't imagine, but I guess I'm about to find out." He rose from the table and took the phone in the next room. "Deondra, what a surprise," he said in a voice loud enough for everyone to hear. "What's this I hear about an emergency?"

"I just wanted you to know that I've decided to have the baby." Her voice was firm, cold.

"I see. Perhaps we should meet and talk about this. I could see you this afternoon at church."

The chatter at the breakfast table had died. They were all listening.

"I don't want to talk about it. My mind's made up."

"Deondra, I don't know what to say. I think you're making a big mistake."

"Goodbye, Reverend."

It seemed he had another problem to deal with now.

"What was the emergency, sweetheart?" asked Monique casually as he took his place at the table.

"Deondra called to tell me she's leaving the choir. Something about boy troubles. She sounded pretty upset. I'm sure I'll be able to talk some sense into her once she calms down." He flashed a toothy grin at his adoring family, without a care in the world. "Now, let's eat!"

Gaines Shockley was feeling particularly proud of himself that morning. His co-workers had all grudgingly offered their congratulations. Jealousy was a common theme among the staff reporters, and the old dogs couldn't possibly be happy that the young pup was scooping them right in front of their very noses. The assistant editor of *The New York Herald* even called personally to compliment him. The paper had a reporter in town covering the story, but she was reporting the same generic crap as everyone else. Shockley was the only reporter so far to get an exclusive interview with Tyler Marshall and now, Elvis Patterson. He got the distinct impression that the *Herald* was looking at a staff addition, and he planned to let the editor know, in no uncertain terms, he was available. For someone his age to land a job at one of the major New York papers was almost unheard of. For the first time in his young career, he could see his efforts were paying off. There was a light at the end of this tunnel.

Just when he thought his luck couldn't get any better, the phone rang, and he heard the voice of a middle-aged woman. "I just thought you should know you got your story all wrong today."

"How's that?"

"You made that awful man sound like an angel. Like he's some kind of victim or something. He's been abusing that child for years. She even had to abort his own child once."

"Who is this?"

Gaines sensed the hesitation. "A friend. If she had that surgery you wrote about, it was because he forced her. She wouldn't have done that to herself."

"How do you know this?"

"Because I reported him to DFACS over a year ago. She admitted to them that her father got her pregnant, but before it went to trial, she had an abortion and recanted her story. She only did that because she was scared to death of him, scared of what he might do to her...or her mother."

"I'd like to help, but I can't do anything with an anonymous tip. I need some concrete evidence before I can act on it."

"What would you do with the information?"

Shockley's mind was racing. "See that this guy is brought to justice. If we could prove he forged the documents for his daughter's surgical procedure, he'd be looking at a felony conviction. The girl would be an adult by the time he got out of prison. She would be protected."

"I have some paperwork, but I can't tell you how or where I got it, and I can't have my name connected to this in any way."

"That's fine. I'll protect you as an anonymous source. Any information covering child abuse or medical records is confidential and is not subject to Georgia's Open Records Act, so I can't use the specific information you give me. But I would like to see it in order to validate your credibility as a source. When and where can we meet?"

Gaines heard silence on the line for what seemed like an eternity before the woman spoke.

"I could meet you on my lunch break at noon tomorrow in Oglethorpe Square..."

"Perfect! I'll be sitting on the bench, wearing a white shirt and yellow tie. See you there." He hung up the phone before she had the chance to change her mind. Finally, it seemed, he found the perfect victim.

After meeting his source during the lunch hour, Gaines made a beeline to the newspaper's office building downtown and barged into George Hawthorne's office without knocking. Hawthorne was not only the editor he was the son of the owner, Della Hawthorne.

"There's no way you can use that information, Gaines. It's confidential and protected," he said after Gaines gave him the background for the story. Hawthorne was old school, conservative, cautious and risk-averse. He would never make a decision that might put the family birthright at risk.

"I'm not using it. I barely even looked at the file. My story is based on information gleaned from a confidential source. I just peeked at the file to make sure she was credible. This woman is a neighbor of the Pattersons. She is in a position to know what goes on in their home. She's clean as a whistle. The story checks out, George."

"Even if it checks out, what's the point, Gaines? What does any of this have to do with Fresh Start?"

"Because it establishes the girl as the victim. She's a victim of child abuse, and now, thanks to Fresh Start, she's the victim of forced sterilization. She had no say in any of this. It was all done to her against her will by her monstrous father and a hopelessly misguided philanthropy. George, this story has Pulitzer Prize written all over it."

"It has lawsuit written all over it is what it has. I can't allow this paper to take on that kind of risk. I'm sorry Gaines."

"George."

"Gaines."

"If that's your final decision, George, I'm afraid you're not leaving me a choice. I will find a paper that will run this story. A paper with some balls."

"Is that some kind of threat?"

"Not a threat. Consider it a promise."

On page four of the following morning's edition of *The New York Herald,* a story ran under Gaines Shockley's byline:

Abused Girl Victim of Forced Sterilization

"A sixteen year old girl in Savannah, Georgia was forced to undergo a sterilization procedure by her abusive father according to a confidential source close to the family. The girl was pressured by her father, Elvis Patterson, to undergo the surgery in exchange for a fifteen thousand dollar stipend offered by the controversial Fresh Start program. Critics assert that the program takes advantage of poor, uneducated people, notably minorities, and preys on their desperation.

Fresh Start staffers claim Mr. Patterson forged a document authorizing the procedure, and they refuse to pay the stipend, although they have offered to reimburse the family for the cost of any reversal procedures, should they so elect. Mr. Patterson, according to the source, has a long-standing history of child abuse, which culminated approximately a year ago when his daughter was forced to have an abortion to prevent an unwanted pregnancy as a result of the incestuous relationship between the two. It is speculated that, in addition to the financial reward, Mr. Patterson may have been motivated to force his daughter into sterilization in order to avoid any further pregnancies.

This tragic occurrence brings to light renewed questions concerning the devastating effect that Fresh Start is having on the citizens of Chatham County, Georgia. The controversial program has stirred racial unrest and, some say, forced its citizens to put a price tag on their own morality. For this young Patterson girl, it was a steep price indeed."

Dark rain clouds were beginning to form in the sky, and a cold, damp wind blew suddenly as if from nowhere as Jennifer Patterson walked to school that morning, oblivious of the article. *The Herald* wasn't distributed in town, and the Pattersons had no access to the Internet. The day before had been tough with the article in the local paper, but she made it through. Even though her name wasn't mentioned, it was obvious the article was about her since it was her father who was interviewed. The kids at school seemed more curious about the operation than anything, asking her a hundred questions about what it felt like. The truth was she hadn't felt a thing. She simply fell asleep, then woke up and went home.

Today, something seemed wrong as she entered the school. Kids were looking at her funny, whispering behind her back. She checked herself in the mirror in the girls' bathroom but didn't notice anything wrong with her appearance. As she walked into her first period class, the noise and chatter of the students fell eerily quiet. She felt thirty pairs of eyes staring at her, but whenever she attempted to make eye contact, they looked away. The final bell rang as Mrs. Murdoch, the English teacher, entered the room.

"Jennifer, may I speak with you for a moment?" asked the teacher, motioning to her in the direction of the hall.

"Yes ma'am," she said, consciously aware of more stares and whispers from the class. The door closed behind them, leaving them alone in the deserted hall, posters of the upcoming school play lining the walls. "Jennifer," said Jane Murdoch, "are you aware of an article that ran in one of the New York papers this morning? It was about your father and mentioned you, his daughter, but not specifically by name."

"No ma'am. Was it an article like the one in yesterday's paper?"

"Sort of. I think you better come with me." The teacher led her down the hall to the teachers' break room, which was empty. Jennifer had never been inside this room before. There was a large sofa and several comfortable chairs. Soft ambient light from various lamps lent the room a warm, cozy atmosphere. Jane Murdoch motioned for Jennifer to take a seat on the couch and sat down next to her. Within moments, the school principal, Ellen Ross, and the school's guidance counselor, Lee Hussing, joined them and took seats opposite them.

Jennifer found it hard to catch her breath, like she was choking on air. "What's wrong? Why am I here?"

The teacher and guidance counselor both deferred to the principal, the senior faculty member present. "Jennifer," said Ellen Ross, "there was a newspaper article printed today about you and your father. Some of the wire services picked up the story and ran it on the Internet. I'm afraid it says some pretty awful things."

"What kind of things?"

"I don't want you to get too upset. Often times the media presents things as facts, without properly checking for accuracy. Unfortunately, in today's society, we can't always believe what we read in the newspaper or see on television."

She felt panic creeping into her voice. "What did it say?"

"I've got a copy with me," said the principal, pulling a folded sheet of paper from her coat pocket, "and I'm going to let you read it in a moment. But first I want you to understand that there are a lot of people who care about you very much, and you can lean on us for support whenever you need it. After you read this, we can all talk about it if you want. Okay?"

Jennifer managed to nod her head slightly as the principal handed her the article. The paper felt cold in her hand, lifeless and rigid. As she began to read, tears welled up in her eyes and cascaded down her cheeks, leaving wet splotches on the paper. Her body was shaking uncontrollably by the time she reached the end of the article. "No!" she cried hysterically. "It's not true! It's not true!"

Jane Murdoch wrapped her arm around the girl's shoulder. "It's all right, honey. Cry as much as you want to."

"No!" the girl screamed. "It's a lie. It's not true at all!" Before anyone could react, she sprang upright and bolted out the door, leaving the startled faculty members behind.

"Jennifer, wait!" shouted the counselor, running after her. "Come back, and let's talk about this."

But it was too late. She had too much of a head start for him to catch her. He could only watch as she flew down the corridor and out the side door. "It's a lie!" she shouted again at the top of her lungs for the world to hear as falling raindrops from the angry gray sky pelted her face. She hit the street running as fast as her legs would take her, running from a relentless pursuer she couldn't see, to the safe harbor of a protector who didn't exist. She turned the corner and nearly collided with two women in their mid-thirties, power walking with umbrellas in their hands, barely perspiring and talking about a television program they had watched the night before. They glanced at her with a sullen disregard as she escaped through a neighbor's yard, then another and another until she found herself sliding down a muddy embankment filled with trees and wild undergrowth. The branches stung her face and sharp, craggy rocks left welts on the backs of her legs, as she slid haphazardly to the bottom of the hill.

In front of her ran a small creek, swollen with runoff from the rain and beyond that, a highway that ran past the edge of town. She sloshed through the creek, feeling the icy cold on her bare ankles as she made her way up a slight incline to the curb of the road, hidden from the view of passing motorists by the low hanging pines lining the creek bed.

Slow and deliberate, without hesitation, she walked into the path of a SUV, traveling sixty miles an hour in wet conditions. The driver later reported that he hadn't seen her until the very last moment, not even enough warning to apply the brakes. The impact of the car sent her flying fifty feet from the point of collision where they found her body, smeared in a grotesque mixture of blood and mud, clutching a rain-soaked sheet of copy paper in her cold, lifeless hands.

CHAPTER FIFTEEN

Tyler glanced at the clock on the microwave in his kitchen. *Two forty-three.* The precision of the number soothed him, provided evidence of structure and order in the universe. In seventeen minutes, schoolchildren would gleefully escape their rigidly disciplined day for the relative freedom of home. In two hours and seventeen minutes, the roads would become thick with traffic as workers embarked on the return trip of their daily commute. Somewhere across the ocean to the east, the sun was setting at this exact moment in time. Farther east, children were saying their bedtime prayers. Farther still, bars were announcing last call to anesthetized patrons. Time was the great order keeper of a chaotic world, all the vitality and wonder of life on this planet boiled down to a brilliantly ritualistic schedule. *Two forty-four.* The time comforted him. The problem was that he had no idea what day it was.

The last thing he remembered clearly was right after the call from Charles Mosely, the police chief. *There's been an accident...a bad accident. At this point, we're treating it as a suicide. I'm sorry Tyler.* Sorry.

After the call, Tyler left the office in a hurry and drove straight to Fun Times Package store. He needed a grocery cart.

"Are you having a party?" asked the cashier, all too friendly.

"Nope, just me."

After that, it was pretty much a blur. He vaguely remembered calling into work at least once to advise that he wouldn't be in. He remembered Annie's tone, hesitant, full of pity, the voice of a dear friend to someone who's just been diagnosed with terminal brain cancer, but perhaps he had dreamed that. In his alcoholic stupor. It was difficult to tell when the dreams ended and the nightmare of real life began.

The girl. Of course, it was all about the girl. It was so simple, really. *If only I'd given the father the money.* There wasn't much more to it, no long, drawn-out conjectures of what could have been, might have been. He knew. He killed her just as if he had driven the vehicle that whacked the last breath from her body. Was it pride, ego or some misguided sense of morality? In the end, it didn't matter. She was dead.

The story was front-page news in the local paper. He saw the headline but couldn't bear to read the article. He already had a pretty good idea of what it said anyway. His cell and home phones rang non-stop for a while: Annie, Don Abbott, Charles Mosely, his mother and pretty much all of the major news organizations. He did not answer any of them. Strangely, the phones had been quiet lately. *Maybe it's Saturday...*

The one person who did not call was Mara. She'd been close to the girl and against Fresh Start. She had advised him to shut down the program, and he hadn't listened. If there was anyone who could say, "I told you so," without prevarication, it was Mara. Tyler felt a perverse urge to hear those words from her, to be punished for his sins, like a penitent monk practicing self-flagellation.

By eight o'clock in the evening, he sobered up enough to shower, shave, clear the alcohol from his breath and make the five-minute drive to her apartment. She answered the door in her tattered robe—the one that was always a turn-on for him. Her hair was astray, like she'd been sleeping, and her eyes were glassy and distant and seemed to look right through him. She was different, transformed somehow in a way he couldn't quite place. He wanted to reach out for her, to hold her close to him, to feel the warmth of her body thaw the winter coursing through his veins, but the thought of rejection intimidated him, and he resisted the urge.

"I have to talk to you," he managed. "About Jennifer."

Her voice was cool, emotionless. "I'm not ready for this right now, Tyler. Maybe later."

"I won't take long. There are just a few things I need to say. Please Mara. Can I come in?"

"Call me tomorrow. We'll talk then."

He glanced at her bedroom door. She had shut it behind her, something she didn't usually do. "I know Annie's here," he said, his voice rising. "I saw her car in the parking lot."

The door cracked open, and he saw Annie's silhouette in the dim light. She was naked except for a thin bed sheet wrapped around her torso. "I…I don't understand," he said to Mara.

"I'm with her now, Tyler."

"You mean…?"

Mara nodded, compassionate but firm. "She's always been drawn to things you take for granted. You should know that by now."

"That's what I came here to talk to you about. I wanted to tell you how sorry I am about Jennifer. I should have listened to you in the first place. I was hoping you'd forgive me eventually."

"You just don't get it, do you? It's not for me to forgive you for anything. I don't blame you one bit for what happened to Jennifer. It would have probably happened anyway sooner or later. I've spent enough time around kids like her to understand that. You just happened to be in the wrong place at the wrong time, kind of like the driver of the car that hit her. No one pushed her into that car's path, except maybe her low-life, scumbag, excuse of a father. What I can't deal with is you running away from me every time things get uncomfortable for you. I'm a pretty strong woman, but I need someone to comfort me every now and then too. This was a very emotional event for me. I allowed myself to get too attached to this girl, and now I'm paying the price for my poor judgment, but Tyler, it's been four days since I've heard from you. It makes me wonder where I am on your list of priorities. From the looks of you, I'd say at least a couple of notches below Johnny Walker."

"I know I've got a problem, and I'm trying to deal with it. I could use your support."

"I'm sorry. I hope you work through your issues, I really do, but right now I need someone strong, someone who'll stand up to injustice in the world with me and fight back. That's who I am. I know that about myself. That's not who you are."

"So that's it? You dump me and start dating her?"

"The word dating sounds so parochial. Annie and I are together tonight. We're both okay with that. Who knows about tomorrow? All I know for sure is that there's no you and me in tomorrow. Goodbye Tyler."

Tyler watched the door shut and heard the chain lock from behind. He'd come seeking absolution of a sin but was leaving with an extended list. He was confused, chastened, embarrassed. And craving a drink.

The following afternoon, Monday, Mara looked up from her cubicle to find Quinnette Rose hovering over her, a panic-stricken look on her face. "What's wrong, Quin?"

"It's Deondra. She just called and sounded hysterical. She wouldn't tell me what's wrong, but she said she needed to talk to you right away, in person. I'm sorry to do this to you Mara, but she sounded so...desperate. Will you come home with me and talk to her?"

"Of course I will. It's almost quitting time anyway. Let's go."

Mara drove them both to the Roses' home. They beat the rush-hour traffic and made it in ten minutes. They found Deondra home alone, in her bedroom, tear streaks glistened on her face.

"We're here baby," said Quinnette. "I brought Miss Mara with me. Now tell us what happened to you."

"Could I...could I talk to Mara alone?" the girl asked her sister.

"I'm your sister, Deondra. You can say anything to me. You know that."

The girl shot a worried glance at Mara. "Please, Quin," she pleaded.

"It's okay, Quinnette," Mara said. "Just give us a couple of minutes. We won't be long."

Quinnette left the room grudgingly, not happy to be excluded from the conversation. "I'll be right outside if you need me."

They both watched her go and shut the door behind her. "What is it, honey?" asked Mara. "What's wrong?"

"Last week, Reverend Johnson sent a couple of his bodyguards to pick me up after school. They said they were taking me to see the doctor, only I didn't have a doctor's appointment. They grabbed me and tried to stuff me in their truck, but the crossing guard saw them, and they took off. I was so mad, I called Reverend Johnson at home and told him I was going to have the baby, with or without him."

Mara nodded. "Quinnette told me you decided to have the baby. You know, we'll both support your decision. So what did the reverend say after you gave him the news?"

"He wanted to get together and talk about it. I told him I didn't need to talk about anything. Anyway, today after school, those same two guys were waiting for me down the street from school property. They grabbed me and threw me in the cab of their truck, and they did this," she said rolling up her right sleeve and showing off a deep bruise on the inside of her arm. "Then they drove me to the church and carried me through the back door up to the reverend's office."

"Oh my god!" said Mara. "Then what happened?"

"The reverend told me I had to have an abortion. He said having the baby was not an option. He told me if I disobeyed him, I was disobeying God, and God would punish me."

"Did he say how God was going to punish you?"

Deondra nodded. "He said I could get hurt, and the baby might get hurt too. He said he couldn't protect me if I went against God's will."

"Did he say he would hurt you?"

"No, not directly, but those two men, James and Rodney, were there and they were smiling the whole time like they were enjoying it. I'm scared, Mara," she said, wrapping herself around Mara's waist. "I'm really scared."

Mara held the girl in her arms and patted her back reassuringly. "There's no reason to be afraid. I'll protect you. Tell me, Deondra, do you still want to have the baby?"

"Yes. I think so."

"Well if you do, that means we have to tell your sister about Reverend Johnson. And we'll need an attorney to make sure that the reverend stays away from you and doesn't do anything to hurt you. A friend of mine is an attorney and would help us if we asked her, free of charge. Are you okay with that?"

"I guess so."

"Then it's settled. How about we bring Quinnette in here and fill her in on the details? After that, we'll call my friend. She'll know what to do."

Annie's head felt like it was about to explode. The past several days at the office had been crazy. First, Tyler disappeared immediately after word of the Patterson girl's death to go on a drinking binge. Today marked the third consecutive workday he'd been absent. Elvis Patterson announced that he intended to sue *The New York Herald* as well as Marshall & Marshall for the death of his daughter, though no papers had been served as of yet. Annie had spoken to *The Herald's* law firm—they seemed spooked and anxious to settle. She couldn't blame them. The public release of protected and confidential information was only a misdemeanor from a criminal standpoint, but if Patterson's attorneys could prove this action led to his daughter's suicide—not a stretch by any means—*The Herald* could be faced with severe civil penalties. Without Tyler to consult, Annie had no choice but to proceed on her own, and she was taking steps to file forgery charges against Elvis Patterson to give her bargaining power down the road. She was handling her own client load now as well as Tyler's, telling his clients that he was on an extended leave of absence, having absolutely no idea when or if he planned on returning to the office. As the headlines in the news continued, the firm's clients were uneasy and needed constant reassuring, something that proved more difficult in light of the sudden disappearance of the firm's managing partner.

Fresh Start traffic continued to pour in, each news story serving as free advertising for the program. At this point, there couldn't possibly be a remaining soul in Chatham County who had yet to hear of the program. Annie had dictated much of the Fresh Start responsibilities to Geena, who time and again proved her worth. She offered her a permanent position as administrative assistant and took her shopping over the weekend to buy some more suitable clothes and saw to it that she also had a beauty makeover to make her more presentable for the new job. Goodbye goth girl.

The protestors were becoming an increasing problem. The locals rejoined the fold after Jennifer Patterson's death—the tragic incident served as a rallying point for the anti-abortion camp. There were, at times, over two hundred picketers outside the office, and they seemed to grow bolder by the day. Geena fielded two anonymous death threats on Friday, and someone threw a rock through a side window over the weekend with a cryptic note attached, "Baby killers must die. Gays too!"

Finally, there was Mara, a situation equally surprising and complicated. It had started innocently enough. Mara was upset about Jennifer Patterson's death and needed a shoulder to cry on, and one thing led to another. Annie wasn't ready yet to deal with her feelings for Mara. Mara cynically accused her of Tyler envy, of coveting the trappings of her boss's life—law degree, social stature, partnership in the firm and now girlfriend. Annie wouldn't honor that statement with a response, but she didn't deny it either. Mara might be off base from time to time, but she was a truth teller if nothing else. For now though, Annie was more concerned with Tyler. She felt in some way like she'd betrayed him, even if it was his weakness and chronic indifference that made betrayal inevitable. Their relationship had withstood years of uneasy accommodation, she pushing him, demanding more, he making excuses, offering less. She wasn't sure if it would survive this.

Annie's cell phone rang, Mara calling from her cell phone. "Hey baby," she said, in her sexiest voice.

"Annie? Hi, this is Mara Dressler. I'm here with a couple of clients of mine, and we've got you on speaker phone."

"Oh, I'm sorry," Annie recovered. "I thought you were someone else. What can I do for you, Ms. Dressler?"

"I've got Quinnette Rose with me and her younger sister Deondra. Quinnette is a co-worker of mine at DFACS. We could use some legal advice. I told these ladies you might be able to help."

"Of course," said Annie. It was obvious to her that she wasn't supposed to know anything about Deondra's fling with Thaddeus Johnson. "Why don't you tell me the nature of the...issue."

Mara related the majority of the story, with Deondra interrupting occasionally to clarify certain details. Quinnette didn't say much—she seemed to be in shock. Annie assumed she had only recently found out who the baby's father was.

"I see," Annie said when Mara finished. "I think I can help, but it would be better if we met face to face. I'm afraid Deondra's legal guardian will need to be present at that time. Will that be a problem?"

Annie could hear Deondra whispering. "I've got to tell Momma? She'll kill me! Then she'll kill Reverend Johnson!"

"Deondra, she's going to find out eventually," said Mara.

"I don't think this is such a good idea..."

"Don't worry about Momma," said Quinnette. "I'll handle her. You can't back down now, Deondra. You've got to trust these people, and let them help you."

Annie could hear hushed voices speaking at the same time, but couldn't make out what they were saying. Mara's forceful voice broke through the muted chatter.

"Annie, I'm afraid we're going to have to get back to you on a date and time for the meeting. There's one other thing. I'm afraid the Roses don't have a lot of money."

"That's okay. I'm willing to take this case pro bono. It sounds to me like Deondra's in a tough spot and could really use some help. I look forward to meeting you all soon."

"Thanks, Annie," said Mara, "from all of us. You're a real life saver."

The doorbell woke Tyler up. He'd been sleeping on the couch, wearing yesterday's clothes. *Or was it the day before?* ESPN was showing highlights of last night's baseball games and cures for erectile dysfunction during the breaks. The sunlight streaming through the windows intensified in the prisms of empty beer bottles scattered throughout the room, refracting rays of amber and emerald green to the ceiling and walls of the room, creating a peculiar Bacchanalian rainbow. The doorbell rang again. *Probably some kid selling Girl Scout cookies.* Had he realized that it was ten o'clock on a Tuesday morning, he might have thought of a more logical alternative but regardless, he had no intention of moving from the exile of his couch. An insistent knock replaced the doorbell, loud and demanding, reverberating in his fractured skull.

"Go away—nobody's home," he shouted into a sofa cushion. He heard the distinctive jingling of keys and the front door lock releasing from its chamber. He jumped from the couch, startled. "What the...?" he said as the door opened, revealing a gray-haired man wearing a sweater vest and khaki pants. "Dad? What are you doing here?"

"I thought I'd come by and check on you," said the old man walking past Tyler into the den and surveying the damage, "to make sure you haven't killed yourself, although it certainly looks like you're giving it your all."

"Dad, you just can't barge in here like this without calling first. I'm a grown man now, and I've got a life..."

"Grown man? Really? Is this what grown men do, drink themselves into a stupor? Poison themselves with alcohol? Shirk their responsibilities to their family and co-workers? Is that what you call being grown up?"

"Please, spare me the lecture. I've heard enough of those over the years."

"You're absolutely right, and obviously you weren't listening to any of them. They say the definition of insanity is repeating the same actions and expecting different results. Maybe you and I are both guilty of that. In any case, I didn't come here to lecture you."

"So why are you here then?"

"Have a seat, son." His father motioned for Tyler to sit on the couch while he went into the kitchen and found a trash bag, which he proceeded to fill up with empty bottles. The high-pitched clank of glass colliding with glass caused Tyler to flinch involuntarily each time. Once the bottles were cleared from the room, his father took a seat in the leather chair opposite him. "Regardless of what you may think, I've always wanted the best for you, Tyler."

"You always say that, but…"

"Please," said the old man, holding up an open palm, "let me say what I came to say. I've always wanted what was best for you, but the critical error I made in that equation was thinking you were like me, that deep down we wanted the same things. I wanted a son so badly to carry on my family's lineage, to perpetuate the line of my ancestors, great and noble men. Leaders. Then your mother and I found out we couldn't have children, and I was devastated. When you were born, it was like a miracle happened. By then, I had spent years imagining what my son would be like if I had one. I was middle-aged when you were born and much more set in my ways. I had lost the naiveté of a young father, who still believes in a world of promise and hope. I was pragmatic, cynical and battle-hardened. Perhaps this was the legacy I left you."

"Please don't take this as an apology because it's not. I'm proud of my accomplishments in life, and I don't have any regrets. I'd do it all over again in a minute. It's just taken me a while to realize the son I dreamed of could never really be. We might share certain physical or character traits, but he would be his own man, apart from me. I never gave you the chance to be your own man. I never trusted you to make your own decisions in life, and I understand now, because of that, I failed you as a father."

"It may be too little too late but starting today, I intend to honor my obligation to you, son. I want to pledge two things to you. I will always support your decisions regardless of my own personal views, and I will always be proud of you, no matter what."

Tyler felt a solitary tear cascade down his face. "You've never told me that before—that you were proud of me."

"I know, son. I'm sorry." He stood from his chair, and Tyler saw him, not as the strict, demanding patriarch of his youth but as a peaceful, reflective man at the twilight of his life. Tyler rose to hug him, an awkward embrace—it was the first time Tyler could remember hugging his father—but he felt his body relax as tension released through his pores. "I love you son, and I'm proud of you. I don't want to lose you. I need you to take better care of yourself."

"I will, Dad. I promise."

"I want to help anyway I can."

"Okay." Tyler wiped his face as they broke their embrace.

"There's something else I came to tell you, son. I'm afraid I've kept things from you that perhaps I shouldn't have. I want us to start today with a clean slate, so I need to level with you about something."

"Sure, Dad. What is it?"

"I'm the ringleader behind Fresh Start."

CHAPTER SIXTEEN

Tyler was stunned. "Excuse me?"

"I put the program together, raised the money and recruited the four men who approached you about acting as trustee, at my suggestion."

"Why?"

"Because I believe in it. Because I believe it will change the world. Poverty begets crime and disease and ignorance and ultimately, more poverty. All of the social programs created to break the cycle of poverty—and I'm not just talking about here in the U.S. but all over the world—have done nothing but create a life of dependency for the very people they're supposed to be helping. This may be a radical solution to the problem but based on the results we've seen so far, it's an effective solution and, in the long run, a relatively inexpensive one as well. The institutions backing us right now are interested in implementing this plan across the globe. I'm not being dramatic when I say this could change the course of history."

"Why did you keep this a secret from me? Why couldn't you just tell me you were involved?"

"Reverse psychology. You never would have agreed to participate if you knew I was involved. I'm guessing one of the reasons you did agree was because you thought I was opposed to it. Am I right?"

Tyler shrugged. "I still can't believe this. Why me?"

"I picked you because I saw you sleep-walking through life without a purpose. I thought this would light a fire inside you, maybe give you something to be passionate about. It seemed to have worked, for a while anyway."

"I suppose. I underestimated the passion it would stir up. Too many people have been hurt."

"The Patterson girl incident was unfortunate, but you can't beat yourself up over it. It wasn't your fault. If you look at the history of the world, some of the most profound life-altering events have involved great sacrifice. It comes with the territory I'm afraid. We must have the resolve to fight our way through the difficult times if we expect to realize our dreams."

"I don't know, Dad. It might be your dream, but it's not mine. I just can't do it anymore. Maybe I've lost the resolve to fight, as you put it."

"What if I told you that within two weeks, we'll reach an agreement with Thaddeus Johnson for a cessation in hostilities? I think that's a goal within our reach at the moment."

"It's not just him, it's everything. I'll carry the guilt of that girl's death to the grave with me. While we're being honest with each other, I'm seriously considering leaving the firm, leaving the practice of law altogether. Maybe you should find someone else."

"While I may be disappointed, I can't say I'm surprised. And if you decide to do that, I'll support you one hundred percent. Can I ask you a question?"

"Shoot."

"I understand Annie's been helping you with the program. Do you think she's capable of taking over as trustee?"

Tyler pictured Annie wearing nothing but a bed sheet in Mara's apartment and Mara's words. *She's always been drawn to things you take for granted.* "I think she would do a great job, probably better than me."

"I was thinking maybe we could make her a partner in the firm. That way, if you decided to leave, she could take over as managing partner. Would you have any objections to that?"

"None whatsoever. She's earned the opportunity."

"It's settled then. If it's okay with you, I'd like to talk to her this afternoon. It's important that we maintain continuity in the eyes of our clients. I don't mean to pressure you. I know you've got a lot on your mind right now, but when do you think you might be prepared to make a decision on your future with the firm?"

"How about right now?"

"Are you sure?"

"More than I've ever been about anything in my life. Thanks, Dad," Tyler said as he hugged his father tightly.

"For what?"

"For giving me the opportunity to find myself. For helping me find peace."

It was dark outside by the time choir practice ended. The moon and stars were hidden from view by the low cloud cover settling over the city. Deondra set off on foot for home feeling surprisingly optimistic for the first time in days. Quinnette had talked to their mother the day before, and she seemed to have taken the news about the pregnancy relatively calmly, with no screaming or shouting. Tomorrow, all three of them and Miss Mara would go see the attorney after school. Quinnette said they might get a restraining order on Reverend Johnson and James and Rodney so they couldn't hurt her or even come near her. She said a judge would make sure they kept their distance.

She was thinking of names for the baby when she turned the corner onto a dimly lit street. It wasn't normally so dark on this road. Deondra looked up and saw one of the streetlights was out. It looked like someone hit it with a rock. There was broken glass scattered everywhere. She walked by a side street on her left, really no more than an alley, and out of the corner of her eye she saw a parked truck with its lights off. As she passed the alley, she heard a motor rev behind her and the squealing of tires. She turned quickly to her left in time to see a dark truck, coming toward her fast with its bright lights on, momentarily blinding her. The last thing she remembered before impact was the distinctive Cadillac logo on the chrome grill.

The truck struck her head on as she turned directly into its path, knocking her ten feet to the curb. A witness, who lived in a loft apartment above the street, heard the squealing tires and subsequent collision and watched from the window as the truck stopped, idling, as if to survey the damage to the young girl lying motionless in the street. Seemingly satisfied with the results, the truck drove slowly and deliberately to the next intersection where it came to a complete stop before turning right and merging into traffic. The street below the window where the witness was watching was too dark for a positive identification of the truck, but the well-lit intersection was not. It was a blue, late model Cadillac Escalade, and the first two letters of the license plate were AE. According to the witness, there were two passengers in the truck, both African-American males.

An ambulance arrived on the scene within five minutes and took the girl, still alive, to Savannah Regional Hospital, where she underwent emergency surgery. Quinnette and her mother arrived at the hospital five minutes after Deondra was admitted to surgery. The duty nurse told them that, in addition to head injuries,

Deondra suffered a broken collarbone, two fractured vertebrae, a broken leg, fractured wrist and broken femur. She was listed in critical condition. There was no word on the status of the baby. Quinnette called Mara from the hospital to give her the news, although she knew nothing about the eyewitness account at that time.

"Who was that?" asked Annie, sipping a glass of champagne. They were out to dinner, celebrating Annie's recent promotion when the call came.

"That was Quinnette Rose. Deondra was the victim of a hit and run accident tonight. She's in critical condition at Savannah Regional right now."

"Oh no! What about the baby?"

"They don't know anything yet. Annie, you don't think...?"

"I think at this point, we've got to assume the worst."

"What do we do?"

"Yell for help. I'll be right back," Annie said, as she got up from the table.

"Who are you calling?"

"The police. I think they need to know about Johnson's connection to Deondra. She told you he threatened her."

Mara hesitated, fearful of betraying Deondra's confidence, but she knew the course of action Annie was suggesting was appropriate. "If you don't mind, I really think I need to be at the hospital right now, and besides, I don't feel much like celebrating. Can I take a rain check?"

"Of course," said Annie. "Call me as soon as you hear anything." After Mara left, Annie sat back at the table and took another sip from her glass. Disaster or not, she earned this bottle of champagne, and she intended to finish every last drop. Deliberately, she hit speed dial on her cell phone. "Hey, it's me. I think our problem may be solved. Yes, I thought you'd be pleased to hear that. I'll keep you posted. Bye."

The Georgia Department of Motor Vehicles database reported only two blue Cadillac Escalade pick-up trucks registered in the metropolitan Savannah area. Only one had a license plate beginning with the letters AE. It was registered to Community Church of the South. The Savannah Police Department received an anonymous tip that Deondra Rose was carrying the Reverend Thaddeus Johnson's child. Police immediately notified Savannah Regional Hospital, who took the extra precaution of securing a DNA sample from Deondra Rose's unborn fetus.

Though her baby did not survive the surgery, Deondra regained consciousness shortly past midnight. Her statements, along with those of her mother, sister and Mara, prompted police to issue warrants for the arrests of Thaddeus Johnson, James Ribbons and Rodney Gunn for attempted murder of a minor and voluntary manslaughter of an unborn child. Within days, police would establish a DNA match between the unborn fetus and its reluctant father, Thaddeus Johnson.

The Thaddeus Johnson story dominated local news coverage over the next several days. Members of the congregation expressed shock that their spiritual leader could be guilty of such a heinous act, suggesting that the two security men may have acted on their own accord, without the reverend's knowledge. Strangely, none of the flock denounced the extra-marital affair with an underage girl, like it was no more newsworthy than a speeding ticket. The NAACP issued a statement supporting the reverend's right to "vigorously defend himself" as guaranteed by law. After the press release stating that Marshall & Marshall was now minority owned and operated, however, the organization sent its leased protestors back to Atlanta. *The New York Herald* made little mention of the story but reported that Gaines Shockley had moved on to seek other opportunities. Most of the coverage focused on Thaddeus Johnson's legal woes and mentioned Fresh Start as an afterthought. As suddenly as the program had entered the public's consciousness, it seemed, it had just as quickly disappeared.

Annie finished an interview with a potential new attorney from nearby St. Marys, a recent graduate from Emory University Law School, who interned at another Savannah law firm over the summer and was interested in living in the area. He was young and energetic and couldn't wait for the results of his bar exam, so he could begin work. *It would be nice to have a little enthusiasm around here for a change.* She escorted him to the door and promised to be in touch shortly, most likely with an offer. There were no signs of the storm that had passed through recently, no banners, no television cameras, no trash and no picketers. She had almost grown accustomed to the circus-like atmosphere, like one gets used to a crazy relative living at home. Outlandish acts become routine after you're properly desensitized. The silence surrounding the office felt like a long lost lover, returning after years away, changed in a way that was neither better nor worse but different somehow. Annie lingered by the door as the young man walked toward his parked car at the same moment Tyler's Mercedes pulled into the parking lot. She watched apprehensively as Tyler stepped out of his car and shook the young man's hand. They seemed to be having an earnest conversation about something, which made her particularly nervous. After a few minutes, they said their goodbyes and Tyler made his way toward the building. Annie had not seen nor spoken to him since the day of Jennifer Patterson's death. She greeted him outside, on the front lawn.

"I just met your new associate," he said, grinning. "Annie, if you were lonely, you could have just bought a puppy."

"Yeah, but this one comes already housetrained."

"So it seems and from my alma mater to boot. Actually, he reminded me a bit of myself at that age."

Annie's antennae went up. "What did you say to him, Tyler?"

"The same thing I tell the groom at weddings I attend. Don't do it! Run away while you still can!"

"Very funny. If you said anything to make him…"

"Relax. I told him he'll be getting a great boss, one that he could learn a lot from."

"Thanks. I really appreciate that. So how are you doing?"

"All things considered, pretty damn well."

"Tyler I'm sorry about how everything turned out with the firm. With Mara. I feel terrible. This isn't how I wanted things to turn out for either of us."

"It looks to me like they've turned out just fine for you. You made partner and got the girl. What's wrong with that?"

"That's not what I meant. I didn't want it to happen the way it did. I feel so guilty about everything, like I've betrayed you somehow."

"There's no reason for you to feel guilty. I don't need anyone feeling sorry for me. It was my decision to leave the firm. I think we both know that was the right decision in the long run."

Annie nodded slightly, not wanting to appear too agreeable. "What about Mara? That must have hurt you terribly."

"I can't say I blame her for leaving me. It is a bit of a blow to the ego though—losing your girlfriend to the other woman."

"So what are you going to do now?"

"I'm thinking of becoming a lesbian. I figure maybe I'll meet more women that way."

"At least you still have your sense of humor. Seriously though, have you given any thought to how you want to spend the rest of your life?"

"I can't think that far ahead right now. I can tell you how I intend to spend the next few months of my life though. I'm taking the boat and sailing down to the Virgin Islands. Maybe I'll start a charter service or something down there. The world is full of possibilities outside of practicing law, and I plan on looking into as many of them as I can. To be honest, I feel like a huge weight has been lifted from my shoulders. I feel free, really free for the first time in my life. I'm as excited about the future as that young puppy you're about to hire, and I've got to tell you, that's a pretty good feeling."

"If this is what you want, then I'm really happy for you, Tyler. I'm going to miss you though."

"I'll miss you too, Annie, but I'll still be around. I still have ownership in the firm. I can't wait to start pestering you with irritating questions about the finances, like my father always did with me."

"Oh great! So I'll be catching it double from two Marshalls? I don't think I can handle that."

"You'll do just fine. You've earned this opportunity, Annie. It wasn't handed to you. The old man thinks a lot of you, and so do I. You can count on my support anytime."

Annie reached out to hug him. "Now you're going to make me cry. Thanks, Tyler. That means a lot to me."

"Now, if you don't mind, I'd like to clean out the stuff in my office and get out of your hair. It just so happened I had a few empty liquor boxes lying around the house, which I used this morning to throw my liquor bottles away, including the ones that weren't even empty. Although I must confess, there weren't many of those!"

As he entered the building, he spotted a striking young woman, nicely dressed at the reception desk, sipping a cup of coffee. "Hi, I'm Tyler Marshall," he said, extending his hand to the startled woman.

"Tyler, it's Geena," Annie said.

"Geena? Oh my God, it is Geena! What happened to the…and the…?"

"We had a makeover," said Annie. "Geena is with us full-time now."

"I'm gone for one week and everything falls apart around here. The next thing you know, there will actually be real clients in here. Are you deliberately trying to make this into a respectable law firm?"

"It won't be the same without you boss," Geena said, laughing.

"No it won't," Tyler agreed. "It'll be much better."

On Saturday, Annie drove out to the Marshall house in Glynn County. Mr. Marshall had invited her to dinner to celebrate her promotion to partner. She arrived several hours early in order to spend a little time with her mother. The Marshalls were still at the club so Annie and Bitty sat out on the veranda, drinking peach iced tea and watching white herons and ibises, partially concealed in the tall, slender grass of the freshwater marsh, stalk their afternoon meal.

Annie studied the lines on her mother's face. She had lived a hard life, full of sacrifice, without much to show for it. She had no IRA, no pension and was still working as a housekeeper well into her seventies. Annie never heard her mother complain, not once, even though her life must have been a terrible struggle, raising eight kids by herself with very little income. Annie knew she inherited her fierceness and resolve from her mother. Still there was an underlying complacency in Bitty, a willingness to accept the hand that life dealt her that Annie could never quite come to grips with. It was the same trait in Tyler that was a constant source of irritation to her. Annie's fire, her ambition, her drive, those all came from somewhere else.

"How's Ty?" was the first question out of her mother's mouth.

"He's doing really well. I think he's relieved, frankly."

"The poor boy lived his whole life trying' to please his daddy. Ain't nothin' good was ever gonna come from that. Boy takes after his momma, always has."

"Actually, I always thought he seemed more like you."

Bitty erupted, a deep, raspy laugh. "Ain't that rich? Maybe that's why we always got along so well!"

"He told me once that you were as much a mother to him as Mrs. Marshall...Cecil, ever was."

"Life is just full of irony, ain't it? He still don't know, does he? About your daddy?" Annie shook her head. "You, on the other hand, turned out just like him, big shot partner in the firm and all. You'll probably be mayor of Savannah some day, maybe even Governor."

"You make that sound like a bad thing."

"It ain't good nor bad—just is. It's in your blood. It's who you are. You can no more fight it than you can fight the tide from coming' up that marsh out there. I bet your daddy's proud of you though."

"You don't talk to him?"

"Not about you, I don't. Wouldn't be respectful to Miz Marshall."

"Momma, doesn't it make you uncomfortable to live with a married couple, knowing you gave birth to the husband's child? That just seems so weird to me."

"That was in the past. Miz Marshall and I made our piece long ago over that. Truth is, if I hadn't gotten pregnant with you, she might never have had Ty. Remember, they didn't think they could have children on account of his exposure to those poisons over in Vietnam. After you came along, they started tryin' again."

"What do you think about moving back to the city with me? I'm making enough money now to buy a bigger place, and you wouldn't have to work any more."

"Annie, this is where I belong. The Lord put me here for a reason. All my kids got their own families, and I keep hopin' someday you'll have one of your own, though you sure are takin' your sweet time. The Marshalls are part of my family. I'm comfortable here. Look out there at that marsh. Have you ever seen such a lovely view? To me, that's what heaven must look like. Why on Earth would I ever want to leave?"

Tyler Sr. and Cecil returned from the club an hour before dinner. "If you'll excuse us ladies, Annie and I have some business to attend to," said Tyler Sr.

Bitty headed to the kitchen to prepare supper while Cecil Marshall went upstairs to freshen up. The elder Marshall guided Annie to his study, a dark-paneled room reeking of masculinity. On the walls were plaques and awards and pictures of Marshall with various dignitaries, including three U.S. presidents. He motioned for Annie to take a seat across from him, at the opposite end of the large, nineteenth century mahogany desk that dominated the room. "So, how are things at the office?" he asked her.

"Everything's going quite nicely at the moment. I have a new associate starting the week after next, an Emory grad. The news media are gone, the picketers have vanished into the night and Fresh Start traffic is back to thirty to forty applicants per day, the vast majority of which are in our target demographic."

"And our good friend, Thaddeus Johnson?"

"Up to his eyeballs in legal troubles. He won't be bothering us anytime soon."

"That was quick thinking on your part to procure the DNA sample of the fetus."

Annie shrugged. "It helps when you have the chief of police and the director of the hospital on your side."

"Yes, and I have no doubt that Judge Murphy will prove his usefulness to us also before this is over. You've done well, Annie. You've kept us on track despite all of the...distractions. Without the information you provided on the girl, we'd still be slugging it out with Johnson in the public arena. He proved to be a worthy adversary, one we didn't anticipate."

"We certainly had luck on our side. I still can't believe he was brazen enough to attack the girl. He must really see himself as beyond reproach."

"Megalomaniacs can be extremely dangerous and unpredictable. Unfortunately for them, however, they're often most dangerous to themselves."

"Yes, well, it couldn't happen to a better man in my opinion. He's getting what he deserves."

"All in all, a smashing success, don't you think?"

"Maybe for everyone except Tyler. I still feel terrible about what's happened to him."

"You shouldn't. You and I discussed this before he was ever approached. We both knew there was a good chance he might stumble or falter along the way. That's been his pattern throughout his life. You and Tyler, my progeny, were both tested by fire. The strong one passed with flying colors, as I knew you would. The weak one must now begin his search to find his place in the world, wherever that may take him. That's not something either of us should feel guilty about or responsible for. And you know he wouldn't expect that of us. You and I, Annie, must be true to our own destinies. Guilt doesn't hold a place for us." He rose from his chair as a thought entered his mind. "There's something I want to share with you. I'll be right back."

Annie heard the door shut behind her as he left the room. Her eyes wandered over the photographs and commendations on the wall, a composite of a lifetime of achievement. *Destiny. I wonder what my wall will look like forty years from now?* Her eyes moved to his desk, neat stacks of paper, everything in its place. Below one thin stack at a corner of the desk within arm's reach, she spied the edge of a colorful legal document, peeking out from below the stack. It appeared to be a title of some sort. Her curiosity piqued, she lifted the stack and took the document in her hands. It was a car title, issued in the state of South Carolina. Across the top of the form, the vehicle identification number, make and model of the car were clearly spelled out. It was a 2014 blue, Cadillac Escalade truck. The vehicle's owner was listed as Timbuktu, LLC.

"This belonged to your grandfather." The deep voice from behind startled her, as she jerked in her chair, clutching the car title in her right hand. "It's a book by Winston Churchill called *Stemming The Tide* and contains many of his post-war speeches," he said handing her the book. She made no move to conceal the car title in her hand. "It's quite rare and very valuable," he continued. "I keep it in a safe upstairs. Churchill signed the inside cover for your grandfather—they were acquaintances during the war. The inscription contains one of his most famous quotes: 'It is a mistake to look too far ahead. The chain of destiny can only be grasped one link at a time.' I want you to have this, Annie."

"I...I don't know what to say," she stammered, taking the book but consciously not permitting her eyes to move from the car title in her hand.

Marshall paused momentarily, studying her reaction. "It was insurance. We couldn't count on the pregnancy being enough to force Johnson to back down, and if the girl refused to press statutory rape charges..."

"Who are we? I don't remember being involved in any decision to try and kill an innocent girl!"

"I didn't see the need to involve you. I wanted to protect you. And the girl's life was never in danger. We agreed on that from the beginning."

"The license plate."

"It was switched with Johnson's plate before the accident and switched back immediately after, before the police even responded to the call. Johnson's truck is parked in the church lot every night, without fail."

"I can't believe this! How in the world can you possibly justify critically injuring a fifteen year old girl, killing her baby and putting three innocent men in jail?"

"We're talking about a program that has the potential to change the very face of humanity. Sometimes the needs of a few are outweighed by the needs of many. It's a great responsibility we bear by embarking on our current course. That responsibility will likely require great sacrifice as well. Your brother couldn't understand that. I hope you can. Your destiny awaits you Annie. Now is not the time to be faint-hearted. I need to know that you're with me until the end. Can I count on you, Annie?"

Annie thought of Mara's words to Tyler the night he discovered them in her apartment. *I need someone strong. Someone who will stand up to injustice in the world and fight back.* Was it Tyler's weakness or his humanity that ultimately drove him away? What would Mara say if she knew the trust she placed in Annie had signaled the death warrant of Deondra's baby and quite nearly, Deondra herself? Tyler and Mara. They were more alike than either of them realized, children of means, harboring a guilt bordering on conceit for all the world's ills. What could they possibly know of her world? Of struggle, of sacrifice? They wouldn't understand, couldn't understand. She was alone, as she'd always been and likely always would be. Perhaps that was her life's burden. She handed the car title back to her father.

"You can count on me, sir. And thanks for the book. I'll treasure it always."

"Please," said the old man. "Call me Dad."

After dinner, they sat out on the veranda and watched the sun sink into the marsh, first yellow, then orange, then fierce magenta, like fiery drops of molten lava. A northeast wind blew gently off the coast, casting wavering dimples on the rivulets coursing through the marsh. They fell silent, each lost in their own private thoughts, as an army of cicadas serenaded them, announcing the coming darkness. They couldn't have been more different: the aging southern aristocrat, his genteel wife, his long-time servant and one-time lover and the by-product of their long ago coupling, but tonight, under the stars, they were a family.

EPILOGUE

I n early December, ten years after the launch of Fresh Start, the National League of Cities hosted their annual Congressional City Conference in Washington, D.C. A light snow was falling outside as the attendees filed into the huge ballroom of the Washington Hilton. They picked at their Pecan Crusted Grouper and Filet Oscar as the keynote speaker, the two-term senator from the state of Georgia, addressed the crowd of city officials. A spattering of gray tinged his hair and slight crow's feet spouted from his temple, but he spoke with a vigor and enthusiasm that belied his age.

"I was once in your shoes, and I know how difficult your jobs can be," continued Quinton Devereaux. "When I assumed my position as mayor of Savannah, Georgia, we were faced with the same problems each of you face every day: crime, poverty, public safety, education, and social services to those in need, just to name a few. We recognized early on, the need for a working plan, a plan that would survive our administration as well as those who succeeded us. I'm proud to look back over the past ten years and see that plan is still in effect and working. Crime is down forty-two percent in that time, and my former police chief, Charles Mosely, is now running the Los Angeles Police Department. Per capita income is up thirty-two percent adjusted for inflation, and the percentage

of city residents living in poverty has declined by fifty-two percent, well below the national average. The city has enjoyed budget
surpluses—unheard of in my day—in each of the past four years.
Twelve U.S. cities have adopted our plan and are experiencing
similar success.

I did not come here today to claim credit for these remarkable
achievements. This was a team effort and others did most of the
heavy lifting. I am here today to honor those individuals to whom
credit is so richly due. I would like to ask the governor of the great
state of Georgia to join me here at the podium, so we can present
the first award of the evening. Ladies and gentlemen, please welcome Governor Anne Burris!"

The crowd greeted Annie warmly with a standing ovation as
she took the stage wearing an elegant, chartreuse Vera Wang evening dress, an election-day gift from Cecil Marshall. Quinton took
her hand in his and raised them both high above their heads as
the crowd continued to applaud the first African-American senator and governor in Georgia history.

Annie motioned for the crowd to take their seats as she stepped
up to the microphone. "Thank you! Quinton and I are especially pleased to be with you tonight to present the Gold Award for
Municipal Excellence. As you all know, the winning cities deliver
the most creative and innovative solutions to our nation's pressing
problems. Of course, we congratulate all of the winners tonight,
but it is our particular pleasure to announce the winner in the
population category of one hundred thousand to five hundred
thousand. I'm sure you can all guess by now, it's our hometown,
Savannah, Georgia!"

"Accepting on behalf of the city of Savannah," said the senator
over the applause of the crowd, "is Mayor Don Abbott."

As Don Abbott gave his acceptance speech, Annie noticed a familiar face lurking in the back of the room. After the presentation,

her security detail escorted her toward the exit and the waiting limousine.

"Please, give me a moment," she said to the agent in charge, as the familiar face approached her from the side.

"Hello, Governor."

"Hello, Tyler. I didn't expect to see you tonight."

"I heard you were in town. It's only an hour drive from our home in Virginia."

"Did she come with you?"

"Afraid not."

"I can't believe she's still mad at me after all these years. I suppose she still thinks I sold out."

"You know Mara—ever the idealist," he shrugged.

"Of course. She's off fighting injustice in the world, wherever it may be. "But you're happy though?"

"Let's see, I'm making little to no money as the local director of Legal Aid, we moved to Virginia to be closer to Mara's family which turns out to be just as crazy as mine, and that sperm I banked ten years ago just got a D in conduct at school. All in all, I'm happier than I have a right to be."

"I'm really glad to hear that, Tyler. You've really found your way."

"What about you, Annie? Are you happy?"

"I've got everything I ever wanted."

"That's not what I asked."

She wore a sad smile, one full of hidden secrets and compromise. "I'm who I was born to be, Tyler. That's all any of us can really expect out of life."

"Mara loved you for your strength, your determination to stay the course despite the circumstances."

"And she loves you for your strength, your ability to remain true to yourself despite what others may think or say. You see, we both turned out as we were destined to be. Momma told me once that my genes could tell me why I am the way I am."

"Bitty told me about Dad and her before she died. She said I had a right to know."

Annie paused momentarily, reflecting. "I suppose that's true. You did have a right to know."

"It helped me understand myself a little better. Understand my parents. You. How long have you known?"

"Since the day I graduated from law school."

Tyler smiled. "I guess you're the son he never got."

"That's not true. He got his son, one that he loved very much. I'm the daughter that grew up to surprise him."

"I guess it all worked out for everyone in the end," Tyler said. "It's good to see you again, Annie."

"Same to you. Look me up if you're ever in Atlanta. There are plenty of extra rooms in the Governor's mansion. Tell Mara…"

"Tell her what?"

"Tell her I'm sorry."

Tyler watched her walk out of the hotel into the falling snow, a guard at each side. It seemed like a dream to him, the kind where someone close to you ended up being a completely different person, alien and unrecognizable. For a moment, he felt light-headed and dizzy, partially detached from reality. A frozen blast blew in from the front door of the lobby, slapping him in his face. He buttoned his coat, wrapped a ski cap around his head and stepped out into the wet, wintry night to make his way home.

www.ingramcontent.com/pod-product-compliance
Lightning Source LLC
Chambersburg PA
CBHW031302170626
46807CB00001B/264